Also by Jack Kelly

Mad Dog
Protection
Apalachin

LINE

of

SIGHT

LINE
of
SIGHT

JACK KELLY

HYPERION

NEW YORK

Library of Congress Cataloging-in-Publication Data

Kelly, Jack.
  Line of sight : a novel / by Jack Kelly—1st ed.
    p. cm.
  ISBN 0-7868-6614-4
  1. Police corruption—Fiction. 2. Adultery—Fiction. 3. Police—New York (State)—Fiction.
  4. New York (State)—Fiction. I. Title.

PS3561.E394 L5 2000
813'.54—dc21

                                         00-038840

Book design by Gabriel Levine

FIRST EDITION

10 9 8 7 6 5 4 3 2 1

LINE
of
SIGHT

I REMEMBER THE NIGHT I first saw her.

I turned up a dead-end street and skidded to a halt in front of a rusted guardrail. I radioed my position, swung the door, and stepped into the thick air. My strobes made the scene pulse. I was sweating.

I had seen the man rising out of the ground, climbing from a sunken railroad right-of-way. I shouted at him. He wasn't about to halt. He took off sprinting, a skinny young man, black, quick.

I took off sprinting.

He cut across a vacant lot toward Our Lady of Sorrows. Broken glass turned the ground into a glittering dance floor where six-foot mullein weeds waltzed with giant thistles.

A cop wears a Kevlar vest and carries a gun and a flashlight, a radio, handcuffs, notepad, keys, pepper spray, two fifteen-round ammo clips, and a blackjack. It's not an outfit for running a hundred-yard dash. I gave it a game effort. Track was my sport in high school. My muscles remembered.

This dude was fast. As he crossed the street under a light his shadow gained on him and went by, stretching out long in front. I was losing ground.

He sprinted into the King Projects along Cawango Street. Mansfield has some evil slums, human warehouses that are all graffiti, garbage, and neglect. He dodged around the corner of a low-rise—I thought I'd lost him.

The chase is the purest form of police work. If you don't like the taste of it, you might as well get off the job. You have to be an adrenaline junkie. You have to possess a hunger to run a man down. You cannot let him get away.

My breath was swelling my chest, crowding my ears. My face glowed with the intensity. I loved it. I lived for those moments.

I glimpsed him turn another corner, hightail it for the far end of the projects. The expressway blocked his path. He veered toward the river, the industrial district. I picked up my pace, pumping my arms. I didn't even know what his crime was. It had come over the radio that he had escaped custody. I was the one in position to head him off.

Oak Hill was a used-up section of town where the bones of the city showed through. Once foundries and factories, now brick-strewn lots. Now scattered car washes and auto body shops and For Sale or Lease by Owner. I could tell we were approaching the river from the cool sewer smell that tinted the air.

I knew this ground the way I knew my backyard. Know your sector—it's one of the rules. You memorize every street and alley, every storefront and garage and convenience store, every abandoned car and every corner where the homies hang. You get it down cold.

The fugitive sprinted along a hurricane fence, ducked under a spot where the wire had been cut and folded back. It was a big scrap metal dealer, acres of old cars, I-beams, engine blocks, heaps of batteries. Ten thousand places to hide, but he wasn't hiding. He vaulted over rusted hulks and around tangles of chrome trim, a real gazelle. He was swimming through air. I went under the fence myself.

Our feet pounded a hollow staccato on the sheet metal. I knew I couldn't catch him, could only pursue. I didn't mind. I was ready to run after him forever. I had a fleeting glimpse of the two of us continuing on, out of Mansfield, across western New York, past Erie, through Ohio and beyond, out over the rolling plains of the continent, cat and mouse.

Great buzzing security lights filled the lot with shadows and artificial glare. They lit the piles of pig iron and tin plate, of used faucets and gutters. They lit him now as he hit the fence on the far side. He climbed, the chainlink swaying wildly under him. If he made it over, he would be gone.

I ran even faster, risked a twisted ankle or worse as I stomped over the hoods of junked cars. I stumbled, nearly went down. I jumped over some old highway barricades, remembering the hurdles I had run sophomore year.

He wore a red basketball tank top, Chicago Bulls, 23. He was picking his way through the coils of razor wire that topped the fence. That slowed him enough for me to catch up.

I hooked my fingers through the wire and heaved myself up. I caught one of his fancy sneakers and yanked. Then I was standing on the ground and had his ankle in my hands. He yelled as the prongs tore him.

He gave way and came down all at once. We both fell. I made sure I kept a grip on him. He didn't make a move, though. Just lay there panting.

To a cop, handcuffs are both a symbol and a useful tool. They symbolize your authority to take away a man's freedom. They turn a wild and unpredictable perpetrator into a manageable package. He was still staring with intense curiosity at the blood on his arms and chest as I snapped the cuff onto his left wrist. He pulled away, but I already had a grip on his other arm. I twisted against his muscles and closed the link.

Still winded, I said, "Whaddaya do the hundred in?"

He was gasping at the humid air himself. Curiosity sparked in his eyes.

"Hundred meters, man. You're fast. You work on it, you could do something."

"The fuck you talkin'?"

I was pulling on a pair of latex gloves because of the blood. "Track and field. You could be a star. Get a scholarship. Put your life together. I'm serious."

For a second, our eyes connected. We were both alive, our nerves stripped. We were both seeing more than an ordinary person ever sees, packing each moment with information. I was telling him something he didn't expect to hear. We were two humans.

A second later the connection was gone and we were looking at each other the way you look at animals in the zoo.

Sweat soaked my shirt. I leaned my hands on my knees to catch my breath. I keyed my radio, announced the capture, and told my location.

I inhaled the smell of old motor oil and smoke and rust. What can you say to a young guy like this? Growing up with an attitude. Hating the world. A stranger, somebody who knows he's expendable.

I informed him he was under arrest and recited the Miranda prayer. To the north I could see the glass facades of downtown, the LoPresti Tower with the revolving restaurant on top. It gave the expense-account crowd a great view of the city while they chewed their prime rib. Could they see the two of us from up there? Could they tell the difference between a cop and a criminal?

In the couple of seconds I mused about it, the prisoner ran. Somehow he managed to get his feet under him and now he was lunging away, running bent over, trying to maintain his footing. It's hard to run in handcuffs, at best you can manage a bobbing stumble. He was game.

I went after him. I reached, just barely touched his back, sent him diving forward into the cinders.

"I gotta give you credit, but don't try it again. Too hot to run. You got warrants? Parole?"

"I didn't do nothing, man. Playing footbball."

"Why'd you run?"

"Fucking cops."

Yeah. Yeah, it's always the fucking cops.

I caught sight of two officers threading their way through the labyrinth of scrap. Jimmy Taggart arrived first, the beam of his flashlight bouncing in front of him. A rookie, born with a square-jawed cop's face and little mouse eyes. I had seen him around the station house, aping the veterans, putting on the swagger. Eager, but already pretending a nonchalance that didn't fit him. Crew-cut hair, crew-cut mind. He was one of the guys on the force who greeted me with a friendly smile—there weren't many.

His partner was Lou Campisi, a sergeant and a dying man. Blood swelled the veins in his face and bulged his eyes, inflamed his florid Italian nose, pulsed at his temples. His gut hung over his equipment belt. Each breath was a weed he yanked by the roots from the bottom of his lungs.

"Good work, Ray," Taggart said.

"Your collar, Jimbo. What is it?"

"We're questioning this suspect and he gives Lou a kick in the knee and takes off like a bat out of hell."

"You okay, Sarge?" I asked.

"Fuck I'm okay." His voice was full of phlegm. He lifted his foot and brought it down hard on the young man's chest. The prisoner rolled onto his side and drew his knees up. "Run from me, you little monkey."

Campisi bragged about having shot three men. He claimed it was a department record. Two of them to death.

I knew he wouldn't leave it at that. He drove a toe into the man's kidney. He stomped him again. I turned to Taggart. He was the one to call his partner off. His eyes met mine for an instant, then drifted up to where the dirty clouds were reflecting the glow of the city.

"Campisi," I said.

Campisi was pulling a blackjack from his pocket. A tap from a convoy like that can deaden an arm. A full swing can snap a collar-bone or fracture a skull.

I put a hand on Campisi's arm and pulled him back. "That's enough."

He glared at me, pointing his finger.

"Don't bone me, Dolan," he said. He smelled like car deodorizer.

"I'm suggesting the prisoner is subdued."

"You're suggesting? I'm suggesting these mokes think they can run. I'm suggesting you gotta teach them."

"I won't stand by, Lou."

"Who the hell are you?"

"You want trouble?"

Turning, he muttered something under his breath. The prisoner was vomiting now, adding another layer of odor to the heavy air. We stood over him, beasts gathered around a fallen prey. Campisi lit a cigarette.

The arresting officers hoisted their prisoner to his feet and walked him roughly down a path toward the gate. I followed.

Campisi was a dinosaur, a guy who had put in his twenty but wouldn't let go of the job. Every day he rode around the city and looked at the welfare cheats and drug dealers living the life of Riley while he sweated for a salary that got eaten by bills before he could cash the check. When he had started on the job, cops still got respect, he told us. Back then, when you told somebody to move along, they moved. Now it was a vacant stare and a curse in the throat. Why should you follow the rules when nobody else did? I understood the feeling. A lot of cops thought that way.

When we reached their patrol car, Campisi very gently put his hand on the prisoner's head and guided him into the backseat. I rode back to my car with another officer.

It didn't cool off much the rest of the shift. The air was still blood temperature when I parked my cruiser near the station. I took a shower and put on my street clothes. I carry a little Walther in an ankle holster. It used to be, an officer was expected to respond twenty-four seven. A cop was like a priest, always on duty. The union got rid of that. Now you could pretend to be a private citizen after your tour. But like most cops, I felt naked unarmed.

I ran into Frank Kaiser as we were both leaving the station house. I told him about the collar.

"What was the idea, running?" he asked.

"Cops, you run. Wouldn't you?"

"If I was him." He barked a laugh. "Question is, Why do you want to sweat your ass off?"

Kaiser was a detective, six years older than me, bristly hair going gray, carrying a couple extra pounds of hard fat. His eyes, way up under his brows, got lost in shadow. He led the major crimes squad, which operated out of our station. He was my best friend.

"I keep telling you," he said, "go for your gold shield. You've got the smarts, you know procedures, you're good with the law."

"I like to sweat."

"Think about the long term."

"Why?"

He shook his head. "How about dinner tomorrow? I want to talk to you."

I hadn't connected with Frank lately. Something in his voice told me it wasn't a casual invitation. I said I would look forward to it.

I drove home and walked up the steps of my old peeling-paint Victorian house. The screen door groaned and slapped shut after me. Inside, I could smell my whole life—old shellac, the ozone buzz of electricity sliding through cloth-covered wires, the refrigerator smell, the mothball smell, the damp-basement smell. I imagined I could smell the wool of my father's uniform, the pomade he used, the shoe polish. Smell stale fragments of my mother's cooking.

The house was a Ray Dolan museum. The leg of the dining room table bore the gouge of a collision with a friction-engine police car hurled in a six-year-old's fantasy of a crash. The kitchen drawer still held a Boy Scout's jackknife. On the wall, in a Woolworth frame my mother had bought, hung a blue ribbon for target shooting I had won in eighth grade.

I went to the freezer and took out the bottle of Cuervo. The viscous fluid lit up my insides with a musty sigh. I said a little prayer to the god of goof.

I'm not a heavy drinker. Let's put it this way, I'm not an out-of-control drinker. Use it, don't abuse it. But change was in the air and I was determined to get a little fogged.

I opened a long-necked Pabst and washed down the sooty taste of the tequila. For he's a jolly good fellow.

Sometimes the house seemed foreign to me, as if I had gone through familiarity and out the other side.

The cat wanted his food. Cairo, solid black with a white bow tie. He looked at me as if he knew something. He complained. I scooped him out some mackerel-smelling goo. I washed the spoon and the can, set them to dry in the rack.

I moved my telescope onto the back lawn.

All changed now, from when I grew up. Developers had erected a tract behind my house, what they called executive homes, big facades packed together on winding streets, landscaped with neat weeping birch, shouting money in plate brass and federal-style trim. The houses butted up almost to my back door. People were always moving in and out of those houses. Corporate people following the job, the career path. Moving to another home in another development in another city just like this one.

I owned a four-inch refractor telescope with some good Japanese optics, sidereal drive, German equatorial mount, 144-tooth worm-lapped gears, 1,000 mm focal length. You can see 2,000 stars with the naked eye, 400,000 with a top-shelf amateur setup like that.

The sky was good that night. Not much haze in spite of the heat. A hill shields me from the light of downtown Mansfield, which ruins the sky to the west. Every year, they're putting in more malls with sulfur-lit parking lots, more of the big argon security lights. Pushing back the darkness.

I peered up the velvet tube. Betelgeuse, a red giant, five hundred times the diameter of the sun, a star on its last legs, a star that would fuse to iron in its core before finally collapsing on itself.

Man is the only animal that is afraid of the dark.

Once, behind a few drinks, I went out with a .22 target pistol and started plinking streetlights. I must have walked ten miles that night. Aim and fire and open a pool of darkness. Very satisfying. I was fighting pollution.

Afraid of the dark. Maybe they have good reason, I don't know.

A jolly good fellow . . . That nobody can deny.

I shifted to the Pleiades and studied the nebulosity that surrounds the cold sisters. Seven virgins, seven swans, light a thousand years old.

I like the sky. I like to know where I am in the universe, like to think about light-years of darkness. It gives me perspective. The telescope is a keyhole on a passionate, silent world. Birth and death in slow motion. I lose myself in it. That's the best you can say about anything you do, isn't it; to lose yourself.

High mare's tails were seeping across the sky now, ghostly clouds that drew a veil. I moved the telescope inside. I opened another beer and sat on the steps of my back porch.

Everything quiet. Breathless, even the crickets falling still.

For he's a jolly good . . . it was my birthday. Thirty-five. I was at the exact midpoint of my life. The fulcrum. No, every moment's a fulcrum. That was one of the rules, or should have been.

A light was shining in an upstairs room of the house behind. I sensed movement. I looked. The thin curtains undulated softly.

The glow was caramel-colored. A figure, a woman, moved past the window and disappeared.

I looked away. I'm no Peeping Tom.

Somewhere, someone knows your desires. Somewhere, out in that blackness, everything is possible. Somewhere, your fate awaits you. You don't have to go looking for it. It comes to you. It's yours.

She reappeared. I could only see her silhouette against the filmy drapes.

What's the harm? Let her close her blinds. I watched.

She had the window open. A breeze wafted the curtain and gave me a glimpse of her thighs. My thumbnail scraped the label from the sweaty bottle.

Her shadow made a gesture, hands lifting to push her hair back.

In the distance, out on the highway, a siren sliced the night air like a razor.

She moved. The light went out.

THEY SAY THAT IF YOU STAND at the bottom of a well in the middle of the day and look up, you can see the stars. The sky is black and you can see the stars.

I met her the next morning.

A house like mine needs regular maintenance. My father was good with his hands, but he never bothered to keep up with the sagging gutters and rotting eves.

Saturday morning and I was gnarling paint off the gingerbread on the back porch. When I tackle a job like that, I do it right. I blister the paint with a butane torch. I scrape and sand and wire-brush it down to the bare wood. Then shellac primer, two coats of oil-based enamel. Like new. I want it to last.

But I'm always fighting a lazy streak. I'll work at it like a demon, then it sits half finished and a year's gone by, who knows where.

The close heat made my skin prickle. The ladder rung pressed my instep. The hazy sun focused on bits of chrome and aluminum and glass and set them gleaming. The water in the pool of the house behind mine ricocheted a bright sheen.

Their son wandered out and smoked a cigarette on the patio, a teenager with the uniform of rebellion—buzzed crew cut, baggy jeans, tattoos, a heavy load of attitude. Who would fardels bear, huh? This kid would. He slouched in the shade reading a paperback for a while, then disappeared.

Next, the husband. A big guy, big face behind the sunglasses; his walk suggested the mincing gait of a man with a hangover. He had been in a gym once, but now his definition was clouded with fat. He carried a can of Bud in his hand and a *Wall Street Journal* under his arm. He didn't look at me.

The wife emerged behind him. Black swimsuit, black hair, not tall, lots of curves. She walked with just the suggestion of a limp. She was aware of her looks and at the same time careless, easy in her body.

The husband sat on a patio chair. She idly massaged his neck and shoulders from behind. He caught her arm and pulled her and they kissed. They exchanged a few remarks before he waded into the shallow end and eased himself onto a floating chaise. He yawned, took a swallow from the can, and opened the paper.

It was a perfectly ordinary scene, the everyday intimacy of married life. I couldn't figure why I was watching it with such interest, or why I was holding my breath.

I worked a folded piece of emery cloth into a groove. Out of the corner of my eye I watched her stroll down to where our two lawns joined.

Between us my sprinkler was waving its iridescent hair back and forth—it had been dry that summer. She stood watching it for a few minutes. She danced closer, inside the arc of spray. As the water leaned in her direction she hunched her shoulders and laughed. Her laugh blossomed, a lush flower of a laugh, not tee-hee.

I live my life by rules. You don't borrow money from friends. You don't drink before noon. You don't say what you can't back up.

Rule: You don't mess with married women. It's tempting, sure. Forbidden fruit. He got, I want. But you're only buying trouble and there's enough trouble to be had for nothing.

I've always been a sucker for a pretty laugh, though.

I saw myself climb down the ladder. Saw it from up in the sky, watched myself cross the lawn in her direction.

I picked up some twigs that had fallen from my maple tree. She ran, burst through the curtain of mist, screamed. When she saw me, she flinched.

"Sorry," I said. "I didn't mean to startle you."

"No, it's all right. You're the neighbor. We've been wanting to introduce ourselves."

"Ray Dolan."

She joined me in the dappled shade of the tree. Her small hand was wet and cool in mine.

"I'm Sheila Travis. We just moved in here." She was very tan. The drops of water on her skin splintered the light like glass beads.

"Welcome to the neighborhood."

"I love the heat, don't you?" When she smiled, crescent dimples lit up her cheeks. She was older than I had guessed at first. Thirty-six, I would learn. The shadows of wrinkles touched the corners of her eyes. But her face had an unformed quality, too, that made her look girlish.

"That's Mansfield," I said. "Blistering summers, Siberian winters."

"I was admiring your house."

"The Realtors tell me it's an eyesore."

"Those dopes? It's a real house. I love old houses."

"Maybe you'd like to see it."

"Love to!" She turned and called, "Lance! I'm going to look at his house." The husband put his hand to his ear. She did a panto-mime. He raised his chin, giving her permission. He went back to his paper.

The heat hit me hard as we walked toward my porch. Silent black explosions shot across the linings of my eyes. I heard that low buzz, the one that comes from the center of the earth.

The screen door banged. The dark air inside felt cooler.

"Aw, look at this," she said. She squatted in the hallway. Her backbone stood out, a row of smooth bumps.

"My grandfather went on a safari once. He shot it."

"Darkest Africa, huh?"

"It's supposed to be an umbrella stand. Only I don't own an umbrella." I laughed like an idiot.

"And that's just his foot."

I led her into the kitchen.

"Could I offer you?" I took the tequila from the freezer.

"Oh, no, I couldn't this early. What is it?"

"I call it a Mexican hat dance." I grabbed two beers. I was al-ready pouring the shots.

She bounced her thick eyebrows. "I'll try one, I guess."

"To the heat." We tapped our shot glasses.

"To neighbors." She sipped hers, made a face, and smiled.

We sat at the kitchen table and drank Pabst from the bottle. Her face reminded me of a boxer's. That sounds funny, but a lot of fighters have a combination of toughness and vulnerability in their features, a hard openness that makes them beautiful. Imagine some-thing of that brutality and candor transformed into female prettiness.

"Are you from Mansfield, Ray?"

"I grew up in this house."

"You're kidding."

"Before he lost his money, my grandfather dreamed of making a killing in real estate. My family owned the land all around here. My father died, later my mother had to go to a nursing home. I couldn't hold on to everything. I sold the land, kept the house. Inertia, I guess."

"My family never had any money to lose. We lived in a trailer park when I was little. Can you believe that?"

"Why not?"

"Now I have the American dream."

"Lucky you."

She gave me an understanding blink.

We chatted about the weather and about neighborhood gossip and about which were the good restaurants in town. It was like listening to a conversation through a wall.

Gradually the talk became more personal. I told her about the one time I left Mansfield, my trip to California after my father died.

"I lived in Glendale, near L.A. I worked for an outfit that dismantled old airliners, stripped out the Naugahyde and carpeting, down to the bare aluminum. Those things were ovens in the sun. But the sky was so blue. I didn't even have a phone. The police came to my bungalow one morning. My aunt had been trying to reach me. It was my mother, a stroke. So I came back here, and after a time she died."

The aroma of grass and coconut oil and subtle perfume, of pure newness, hit my nostrils. Her toenails were painted blush pink.

"I always wanted to be an actress," she said. "But I married young, seventeen. I've lived all over, out West, Florida. We moved to Mansfield six months ago, rented a place till we found this. The rust belt. Did you know Mansfield has more scrap metal dealers than any other city? They brag about it."

"I know there are a lot."

"Rust is a form of fire. They say the world is on fire, if only we knew. Whew, this Mexican jumping bean is making me run my mouth."

"Hat dance."

"It's good. We're always moving. My hubbie's a salesman. It comes with the job. Lance."

"What's he sell?"

"Anything and everything. He has a forceful personality. He's a good provider. What do you do, Ray?"

"I'm a cop."

She couldn't keep her eyes from widening. She smiled again. "The things you must see."

"It's a job."

"I feel safer already. How is the crime in Mansfield, anyway?"

"Stay out of certain neighborhoods, you're all right."

"A mother worries."

"These days you have to."

"Now I'll know who to call when I get scared of the dark."

It was my turn to smile.

I showed her the living room. She lifted a piece of my mother's cut glass and twisted it in a shaft of sunlight to set off bursts of color.

"When I was young, I thought moving was glamorous, something you did if you had money. But moving all the time isn't good for a kid. A kid needs a place to call home, don't you think?"

"Maybe you'll settle here."

"Wouldn't that be nice."

We wandered into the dining room. She went to the window and looked out at her own house.

"You were having fun out there," I said.

She glanced at me in the mirror over the buffet. "Sometimes I feel like a little girl. I can't understand how I got all grown up."

"Time goes by."

"Scary, isn't it. You look at the stars?" She ran her fingers over my telescope.

"I pick out a dot and I see it's actually a galaxy, ten billion stars, each one as big as the sun."

"Isn't that food for thought."

"Or bigger. Hotter. Unknown planets. People who have worked it out a whole 'nother way than we have."

She swung the telescope down and gazed into the eyepiece. She was focusing on her husband. I could see him dozing as he floated in the pool.

"We're having a little party next weekend," she said, "kind of a housewarming. Think you can come?"

"I'd like to."

The world had been holding its breath. Now, as we moved back through the kitchen and onto the porch, sounds began to reach us again. I heard the brakes of a semi out on the highway, the screams of kids playing ball up the block.

She thanked me for the drink. "It did me good. And it's so nice to know there's an armed man around."

"If you need me," I said, "just whistle."

"I'll remember. See you Saturday."

The sprinkler was still shooting rainbows into the sky.

Back in the kitchen I saw that her bathing suit had made a damp print on the cloth seat of the chair. I stared at it until it dried.

MULLIN'S WAS ONE LONG BLOCK from our station house. One long sweet block, because when you were on your way to Mullin's you were done with your tour and looking forward to soaking up some booze in a snug tavern that was as familiar as your own living room.

The smoky air was loud with cops unwinding and self-medicating. The usual neighborhood characters and a few couples filled in the gaps, everyone well oiled.

I was glad to be there, glad for the distraction. I didn't want to think about her anymore, about Sheila. I didn't want to go home and look out my back window and imagine her moving around in those rooms, eating and sleeping, dressing and undressing. I didn't want to fantasize things that might go on between us. I didn't want to think about her, but I did. I couldn't help it.

I had finished my fish fry and was drinking a beer. Frank Kaiser was already on his fourth scotch. He was still ragging me about going for detective.

"I need to be out there," I told him. "I need that anything-can-happen. I need, every once in a while, to be where things are going down right now. You know what I'm talking about. Trying to sort out shit that's in the past, that's not for me."

"You're a dreamer, boy."

"I like to sit in my cruiser and think my thoughts. I don't want to canvass, follow up leads, solve puzzles. I want to coast."

"Coast? You can waste your whole life coasting. Hey, look"—Frank pointed to the television over the bar with his eyes—"they're going on about that perp that had the heart attack. They talk to you yet?"

A girl newscaster from Channel Ten was standing in front of our station house. The word *live* appeared on the bottom of the screen. She was speaking earnestly, but the sound was turned down on the set and the jukebox was twanging out an old Merle Haggard song.

"They talked," I said.

"Campisi says—"

"He's lying."

He stared at me, nodded. "I'm just glad it wasn't one of my stoolies who croaked."

The reporter made her cute face frown to show us this was serious stuff.

Kaiser said, "That kind of shit wears on you. Hell, time wears on you. If I was on the street now, fuck."

Frank had been my first partner. In Mansfield we mostly ran single, but your first year on the force they paired you with an experienced officer. When you spend time with a guy that way, talking time, not-talking time, you develop a bond. When you respond to hairy calls, you learn who the man is with his mask off. You get to know each other all the way through. You can communicate with looks, telepathy.

Frank had taught me to be a cop. He had taught me by-the-book. You start from that, he always said. You get that down. Too many cops, they don't understand the rules, don't have the book by heart. They make it up as they go along. They're cowboys. Or they're guys like Campisi—they make all cops look bad. You gotta have rules.

He taught me well. It's a narrow path and I made sure I erred on the side of being too tight, too straight-arrow. Guys might resent it, but that was the way I did things.

Everybody liked Frank. He had style. Once when he was patrol sergeant, a Mansfield officer, Gary Wilson, stopped a Devil's Disciple, wrote him up for DWI. The Disciples found out where Gary lived. They rode up on his lawn where his little girl was playing, scared her.

Kaiser went down to the bikers' clubhouse with three other cops, all plainclothes. First guy he saw, Frank grabbed him by the hair and jammed the barrel of a .357 in his mouth. How's that taste, pal? You sure you want to mess with the police? The big bad biker peed his pants.

The cacophony of the bar had smoothed to an easy hum. An old Roberta Flack love song drifted in the warm air.

"I thought she was happy," Frank said out of the blue, words he'd rehearsed.

"Elaine?"

"Now I know she's not happy."

"She's happy. Who's happy?"

"No. It's something deep this time. I can feel it, like an earthquake coming."

"Not Elaine. She's solid. You guys are a unit. What is it, fifteen years?"

"Sixteen. That's just it, I know her. I've seen everything about her and now I'm seeing something new."

"People change."

"Exactly."

"But that doesn't mean it's trouble."

"No?"

Those early years, Frank and Elaine and I were family. She was a nurse, the ideal wife for a cop. She had a nurse's instinct for understanding what people needed when they didn't know themselves. She was used to odd hours, and like a cop she didn't mind seeing reality bare naked. She had eyes that looked at you the way you wanted to be looked at. She could tell a dirty joke.

We used to double date all the time. We spent New Year's Eves together. Frank never had much to say about my various girlfriends, except to rate them on an anatomical ten-scale. But Elaine would treat them like pals and give me her opinion, sometimes urge me to pop the question or at least commit—other times to run for my life.

Frank and Elaine organized the cold-cut lunch after my mother's funeral. One night, behind a bunch of margaritas, I told Elaine that I loved her, that if not for Frank . . .

Kaiser jumped up to detective, then quickly to lieutenant. After he became the star of the department, the man who grabbed all the glory cases, we didn't see each other as much.

Frank had to have someone as hard as he was inside, so it was inevitable that he and Elaine would clash now and then. I knew that Frank wanted children and Elaine didn't, and that it was a running issue with them. They fought, but they fought fair. He moved out a couple of times. Once she left for three weeks. But they were the squalls of married life. Of love.

"You know Elaine," Frank said. "Do you think she'd lie to me?"

"She wouldn't lie. Elaine's an honest woman. She isn't the type to set you up. If anything was going on, she'd let you know."

Frank swirled his glass. "No, this is the kind of thing you hide. Wouldn't you hide it? Wouldn't you be ashamed?"

"Where's the evidence, Frank? You know what you always told me: Don't put the big ego into it. Your mind is a light. You shine it into a situation, you cast all kinds of shadows. You have to stay cool. Show me the hard evidence."

"The way she looks at me," Frank said. He had done a lot of thinking about this. "The way she gets undressed. The way she smiles. The way she stands. The way she does this thing with her eyes when I ask her anything. You know. When you've been married, you know. You know."

Frank got up and steered himself toward the men's room in back. I stepped over to the bar.

The girl next to me was just turning her face in my direction. She was holding some kind of fancy drink with a miniature umbrella and a straw. My eyes tightened, her eyes tightened. Not quite a smile at either end. She pursed her lips and slipped the straw between them. She sucked, still looking. She turned away.

She was my type, what I thought of as my type—the long legs, the eyes that danced.

"Kenny, another round here," I told the bartender. I leaned toward the girl. "Could I buy you one? What is that, a kamikaze?"

"Thanks, but no thanks."

A curly-haired man in a blazer was returning to the stool next to hers. My eyes sized him up. Weak mouth, sloppy smile, shaving rash on his soft throat. Other nights I might have challenged him, continued the move on the girl. I got a certain satisfaction out of that when it worked—and it often did. Women liked it, two men vying for the honors, caveman stuff.

Tonight I wanted to and I didn't want to. I let it pass.

A cop has an advantage with women. There are girls who go for the uniform, go for the idea of a cop, tough guy, seen it all, authority figure. They think a cop is as simple and honest as a child. It's an aphrodisiac. So getting in the door is easy. Beyond that was where I always got lost. A few dates, some by-the-numbers sex, an emotional blowup and on to the next one.

I prided myself on my end game. No sentimentality. Pick the right time and cut them off clean. That way nobody got hurt, badly hurt, and you didn't accumulate a lot of baggage.

Tonight I had a funny urge. I wanted someone who could make me stop thinking about a married woman, stop feeling awkward about going home. Maybe I wanted someone who could turn aside my fate. Or maybe I just wanted to get laid.

Back at the table Frank said, "She wants out, okay, but be honest. She wants to spoil all the years we've had, thinks it's just spit, fine. Marriage is strictly a convenience thing, fine. Nothing means nothing, fine. But come out and tell me that's the way it is. Don't hide it. Don't sneak. Don't, I'm the last one to know. I'm not going to be the last one to know, Ray. Believe it."

"You don't know there's anything to know."

"I know. On the job I am lied to by everybody. I swim in lies, like in a sewer. I will not be lied to by my wife. I will not accept that. Understand?"

"Sure."

I understood him. Frank couldn't bear the idea that she was making a fool of him. He could accept that she was cheating, but he couldn't stand to think she was getting away with it. That was what it came down to. Frank was a cop through and through.

"No, you don't understand," Frank said. "You, I used to envy you. One-night stand and good-bye. Slam, bam, wham, damn. That's great. You're a cop, that's the way it should be. I'm a cop. Elaine, she wants more."

"We see things, Frank, and it changes us. You say she's changed? You've changed."

"I haven't changed. I don't know what the fuck you're talking about." His eyes held a lot of pain.

"Take her to Acapulco," I said. "Some beach, some mai tais, a real vacation."

"Why? I go away, I can't settle down. What are you supposed to do at the beach?"

"You don't know how to relax."

"I'm relaxed. My wife's cheating on me, then I'm not relaxed. Okay? Then I'm very not relaxed."

We were getting up to go.

"Who would have thought it would come to this," he said. Self-pity didn't fit Frank Kaiser. He was working it to the bone. The idea of her betrayal both frightened and fascinated him. Men take pleasure in justified anger, especially controlled men like Frank.

We stood outside by Frank's Mercury.

"She isn't cheating on you, Frank. Elaine is a good woman."

"I'm a lucky man."

"Go home, tell her you love her. You love her, she's your life, she's beautiful. When's the last time you said that?"

"We don't talk that way."

"Start talking that way. It's all now, Frank. It's today."

"You don't know shit about it."

"You're doing this to yourself. You understand that?"

"Sure I understand it. I'm not worried about what I'm doing to myself. I'm worried about what she's doing."

"Does she love you, Frank?"

"Yes. I don't know. How do I know?"

"That's what counts."

The air was warm, tinted with the aroma of dark flowers.

"You know what bothers me?" Frank said. "It's not just what she's doing. It's what I'll do if I find out for sure."

For an instant, dropping his intoxication as if it were a Halloween mask, Frank gave me the look—the steely, ice-cold look that went right into the nerves.

"Let me give you a ride home," I said. "You shouldn't be driving."

Frank pointed a finger at me as he unlocked the door of his car. "Hey," he said. "Hey, fuck you."

A WOMAN STRETCHES and a white wedge of her belly shows between shirt and jeans. Or a slit skirt opens and snaps closed. Buttons gape, the blouse a little too tight. A sweater bares a shoulder. She's wearing gloves and a sliver of white skin shows at her wrist. It's the glimpse. It's not nudity that ignites the fire, it's the peek, the flash.

I found myself driving home too fast that night.

The quiet that descended when I switched off my engine became a cathedral of silence. The heat grabbed at my skin. Inside the house, I pulled off my shirt and opened a bottle of beer. I wandered out to the back porch. The steps creaked. Weeds sprouted all along the foundation and had begun to climb up among the railings. No weeds grew around the new development houses.

I waited. Why wait and for what?

All the windows of the house behind were dark, blank. Yet I stared with the bone-deep interest that I usually turned to the stars. Desire and disaster, both words are based on the word for star. I looked it up once.

That night I was a child, caught up in expectation, captivated by the prospect of seeing something new and vital and exciting.

I had sat on these same steps as a boy, had sat here yearning, dreaming of girls, remembering glimpses, long before I had even taken aim with my sex. All the layers. Their house was right where the shed used to be. Where my father . . . Where I found him.

Who wants to grow up? You're a cop, it's no job for an adult. You fool with women like a boy. You let time flow around you the way it does when you're a kid, while you pin your attention to the now. You're thirty-five and where the hell are you? Old enough to sense the finality in everything. Old enough to be turned on by a married woman. Old enough to start playing for keeps.

What is it about the sound of breaking glass? It gets inside your nerves. It sets off alarms you can't ignore.

I was standing. I took three steps across the grass.

The windows of their house stood open. I couldn't make out the words, but I could hear him shouting, his voice a fist. I could hear her answering, pleading. More glass breaking, a tumbler or wineglass thrown against a hard surface.

I waited. It was not my problem. Quiet settled. The squall was over.

Three years earlier I had arrested a Peeping Tom. We had gotten complaints from two different apartment complexes in my sector. Prowler, suspicious person. One party had actually seen him looking into a window. I would drive through these places, checking the foliage. One night I caught some movement, hit it with my spotlight.

He started to run, but when I yelled at him he stopped. I checked his ID, ran it through the computer. I asked him what he was doing lurking around the bushes, eleven o'clock at night, five miles from where he lived. He was at a loss.

"I know what you were up to, okay?" I said. "So let's be out front about this."

"I never hurt anyone," he said. He was a couple of years younger than me, very normal. He worked as an optician, fitting eyeglasses at the local mall. Married, two kids. He admitted he had been at that complex before, and at others, "looking around." He spoke like a man suppressing a stutter.

I handcuffed him.

"Is that necessary?" he asked. I told him it was procedure.

You make an arrest, it's like going on a blind date. Between the paperwork and the wait for processing and arraignment, you're sure to spend a few hours with a person you've never seen before. You get to know them. Sometimes there's no chemistry. Sometimes you make a connection, you talk, the evening's a success. Sometimes you even learn something.

"Why go out and look in women's windows?" I asked him.

"Imagine you haven't, um, um, eaten for a week and you hear of a place where they're serving sirloin with all the trimmings. It's way beyond, um, wanting. It's survival. That sounds f-funny to you."

"Would you like it, somebody gawking at your wife?"

He thought about it. "I don't hurt anybody. I just can't not look."

"I'm afraid it's against the law."

"I'm not a pervert. This isn't a sexual thing. You have to understand that."

"Sure I do."

"I mean, it's not just sexual. I have this idea—I can't get it out of my head—that it's all a charade. Everyone on earth—my wife, people at work—they're all putting on an act for my benefit. They aren't real except when they're with me. It's a lonely feeling. So I watch from hiding and see what happens when somebody's alone."

On some level, I understood what the guy was saying. I understood about looking.

The judge gave him probation, ordered him into a treatment program.

"I don't do it for the enjoyment," he told me. "Good God, I'm afraid all the time. I'm terrified. Do you believe that?"

"You're afraid of getting caught."

He shook his head. "No, of myself."

I was no Peeping Tom. Yet I was sitting in the dark looking at a woman's dark window and I couldn't take my eyes away. No light came on.

That night I lay in bed staring at the ceiling for hours.

HEAT MAKES FOR A good party. It loosens people. It brings them out thirsty and lightly dressed and ready to mingle, ready to dance and get wild. The thick, late-summer air that night pulsed with the tom-tom of crickets. The ripe, waning moon seemed half drunk as it pulled itself over the horizon. My two big maple trees rustled their leaves in the settling breeze, sounding like distant applause, as I walked across my backyard to their house.

Lance Travis gripped my hand and hit me with a hundred-watt smile. He might have played tackle in college—he still carried the bulk and his manner brought to mind the enthusiasm of a frat boy. He was the type of guy who made you feel you were his instant friend. Yes, you were the most important person in the world and he was keenly interested in anything you might have to say. He stood too close to you and liked to touch. I suppose for a salesman these were tools of the trade.

"We're talking politics here, Ray. I was saying I think Catlett's one smart cookie and the sky's the limit. Peter doesn't agree."

Peter was a balding puppy of a man I had seen jogging around the streets of the development. "I just said, to become mayor of Mansfield, you have to get your hands dirty. Dirty hands can come back to haunt you."

"That man could swim in a cesspool and climb out smelling like roses," Lance said. "He's coming here later."

The remark drew a round of anticipatory murmurs and subdued laughter from his listeners.

Preparations for the party had gone on for two days. A tent covered a sizable chunk of their lawn. Inside it, linen-covered tables surrounded a hardwood dance floor. A group of tuxedoed musicians shaped jazz ballads. Japanese lanterns dangled everywhere and strings of white Christmas-tree lights draped the bushes. The caterers loaded long tables with London broil and sugar-cured ham, iced oysters and smoked salmon. Perky waitresses carried trays of champagne. Bartenders mixed piña coladas and gin fizzes. A white-faced entertainer juggled and performed off-color mime skits.

I didn't fit with this crowd; they weren't my people. They were the comfortable, the well-to-do, the lawyers and bankers and entrepreneurs who paid my salary. They were the busy people who knew their own importance, crisp, alert people with conscientious suntans, people who thought they were entitled. They had figured the way to play the house odds. They drove Swedish cars and owned purebred dogs. Landscaping, recycling, white wine.

To them, cops were garbage collectors who cleaned up the unpleasant corners of the gleaming world. We were the zookeepers; we smelled of the punk of the animals.

"You didn't tell us what you think about Catlett, Ray," Lance said.

"He's my boss, so I can't really comment."

"You're with the city?"

"I'm a police officer."

He quickly recalculated his take on me. "Well, isn't that something? Wonderful. Peter, pass the word, nobody offers this guy a joint."

They all laughed again.

Peter's wife was Christy. She bared her teeth at me and asked, "You must have some stories to tell."

"Mostly it's just routine, just a job."

"One tough job," Lance said. "I give you guys a hell of a lot of credit."

He slung his arm around my neck. I don't like being touched. I could tell he was a little toasted already, a convivial drinker.

Peter said, "You can probably give us the inside poop on that kid, the one we've been reading about in the papers."

"I saw it on the news," Lance said. "Don't start on that. Somebody's always second-guessing these guys. Things happen, right, Ray? Things happen in a split second that nobody can imagine."

"You're right, things happen."

"Do you carry a gun?" Christy asked me.

"Of course he carries a gun," Peter said. "Cops carry guns."

"I mean wear a uniform?"

"Sure," I said. "A blue one."

I caught sight of Sheila, her simple halter dress bared her back. She returned my glance over her shoulder.

"What's the going price, fix a speeding ticket?" Lance asked.

"Bribery's a crime, Lance," I said, smiling.

He chuckled. "Since when?"

"The Mansfield police have sexy uniforms," Christy said.

We talked some about crime in Mansfield. Lance drifted away to welcome more guests. People were arriving all the time. The smiles could have cut you to pieces.

I'm not good at parties. I stick to the fringes. I watch people. I only imitate their social rituals, hello how are you. Monkey see, monkey do. Small talk, I fall on my face.

I circled the pool to give myself a little distance. I met Sheila there, on the edge of the darkness. She gave me a look that could have meant anything.

"Having a good time?" she asked.

"You have a lot of friends."

"Lance makes friends. He's good at it."

"He seems to be enjoying himself."

"Mister Life-of-the-Party. Nobody can work a crowd like Lance."

I tried to read her eyes.

"Come here, hon," she said. The girl who approached had rings up the rim of her ear, one through her eyebrow, and a stud in her nose. It was the teenager I had seen on their patio, the one I had thought was a boy—the crew cut had thrown me. Her chocolate eyes and ice cream shoulders contrasted with the boy's undershirt and the baggy blue jeans. She looked about fifteen, pale and cocky and fashionably undernourished. Her breasts, beneath the thin fabric, were defiant, as if adolescence were a trick she resented.

"What do you want?" Her voice still played the belligerent scale of a spoiled child.

"This is Brie," Sheila said. "Ray is a policeman, babe."

The girl folded her arms. "So?"

"He lives in that house over there. He's our neighbor."

"That's great. Cops are always hassling us."

"Jesus, Brie. Be nice."

"Why should I?"

"Time comes," I said, "maybe you'll need a friend. We're not all monsters."

"No? What about that Keshawn guy who got killed? All he was doing was playing football, and the cops killed him."

"What guy do you mean?" Sheila asked her.

It was all over the papers. The young man Campisi and Taggart had put in the back of their police car had arrived at the station in a coma. He died a day later. Apparently he'd had a heart condition. Whether the officers had manhandled him on the way in wasn't clear.

I had had to give a statement to Internal Affairs and to the district attorney's office on my day off. I had told what I saw, about Campisi kicking him while he was handcuffed. The official department story was that the guy had violently resisted arrest, that the officers had subdued him with minimal force. The black community in Mansfield wasn't buying. They had good reasons for their suspicion.

Brie gave Sheila a lurid account of brutality, torture, and murder. I didn't venture an opinion, or mention my role in the case.

"They killed him in cold blood," she concluded. "For nothing."

"We can't judge," Sheila said diplomatically. "We can never judge if we weren't there."

"I wasn't at Auschwitz," the girl said. "Can't I judge that?"

"You know what I mean."

"I'm leaving. I'm going to stay over at Pam's tonight."

"Don't tell your father. You need money?"

She grunted. Sheila produced a bill from somewhere and slipped it to her. We watched her amble away.

One of the caterers approached. Sheila had to go off and see about party business.

The big event was the arrival of the mayor. Richard Catlett was a comer, a golden boy. Not much older than me, he was on a trajectory that local pundits imagined would carry him to the political stratosphere. Nice face, easy smile, sharp mind, fluid voice, attractive wife. His manner said he was a sincere man, a man without guile, a man you could trust.

His presence there put the Travises on the Mansfield social map. Lance greeted him like a long-lost brother and posed for a photo. Sheila kissed him on the cheek and shared a joke. Catlett shook hands all around, bubbling with political pep. Half an hour later he was gone, on to another function, somewhere else to be seen.

Word went around that it was time to eat. I joined the line at the buffet table. I carried my plate to a shadowy corner of the lawn and sat on a folding chair. Others found me and formed a group. Lance joined us. He wasn't eating, only sipping from a large drink.

"Insurance," he said, answering someone's question. "I call myself a financial adviser, but bottom line, it's old-fashioned insurance sales."

Someone asked was life insurance a good investment.

"I don't see it as an investment," Lance said. "To me, my clients, it's a gamble. When I talk insurance, I talk big money. Make your heirs millionaires, if you dare—that's my line. A million-dollar policy is not out of budget if you're knocking down decent bucks."

"You mean work your ass off for your wife's second husband," Peter said. He licked grease from his fingers.

"What are you, a cynic?" Lance said, suddenly angry. The drink was making him volatile.

Peter hesitated, not quite sure how to take it.

To cover the silence, Christy talked about old songs she liked. She sang a Paul Simon tune, "Fifty Ways to Leave Your Lover."

She had a nice alto voice. Several other women joined in on the chorus. Just get on the bus, Gus.

Everyone was sliding toward intoxication. Voices grew louder and more liquid.

Lance snatched back the attention of the group. "Life insurance doesn't excite people, a million bucks excites people. They're afraid of tomorrow so . . . hey."

Sheila had leaned over and said something to Christy, who burst out laughing.

"Hey, what's so funny?" Lance's face was coloring now.

"Nothing," Sheila said. "I'm trying to get people to dance."

"You're interrupting me. I told you."

"I'm sorry, dear."

"You want to dance? I'll show you how."

"Please."

"I thought you wanted to dance." He was on his feet now, throwing big gestures.

Sheila stared at him for a second. She frowned nervously, walked away. Lance forced a laugh and held on to it until a few others joined him. He sat down and started telling a joke about a doctor.

Christy insisted I dance with her. We maneuvered under the tent. The band was playing a swing version of a country tune. Christy was full of life. We cut up a lively version of the two-step.

Sheila danced with Peter. I revolved and she revolved and our eyes met. Her face didn't change, but she looked right at me.

The band fell into a slow ballad, an old Patsy Cline number, "Walking After Midnight." From across the tent, Sheila moved her eyes lazily toward me and let a smile slide onto her lips. I made an excuse to Christy and stepped toward Sheila. Without a word, we came together.

I didn't know where to place my hand at first. Finally, I rested it gently on her bare back, where it glowed.

I could smell her hair. A light sheen of perspiration dampened her skin. I imagined her tasting of salt.

I thought that everyone could see, that everyone knew, but no one noticed a thing. We floated on the music. Sheila leaned her head back and smiled into my face. My lungs were sucking pure oxygen.

We swayed together, swayed and swayed, until I suddenly realized that the music had stopped. I pulled away from her.

"Thanks," she said. She patted my arm as if I were a nobody, as if our dance were a hostess's duty. As casual as a breeze, she turned to other guests.

The stairs inside were softly carpeted, the hallway softly carpeted. I pushed against a door that stood open a few inches. I was stepping inside the dimly lit bathroom before I noticed it was occupied.

"Excuse me."

"Hey, pilgrim." Lance sat on the toilet cover. He was scooping white powder from a folded section of aluminum foil onto a mirror that he held on his lap. Before I could retreat, he said, "You've met Christy, haven't you?"

Perched on the bathtub, her legs crossed, Christy smiled "hi" without making a sound.

"You know Ray's a cop?" Lance was arranging the powder into short lines with a single-edge razor blade.

"Sure," Christy told him. "I love cops."

Lance leaned down and vacuumed a couple of lines into his nostrils. I was interested in this man, this person Sheila was attached to.

He handed the mirror to Christy.

"Better watch it, he'll bust your ass," Lance said. He inhaled tightly through his nose. "He prob'ly don't cotton to folks getting high. You want some, Ray? Good crystal. Make you feel mighty powerful."

"No, thanks."

" 'Course, you wouldn't arrest a man in his own home, would you?" He was staring at me defiantly. The booze had given him an attitude. I ran into guys with attitudes all the time. I ran into guys who took a little dope and it made them think they were king of the world.

I didn't answer. Christy licked a finger, rubbed it across the mirror, then onto her gums. Lance pulled her onto his lap and wrapped his arms around her waist.

"How about corrupting the morals of a minor?" he said. "You a minor, little girl?"

"Sure, a minor, forty-niner." She held out her wrists and tittered. "Put me in handcuffs, Officer. I know not what I do."

Lance started to say something else. I turned my back on him and shut the door.

Outside, the party had shifted gears. The conversations blended into a quavering hum punctuated by rim shots of laughter. Champagne and Absolut had worked their magic, unlocked throats, injected a zing into Republican lungs. Dancers crowded the floor, the band blew a breathless tempo. Certified public accountants were telling last week's dreams to strangers.

I caught sight of a connected guy, a district vice president with the electricians union who had done time on a bid-rigging rap a few years earlier. He kept throwing words out the side of his mouth to the blond snuggle-bunny on his arm.

I convinced myself that I had misread the situation. A cop, a mob guy, we were all just characters invited to give the party some zip. Sheila was just a flirty housewife, nothing more. Nothing was brewing, nothing deep was going down.

Peter grabbed me and began to tell me what being a cop was all about. A lot of people figured they watched television, they knew at least as much about it as I did.

A scream, everybody looked. Lance was pulling on Christy's wrist, urging her toward the swimming pool. She laughed and screeched her protests at the same time.

"When Lance is on a bender," her husband told me, "he's a terror."

He was reeling her in, hand over hand up her arm. He wrapped his own arm around her waist. He hoisted her onto his shoulder. Her dress ripped.

She wasn't laughing now. She pounded Lance on the back and yelled, "Stop it!" He spun her around, stumbled toward the pool. Now her scream bent toward hysteria. Her legs kicked frantically.

The ring of spectators laughed. Peter emitted a few dry yucks.

Lance tottered, tripped, and sat down hard on his can. Christy fell on the apron of the pool. Her face became a crying mask. Laughing, Lance pretended to bite her on the calf.

Peter now wandered over and helped Christy regain her feet. She pulled her dress up to inspect an abrasion along her thigh. Some of the guests gathered around her, half laughing, half clucking their tongues at their host's shenanigans.

Lance rose as if on a ship at sea. Someone handed him a drink and he downed it. He thrust his hips lewdly in Christy's direction. The circle of spectators dissolved; the show was over.

Sheila approached her husband to talk to him. Lance stared at her through lidded eyes. I couldn't hear his words, but the movements of his mouth were ugly.

The party quickly resumed speed. I kept my eyes on Sheila and Lance as they moved toward the bar. Lance ordered another drink. They talked for a few minutes, Sheila's hands pleading.

Lance drank. He turned toward his wife and his face changed. With the quick and fluid motion that drunks are capable of, he swept his arm around her neck. For a second it seemed he was about to kiss her. But as she pulled back, he grabbed his own wrist and yanked her down into a headlock. Clenching her in the crook of his elbow, he grabbed a bottle of gin. He upended it. The liquid wet her hair and her face, splashed onto her back and down her dress. She struggled. They both fell into the table. It collapsed and they went down. The bottles and glasses and ice and little cups of lime wedges and maraschino cherries spilled onto the grass. Sheila broke away from Lance's grip. She regained her feet. He laughed with his eyes closed.

By this time several men had responded and stood poised to restrain Lance, but they weren't needed. He got up and navigated a zigzag path toward the back door. He disappeared into the house.

The party changed tone. One by one, then in flurries, couples discovered how late it was. Baby-sitters needed to be taken home. Early morning duties required immediate slumber. The retreat quickly became a rout.

Sheila accepted their sentiments and thanks, exchanged air kisses and half hugs, told everyone how glad she was they could come, how wonderful it had been to see them.

I meant to join the exodus. I certainly didn't intend to be the last to leave. But when Sheila returned to the patio from seeing the other guests off, I was still there. The musicians were carrying their instruments around the side of the house to their van. The caterers were getting rid of what remained of the food. In a few minutes they were all gone. Sheila turned out the lights, leaving only the lurid glow of the pool.

She shook her head wearily. "I don't know what happens. A button gets pushed and he's a different man. He won't even remember this. I've tried to get him into programs, help him control his drinking, but he doesn't think he needs it."

"Are you afraid of him?"

She stared at me for a moment before answering. "Afraid? I guess sometimes I am afraid. I don't know him when he's like this. Sometimes, Ray, I'm not sure how far he'll go." She clamped her palm over her mouth and closed her eyes and sobbed.

The husband right there, I was tentative. I touched her shoulder. She turned away.

"It's a nightmare," she said through her fingers. "Oh, God."

She had done some serious drinking herself, her emotions were sloshing. She pressed a fist to her forehead and wept openly.

"I told you before," I said. "If you need me, call. Anytime. Okay? Don't be afraid."

She sniffed and licked her lips and nodded. "Thanks," she said. "Christ, I reek."

She fingered her dress and wrinkled her nose at the booze stench. Then in one motion she unzipped and stepped out of it. A second later she was diving naked into the pool.

I held my breath while she swam underwater. She came up and smoothed her hair back and sighed. She walked along the shallow end. She turned to me and gave a little embarrassed smile, as if she'd forgotten I was there. She covered herself with one arm.

"I'll be running along," I said.

"It's okay. I get carried away. I'll be all right. You don't have to—"

We both turned toward the noise that came from the house. She climbed up quickly and wrapped herself in one of the towels piled by the side of the water. The patio door slid back and Brie emerged.

"You're back early," Sheila said, making her voice normal. "I thought you were staying—"

"Pam and I had a fight. She's a bitch. I hitchhiked home." She gave me a sidelong glance.

"Brie, I told you about that. You're taking a terrible chance—isn't she, Ray?"

"There are some bad people out there," I said.

"Why do you let him get like that?" Brie said, pointing toward the house.

"If I had any way to control him, honey, don't you think I would? You know how he is when he drinks."

"It makes me sick. What if I had friends over? It's disgusting."

"It's something we're going to have to deal with as a family, Brie."

"A family?" she said with a sneer. "You people."

I said the appropriate words and began to cut across the yard toward my house.

I glanced over my shoulder. The girl was already heading inside. Sheila nodded good night to me. I could feel her eyes on me as I walked along the grass. When I looked back again, she was gone. Orion was climbing over their house.

"THIS CAMERA CAN see in very low light," she said. "I won't need to turn on floodlights. I won't get in your way."

She folded one of her long legs and faced me across the seat of the patrol car. She flicked a switch on the camera and turned it so I could look through the viewer. Even in the dim light the tiny image of her was luminous. Her lean face smiled at me. She waved.

"Cute," I said. "I hope you're not looking for excitement. This job can be damn boring."

"I know that. We're trying to show a patrolman's actual experience, not the tabloid stuff. We're trying to get some communication going. I think it's overdue, don't you?"

"People see these programs, they think they know what a cop's job is. They don't."

"Maybe not. But I'm going to try and portray what's going on inside your head."

"I doubt if you want to know what's going on inside my head," I said. I gave her the wolf eye, but she didn't respond and I felt stupid.

"Why's that?" she said.

"Forget it. Let's go." I put the car in gear and headed onto the street.

I had seen her on the tube plenty of times—Channel Ten Eyewitness News, Leanne Corvino, perky, athletic, with the pixie hair, the earnest face, the polished voice. She was hard to take seriously— too young-looking maybe, too eager. She wore clothes well and her teeth gleamed in perfect rows.

I was articulate, Captain Barnes had told me. I would make the department look good. A buttoned-down administrator with a college degree and a master's in social work, Barnes had been acutely embarrassed by the incident in his station house. He was anxious to polish our image. He told me I was smart enough to know what not to say.

"This is all public relations," I said to her. "You know that, don't you?"

"Of course I do. We've been trying to set this up for months. Now, all of a sudden. It's the Keshawn Pitts thing—his death, the lawsuit. I covered that."

"I saw you."

"I understand you were there the night he died."

"That's not something I can discuss."

"They say you talked to the grand jury. They say your version was that certain officers seemed to have a grievance against Pitts, that they roughed him up more than anyone's admitting."

I stared at her and let her read what she wanted to in my face. I played the honest cop who's discreet enough to keep his mouth closed.

"Okay, I'm guessing. But people are asking a lot of questions about the police in Mansfield. Racism is certainly a factor inside the department, isn't it?"

"Can I really talk to you or do you just want a sound bite?"

The red light on the front of the camera stopped blinking.

I said, "The people of this city, black and white, want protection. They don't want to be afraid. They hire us to make that happen. It's dirty work. It's always going to be. Who are we? Ordinary working men, working women. Prejudiced? Sure, some of us. Just like the guy in the office or driving the truck. Race comes into it, it's always going to come into it. But we're not all racists. End of sermon."

"I don't think you're a racist. I do think you're playing dumb."

"Meaning what?"

"The guy in the office or driving the truck isn't carrying a gun, isn't wearing a badge. The police in this city have a serious problem. Is that problem a reflection of society? Sure. But a man is dead, for Christ's sake."

"I'm not pretending."

"Yes, you are. You don't trust me. You don't realize you can trust me." She smiled again.

Having her sitting beside me in the car made me acutely aware of all the little things that had become routine. She was curious, asked me questions about what I was doing and why. Suddenly the whole drill was new again. I became self-conscious about the way I did my job.

She also made me realize what a solitary job it was, alone in a patrol car. You're the Lone Ranger, without Tonto. You're isolated in that car night after night. You get used to talking to yourself. Now she filled the space with her presence and with a hint of musky perfume, and filled me with a longing that genuinely surprised me.

The season had taken the first turn toward autumn, the night was chill.

I made a routine traffic stop, glad to perform for her. The Pontiac had swerved too wide taking the turn by the Mobil station on Lansing. Leanne was nimble climbing out. I could feel the stare of the camera as I approached the driver's window, as I went through the license-and-registration check, the initial size up.

"Step out of the car, please."

Hispanic male, five-six, one-sixty, dirty sweatshirt, upper right incisor missing.

He wasn't able to stand, extend his foot, and lean back without teetering. He bogged down reciting the alphabet. I wasn't sure if he could recite it sober. He definitely wasn't sober.

I slapped cuffs on him, gave him his rights, called him "sir." I summoned another patrol car to come and take the prisoner back to the lockup. I was supposed to stay on the street that night.

"You were nice to him," she observed.

"It's no act," I said. "I don't condemn somebody for taking a drink. They respect me, I respect them. The golden rule. Or maybe I can't help putting on an act."

She gave me a look I knew, a little tang in the eyes that was undoubtedly a suggestion, an opening gambit. "What's the key to being a cop?" she said.

"The key? I guess it's to keep your eyes open."

"Awareness, you mean?"

"You ever see a prize fight?"

"My dad used to take me up to the old Armory A.C. He loved the fights."

"Then maybe you know. A boxer lives in his eyes. The whole idea is to look, never flinch, never stop staring at your opponent. That's the most important thing and the hardest. The great fighters, their eyes are always alive."

"And being a cop is like that?"

I nodded. "You don't miss anything. I say the job is boring, but the truth is I'm never bored. Why? I pass a corner, I look. I pass it again an hour later, I'm looking again. What's different? Who's on the street I haven't seen before? Who's spending money, he never used to have any? Why is that door open? Why is that light on, or not on? You look and you look. You're always suspicious. Always glancing at the rearview. Always shining your flashlight into the car you stop. Prying eyes."

"I like that," she said. "Prying eyes. I can use that."

I drove over to Henry Street to assist Emergency Services on a "man down" call. It turned out to be a drunk sleeping it off. The paramedics roused him, got him on his feet. He refused aid, and swayed on down the street fighting some inner storm.

Back in the car she asked me, "Why did you decide to be a cop?"

"I guess everybody's got their drug, maybe it's booze, maybe it's women, maybe it's money. For a cop—for me, anyway—it's the rush. It's those times when the action starts and everything just shines. Does that make any sense?"

"I think so."

"I hate to use the word *beautiful*. But on an adrenaline rush, the world can be very beautiful. It's what I live for."

I pulled into the Taco Bell on Norton. We climbed out of the car and bought a couple of burritos and Cokes and sat on plastic stools at a pebbly concrete table. Night was settling in. The cool air smelled clean.

"I tell you these things because people think cops are clowns. Some are. Some want a license to be a bully. But for most of us, it's both simple and complicated. It's a job."

"Thanks for opening up about it."

"You mind if I ask you something off the record?" I said. "Something personal?"

She rolled her eyes.

"Corvino?" I said.

"Sam? He's my uncle."

"Sammy Two-Fish?"

"He answers for his own sins, which he's doing right now, five to ten in Atlanta. So?"

"Just a cop question."

Two-Fish used to be connected to the Steve Maggadino clan when Big Steve ran everything between Cleveland and Toronto. To people in Mansfield, Corvino was a man to know. Everybody's pal. Terry Ohlson, whom I had gone through the academy with, had gotten caught on Two-Fish's pad and had been dragged before the grand jury and lost his pension.

"How about you?" I asked her.

"I used to pretend to be a reporter when I was four. I was thrilled when they hired me to do the weather—I had taken a couple of earth science courses, so they called me a meteorologist. I did the chance-of-showers-take-your-umbrella thing. Smiled till my face hurt. Finally moved up to features. Now I get to do some investigative stuff. My dream is a job with the networks."

"You like it."

"I like finding out things, discovering the world. Talking to you, for example, it's very satisfying. And I guess there's something about being on television, reaching all those people. It turns me on the way action turns you on."

"You like to be seen."

"I have five sisters, maybe I didn't get enough attention growing up. But yeah, I like the idea of people looking at me. It's a kind of drug. You get on network and it's millions of people, millions of eyes."

Back in the car, the camera formed a wall of glass between us. But every now and then she looked up from the viewfinder and the glass dissolved. She had sweet eyes. A thought began forming in my mind.

"I can see why they chose you," she said. "I figured they would pick somebody squeaky clean to act as poster boy for the department—you're that. But you're also a human being, Ray."

"Let's not exaggerate."

"We should stay in touch. Being a reporter is all about connections."

"A patrol cop?"

"You know things. I mean it. We definitely have to see each other again. I like you." She had the direct friendliness that you see in a lot of Italian girls. All the gear wheels inside me turned another notch.

"How do you stay detached emotionally?" she asked for the camera. "How do you keep the job from—"

The radio crackled. "Sector seven patrol, we have shots fired at 719 North Fremont."

I snatched the mike.

"Patrol one seven responding. I'm on Hardwick, at the corner of Alston."

Two other units announced that they were heading toward Fremont. I turned on my light bar, hit the siren.

"You may get a juicy one after all," I said.

"Tell me." She hefted the camera.

"It's the type of call you don't know what you'll find—somebody shooting firecrackers or two people dead."

I whipped around a corner, killed the siren, floored it.

"How far away is it?"

In the middle of a block of dirty houses I pulled to the curb.

"We're here."

I DIDN'T SLAM the car door. You need a delicate touch in a situation like that. Everything quiet—everything light. I could hear the creak of my equipment belt as I climbed out.

Sensations were cascading. Time had speeded up and slowed down.

"Stay by the car."

She didn't stay by the car. She followed me up the steps, balancing the camera on her shoulder as she ran. I didn't take the time to argue with her.

The world went technicolor. A dirty rubber doll lay on the top step, its hands in an Egyptian dance pose. One blue eye stared wide open, the other winked at me. Half of its lemon hair was missing, leaving rows of pinholes on its scalp.

Eight mailboxes on the front porch told of eight apartments. The boxes were rusted, the names scrawled on masking tape. A Coke can clogged with wilted dandelions perched on the edge of the railing.

I laid my back against the wall and reached over to try the door. It swung open easily. I took a deep breath. The outside air was perfumed with the umber smell of early autumn. A dirty moon was rising through the trees across the street.

I crashed inside, gun first, safety off.

A gray-haired black woman in a pink satin bathrobe looked out the door of an apartment, her eyes stretched.

"He's upstairs," she whispered. She slowly nodded her head, agreeing with herself.

I mounted the staircase, through the odors of cooked cabbage and wet cigarette butts and pine-scented linoleum. Obscene hieroglyphics were gouged into the turquoise plaster. A halo of white fluorescent light shone down from over the top of the stairs and lit a scene of chaos—several women, half a dozen kids, three men, all talking and dancing and waving their hands.

Leanne came right behind me. I could feel her.

Two of the women ran to meet me. I lowered my pistol to the side of my leg. Husband, ex-husband, little girl, wife, order of protection, son of a bitch, warned him, kill himself, if he hurts her—they went on and on.

"Who's involved?" I asked.

They pointed to an obviously excited white woman, slender build, ponytail, barely twenty behind the midnight eyeshadow and the lipstick. A pretty face but one whose prettiness was all in its youth—in five years she would fade into the wallpaper.

"He has my daughter!" she gasped. She pointed toward the next apartment.

I motioned everyone back and moved toward the open door, keeping concealed behind the jamb. "Who is he?"

"He's going to kill her. He said he'd kill her and he will. Oh God, Mimi. He ain't kidding, Officer. He's a goddamn lunatic, show-off *dickhead*!" She tried to get past me and yelled into the apartment with a voice that seemed too large for her. She was strong, surging with the energy of high excitement.

I felt as if I knew her, somebody who rushes into adulthood too fast, who overnight has a kid, a faithless boyfriend, money problems, and dreams that she carries around in the pockets of her Wal-Mart clothes, gradually wearing them out.

"He fired the gun?"

"Fired it? He fired it three, four times. If he hurts that kid, I won't just kill him."

"He's armed now?"

"Sure he's armed." She called, "Mimi? Are you all right, hon? Mommy loves you."

I said, "He's your husband?"

"He ain't my husband. I told him, stay away from here. Just stay away. He says it's his kid. That is not his kid and he knows it. He don't have any kid. He never gonna have a kid, ever."

"Where is he?"

"In the bedroom. He's got her, says he's gonna kill her, kill himself, nobody can stop him. Please help me! Please, she's all I got."

"What's his name?"

"Danny." I had to hold her back again. "They're going to kill you dead, you son of a bitch! You're going to hell, what you're doing. Eternity, you hear me? *Eternity!*"

A gunshot split the air. Several of the onlookers screamed. I spoke into my shoulder mike. I briefly described the situation, told the dispatcher I was going to try to stabilize things. I glanced at Leanne, who was intent on filming me. For a second she looked away from the viewfinder and met my eyes. Her face was ecstatic.

"You stay here," I said to the mother. "Do not come into this apartment. I'm going to talk to him. I want everybody to keep calm."

No, you don't do it this way. You wait for backup. You wait for hostage negotiators. You don't cowboy it.

I went in.

A ratty couch covered with a stained green fabric. A smell of diapers and despair. A bureau with the drawers hanging open, a broken mirror on top. Beer cans, potato chip bags, dirty clothes, overflowing ashtrays, toys. A child's jigsaw puzzle, a map of the United States, half the pieces gone. I had seen a hundred apartments just like it—it was where poverty lived. To the right a kitchen area, sink, stove, under-the-counter refrigerator. To the left an open door.

I hugged the wall moving toward the bedroom.

A noise from behind. I jerked around, pointed the gun. Leanne had ducked around the edge of the apartment door with her camera. Okay, they wanted public relations, they were getting public relations. I wasn't responsible for her.

I edged closer to the door.

"Danny?" I said. My voice was dead calm.

A long pause. "Whaddaya want?"

I urged him to keep cool. Nobody wanted to hurt him. Everybody just wanted this thing to wind down, no real harm done. Not yet.

Behind me I could hear other officers arriving. I held up my hand to signal to them.

"We need to talk this thing out, Dan."

"Talk to her," he said. "She's the one. You're the one, you fuck-ing *bitch!*"

"We will talk to her. Right now, I want to get straight with you. This isn't about her. It's you and me."

I heard a child whimper, say something. Leanne had moved closer behind me

"I'll kill her!" the voice shouted.

"You don't need to kill anybody, Danny. We can talk. You and I can talk. Okay?"

I was desperate to resolve the situation. I had gone in there against all the protocols. The only way to redeem myself was to make it come out the way I wanted, to force my will on the situation, to be a hero.

"Danny, I need to come in there with you, okay? I'm putting my gun away. We don't need guns here, you and I. I'm going to trust you, man. This is not about guns. Okay? Just lower your weapon, don't point it at anybody."

I tucked my pistol back into its holster. Slowly, step by step, I rounded the doorjamb.

The man was sitting on a rumpled bed, his arm around a girl, maybe four years old. The big stainless revolver he held to her head made her look tiny.

His eyes met mine, dropped. Something in him, maybe, was still capable of shame. He said, "She claims she was going with him all the time. She wasn't going with him. This is my kid. I know Mimi's mine. She's telling everybody."

Skinny, tattooed, wispy beard. The gun looked like a big Colt, maybe a Python, an ego piece.

"You've got a legitimate complaint, Danny. We can talk about that."

"She's not going to have this kid. She'll bring this kid up hating me. That ain't right. Hate her father?"

A television on the dresser against the wall was flashing color.

Every few seconds a spasm of laughter spilled out. The little girl was watching the familiar movement. She whimpered, her eyes raw.

"Mimi knows you love her. Don't you, sweetheart? You love Daddy, don't you?"

Her eyes reached around to try to see the gun. She pressed her lips together and nodded.

"People care about you, Danny. People care what happens to you."

The little girl looked at me for the first time. She was struggling to keep a cry inside.

"I want my rights," Danny said. "I've got rights. Right is right."

"You'll get your rights. That's what we're here for. First we have to ease out of this situation we've gotten into."

"You don't know what I'm talking about."

"Sure I do. I have a little girl of my own," I lied. "She's not much older than Mimi. Her name's Jennifer. I know how you can love somebody so much it hurts."

I could see the girl's little chin trembling.

"She's got the cops on her side. She's got everything. I'm going to fucking show her."

"That's not going to solve anything," I said. "You're not going to teach anybody any lessons. That's just what she wants."

"I've fucking had it. You don't know what pain is."

He cocked the gun.

Mimi put a strand of her blond hair to her mouth and sipped it. She glanced at me, then back at the television. She gave her shoulder a shrug where the underside of the revolver was digging at her.

"Danny." I took a step forward.

"Stay away. You get the hell away."

"Sure. I'm staying away. I just want you to uncock that gun. We don't want any accidents."

"You don't get it, do you? I am taking Mimi with me. I am leaving her *nothing*!"

"You want to be with your daughter. I'll arrange for it to happen. I'll personally make sure. Okay, Danny? I give you my word."

The odd thing was, Danny was watching the television, too. He couldn't help it.

Now he looked at me. I could see that he was caught between hopelessness on one hand and the seduction of notoriety on the other. Suddenly, everybody was paying attention to him. He enjoyed that. He was calling all the shots for once in his life.

A commercial for precooked gourmet entrées came on. "Dee, dee, dee, dee—licious."

"Fuck her," Danny said. "I'm nothing? It's not mine? I'm out of the picture? She'll see."

He had the child by the neck now, his thumb jabbed under her ear. She closed her eyes and began to sob. The barrel of the revolver pressed against her temple.

I calculated the space between us. Two steps.

"Danny!" I put a lot of authority into it. "Put the gun down. Put it down now!"

He swung the barrel casually toward me. He was hyperventilating.

"I'll give her. Something. To remember."

For a fraction of a second, the pistol wavered. He had lost his focus. He wasn't sure of his next move.

"Look at me!" I said.

Danny moved his eyes.

My foot was planted. I vaulted forward. I landed with my knee on the bed, my hand wrapped around the top of the gun and jammed against the hammer.

Mimi screamed.

Danny breathed into my face. His eyes were weak. He lowered them.

"Go to your mother, Mimi," I said. "Go on now. Let her go."

She looked around at him for permission, her eyes so vulnerable it stabbed me right in the chest.

"It's okay," I told her. "Nobody's going to hurt you."

She slid down, ran through the door.

In an instant the room was full of cops. They had Danny on the floor, hands cuffed behind his back. One of them took the perp's gun from my hand, unloaded it, slid it into a plastic bag.

I needed to sit. I brushed a pile of dirty socks from a chair. I was in a zone where all the sounds around me blended into a blur. For a few minutes, my nerves shorted out, I just couldn't get a grip.

When I closed my eyes, they suddenly burned with tears. I pressed a fist against the side of my nose and held my breath.

Then cool light fingers touched my neck.

"You okay?" Leanne said.

"Sure."

She put her camera down. She squatted beside me, squeezed my hand.

They were taking Danny out. I stood and followed. I wanted to see it through.

Two television news vans had picked up the action on their scanners and were staking out the front of the house already, interviewing bystanders. We led Danny out the back way to an alley behind the house.

I was glad to breathe the air.

Danny had a stunned look on his face as they dumped him in the backseat of the cruiser.

"Danny," I said, leaning in. "One thing."

He looked. I slammed my fist into his belly. He doubled over, retching, gasping for breath.

"How does it feel to be helpless?"

I pulled him up by the hair, hit him in the torso three more times.

"Like a little child," I whispered to him. "Just like a little child."

I ducked out of the car and slammed the door.

"I'll cut that part," Leanne said, turning off the camera.

"I trust you."

"This is real news. I have to get back to the studio. This is going to be so powerful. Can we talk later?"

"I'm down at Mullin's after work."

"Wait for me."

"A MANSFIELD POLICE OFFICER put his own life on the line this evening to save the life of a four-year-old girl. I was riding with Officer Ray Dolan when the call came in. We're going to show you highlights of this dramatic incident from the moment it began until its startling conclusion."

I had never seen myself on television. I didn't really look like that, did I? That nose? That wasn't the way I talked, the way I acted. It was somebody playing a role, a Ray Dolan imitator.

I sipped my beer and watched the screen at the end of the bar. Some laughs of recognition sounded when the thing started, then the place grew very quiet. I knew what was coming, but each event surprised me—the arrival, the jerky run up the stairs. It was edited so that it all came in a terrible rush.

I cringed at my bravado—racing in there like that went against all the rules. Mister Macho Man. It was a cowboy stunt that they should show to every rookie in the academy—a perfect example of how not to do it.

Yet I was secretly glad I had done it. Everybody wants the light to shine on him sooner or later. Everybody thinks he deserves it.

The odd thing was, sitting there watching it, I was thinking of Sheila, watching myself through her eyes. I wanted her to see this. I wanted her to be excited by it. I wanted her to admire my heroics.

Leanne kept the camera focused on me. I sounded calm, convincing. I said all the right things to the guy, really put it over on him. I sounded like someone you could trust, the voice of reason.

I watched myself step into the bedroom. She had not gotten an angle to see inside. You heard indistinct voices, then the little girl ran out.

It was over. She filmed me with the revolver in my hand. From there she cut to Mimi crying in her mother's arms as the two of them pirouetted around the shabby apartment.

"We go to the movies these days looking for heroes," she said, talking into a microphone outside the house. "But sometimes we forget that there are real heroes walking around among us. Because of Officer Dolan's courage and dedication a little girl is asleep in her bed tonight."

The picture switched back to the anchorman. The bar exploded in shouts and clapping. I shook my head.

Guys came over to me, guys I knew, cops I had only spoken to in the code of kidding we used in the station house. They shook my hand, they patted my back, they told me in all seriousness that I was a hero. That I made them proud. That what I had done was something, really something. Everybody wanted to buy me a drink.

I was still riding the action euphoria. It made me restless, made my eyes hungry, burned the alcohol inside me.

I turned, sensing. She had just entered. I watched her make her way across the bar, her face glowing with her triumph. I made a decision—the decision made itself. She would be my salvation. She would keep me from straying, keep me from the near occasion of sin. I told myself this almost joking, yet understanding that it was serious, that something important was playing itself out.

I ordered her a drink and we moved to a booth against the far wall. I would be honest with her, I decided. I would not just put on the habitual shining armor of charm that had carried me through my various conquests.

"You got it wrong," I said. "I'm no hero."

She laughed.

"I mean it. I screwed up tonight. I didn't follow procedures."

"You followed your gut feeling, your heart."

"It was all wrong, a cowboy move."

"You had to act fast."

"The rules are, you secure the scene, you send for hostage negotiators."

"The hell with rules. You saved that girl's life. You're a good man, a good cop."

Her sincerity annoyed me. "You think you know me?"

"I think we've been through something together. Plus, I checked on you before we went out. I looked you up. Your father was a cop, right? Sergeant Edward Dolan?"

"That's right."

"And something bad happened."

"You could say that."

"And you don't want to talk about it."

"It's common knowledge. He was stupid enough to take a bribe in an election year. Reprimanded, busted down to a beat. He wasn't a bright man, Teddy Dolan. Just a dumb Irish cop. But he worked his ass off to make sergeant. And he was a good cop. A good, underpaid cop who did what they all did. If you didn't do it, you were a holier-than-thou asshole. But the politicians, they had to make an example."

"I'm sorry to bring it up."

"No, that's all right. He deserves to be talked about." The events of the evening, the drinking, had loosened something in me. Words wanted to be said, memories wanted a breath of air, wanted light— they were tired of only sneaking out of the dank basement during nightmares. "We had a shed out in back. My father went out there— this is about five months after the scandal. We thought he was adjusting pretty well. I heard a shot. He used to do a lot of target practice, but not at night. I ordered my mother to stay in the house. It was the only time I ever ordered her to do anything. I knew what I would find. He was dead." I had never told this to a woman before. I pushed my tongue around in my mouth, surprised at the razor blade caught in my throat.

"Oh, Christ. That's hard. That's very, very hard. I'm—"

"I swore I would never become a cop, never live in Mansfield."

"What happened?"

"Wheels turn. I came back to take care of my mother. I got a job with the Pinkertons. I found out I liked it, liked the boredom, liked cruising the parking lots of factories, checking doors. I took some courses in law enforcement at the community college. It happened."

"Nine years on the force," she said, "six citations for bravery and meritorious service."

I shook my head. "Tonight, I put that kid in a lot more danger by walking in there. I got lucky."

"Maybe that's what being a hero's all about, luck."

She flashed me that perfect smile. It was the smile of a June day.

"Anyway," she said, "getting that footage was a hell of a boost for my career, sweetheart." She was being honest with me, dropping the pose. Good.

We talked the way people do who have something in common but don't know each other. I told her about going joy riding as a teenager, how it seemed natural a cop's son should raise a little hell. She told me about her big Italian family, how each of her sisters had at least three kids.

Then it was time. We had both had enough to drink, we were primed, colors were bright, the future was beckoning. I invited her to my place for a nightcap.

We drove out in separate cars. She was surprised I lived in the big rambling house.

"I would have thought an apartment was more your speed, a bachelor pad. This place is great. It has a real personality."

While I made her a drink I talked a little about the stars, my interest in astronomy. She was enthusiastic, wanted to look right away.

The night sky was clean. She hugged herself while I set up the telescope and aligned it. She leaned over to look. She sighed and said, "My God."

I talked about red giants. "After tens of millions of years they collapse in exactly one second. Then they explode. The light they give off is a supernova, brighter than a billion stars. Sometimes you can see it during the day, it's that brilliant."

She told me how amazing that was. I brushed her smiling face with my knuckles. We kissed, lightly at first. I cupped the seat of her blue jeans. She leaned into me, trusting, a little drunk. I touched my fingers to the back of her neck, and felt her arms go around me, and looked over her shoulder at the dark windows of Sheila's house.

I had been half expecting her to appear at her window. I was aroused and ashamed and afraid. Ashamed of what and afraid of what I couldn't have said.

I had to return to bring the telescope in; Leanne stepped out to her car. She carried the video camera and a tripod to my bedroom.

She plugged the camera into my television, handed it to me, showed me how to work it. The bright, luminous image of her did a quick dance in the viewer. I zoomed in and out comically. She struck a pose. We laughed. She dropped her leather jacket to the floor. I worked the focus. She dipped her chin and smiled at me coyly. Her fingers danced down the front of her shirt. She turned her back, bared it. Her shoulder blades floated.

I put the camera down. She stepped toward me. We kissed in earnest. While I undressed she mounted the camera on the tripod.

"It adds a certain spice, don't you think?" she said. "Like having the eye of God on you."

She panned down me, zoomed. My bucking, mule-faced cock filled the screen. We both laughed. It was a good note. For some women laughter breaks the spell. It was healthy, I thought, to laugh.

She stretched her high-jumper's body along the bed. She squirmed a little, making the springs jingle. She was watching the screen. She waved at the camera with her toes. The bed groaned in protest as I climbed onto it.

It was not like watching yourself in a mirror. Those eerie people wrestling on the tube were more remote. Their actions seemed a parody of what we were doing.

Because of the light, our eyes were dark shadows. On the screen, her small breasts and slim hips looked even more girlish. I gripped her, pinned her, held her wrists as she writhed beneath me. I was surprised by the strength of her slender arms.

I thought of all the guys who had undressed her in their minds while they watched her on the nightly news. It fascinated me, the idea of this pretty face being flashed over all those television screens, ten thousand images of those eyes scattered around the city. She was a star.

I never forgot about the camera. I couldn't lose myself, couldn't forget myself. We went through all the motions, but we went no further.

Later, I looked over at the television and saw two spent bodies sprawled across the wrinkled sheets. I rolled my head back toward her million-dollar smile. She kissed me on the eyes. Drained, I fell into darkness.

I awoke in some dark corner of night. Leanne was asleep beside me. She had turned off the TV and covered us both with a quilt. Now her slack lips were young in sleep.

A quick flash of the hostage scene sprinted through my mind, the little girl staring at him, her captor's whining voice, the big efficient pistol.

I needed to get up. I found myself in the spare bedroom. I didn't go there, didn't plan it. It happened the way things happen in a dream.

I stood close to the window and waited. Watched and waited.

Her light. Why now? A glimpse of her moving like a caged animal.

Why did that sweet and supple body in my room, the one whose warm breath had just now merged with mine, seem so distant? My salvation. Why was I drawn to this window? Why did the sight of Sheila's distant form scald my eyes?

She moved into view. I couldn't make out her face. She stopped, casually lifted her leg, propped it on something. She poured lotion into her hands and smoothed it along her calf and thigh.

Rules. Of all the pleasures, I thought, letting go of the rules is one of the deepest. You tie yourself down with rules. So many possibilities bloom when you stop clinging to them that it takes your breath away. It frightens you.

I was frightened. Terrified. Entranced. Shivering. I was gritting my teeth, straining to look, to see more, to take in everything, to possess her image.

Sheila passed in front of the window. She stopped. She lifted her hands to her hair. The robe fell open. It was a simple, absolutely innocent gesture, a gesture that touched me inside my bones.

The night dissolved. I must have stood there for an hour. Maybe longer. Long after her light went out. I stood there, looking out at nothing, my empty eyes yearning for Sheila.

RAIN IS GOOD on a stakeout. People don't look around; you can sit practically on top of them and they won't see you.

The drops were drumming softly on the roof of Frank Kaiser's Sable, a steady autumn rain. We had parked on a street in the peaceful north side of town, across from the brick buildings of the state college. We waited. A soiled evening was settling in.

Frank had the attributes of a good detective. He was smart, but it's possible for a detective to be too smart. A detective needs to be able to understand stupidity. Frank had the knack of thinking like somebody with limited intelligence. He could slow his thoughts, see connections that a typical street criminal might make, see the logic in absurdity.

And he was relentless. You couldn't wear him down. Years back, somebody slit the throat of a Culver Avenue prostitute on the Fourth of July. Kaiser kept the case open for six years. He developed evidence and cleared that murder after even her own family had forgotten her.

"I've worked a thousand stakeouts," he was telling me now. "I like it. Some guys, they fall asleep, they can't keep their attention up. You look away five seconds, just to ease your eyes, your man could be gone and you spend the rest of the night looking at nothing. For me, it comes natural. All you need's an iron bladder and an imagination that doesn't run away with you. You need to get inside of time, not anticipate. It could happen six hours from now, or it could happen in an instant. You climb inside of time and you wait. You're ready."

He was talking like this to keep away from the reason why we were there. He told me a story about a case I vaguely remembered, a woman who was afraid her husband was going to do her. Jealousy was involved, and quite a lot of money. Frank found out the husband had met with a contract killer and planned to see him again to firm the deal. So he tailed the husband for three days, stuck with him everywhere he went. The last day—it was raining—Frank followed him to a gun shop. Maybe he had changed his mind and decided to do it himself. He came out with a package and drove home. He parked the car in his garage but didn't come right out. Suddenly, boom. Frank ran inside, the guy is dead, shot himself.

"You never know," he said now. "Most guys, they kill her first. You have to give this one credit. All he was doing was making a mess for the wife to find. Look-what-you-made-me-do kind of thing."

I nodded. Suddenly he seemed to wake up and said, "Oh, shit. What am I fucking talk about?"

He meant because of my father. I said, "It's okay, Frank. It's all scar tissue. You can talk to me."

"I'm not thinking. This thing . . ."

"What is it, exactly? What are we doing here?"

A couple of college girls came out of the classroom building across the street.

"You'll see, get ready," Kaiser said. "Watch. Here, take a close look." He handed me a pair of binoculars.

More students emerged, a crowd. I glanced through the lenses. Most of them were kids. They wore sneakers and jeans, lots of sports logos, knapsacks. They were running, holding jackets over their heads.

"I see nothing, Frank."

"Wait. I've watched them before. I'm here every Tuesday and Thursday night. You'll see."

The school door closed. I said, "Is this about Elaine?"

"Hey, you're not watching. What did I tell you? One second, you miss the whole show."

I raised the binoculars again and recognized her through the glass door even before she came out. I knew Elaine's walk.

The man first. He opened an umbrella and held the door for her. Dark hair, dark complexion. An Indian or Pakistani, maybe. Slender, amiable, full of smiles. He took her arm and made sure the umbrella was over her.

"There," Kaiser said. "You see? There it is."

"I see. So? They're friends. It's raining."

"Friends? That's Elaine. That's the woman I'm married to. Friends? He's banging her. He's banging my wife. I swear to God, Ray, this is no joke."

I continued to watch as they walked toward the curb. The man's mouth was moving. I could imagine the musical lilt of his voice. Elaine was taking it in. He was telling her something interesting.

"He's her goddamn teacher," Frank said. "Tariq Patel, they're all named Patel. Ph.D. in psychology from the University of Rochester. Thirty-nine. Never married. Eleven years at SUNY Mansfield. Tenure, a job for life. Owns a big brick house on Lockport Avenue, a hundred-and-eighty-thousand-dollar mortgage. Teaches the psychology of gender roles. Nice touch, huh? Five credit cards. Cellular phone. Bought the Volvo last year. And get this, his brother was indicted two years ago for tax fraud, runs a gasoline wholesale business. This Tariq was questioned, claimed he had no knowledge of the case. But he had loaned the brother a shitload of money."

"You see him walking with her after class and you go into it that deep?"

"Don't bullshit me, Ray. Look at them."

He was right. There was nothing specific you could point to, but you could tell. They were together in a way that wasn't casual.

Elaine was my age. I could imagine her thinking what I had been thinking lately, thirty-five, turning a corner in life, need to pick up the pace. Maybe for women it hits even more deeply. For a man, money and know-how can still draw the babes. A woman's ammo gets used up faster.

"Keep looking," Frank said.

They were climbing into a Volvo station wagon. Through the binoculars, in the dim interior, I could see them kiss, the quick candy kiss of new lovers.

I remembered a time, it must have been two summers before, when I had gone fishing with Frank and Elaine out on Lake Erie. Frank wasn't a fisherman, but he loved boats, and Elaine was enthusiastic about hooking the big bass and walleyes. Frank had rented a small cabin cruiser and we had passed the day fishing and drinking beer—a replay of the old days when we used to spend so much time together.

But I had sensed a tension that surprised me. Elaine was happy, but happy in herself. They weren't sharing. Their bickering now had more acid in it, like a skirmish before a big battle. At the time, I had tried to ignore it and enjoy the water and the sunshine.

We had all gotten sunburned. As we were driving home, Frank's pager had gone off. He called in. They wanted him to take a homicide, a shotgun robbery of a Friendly's. He dropped the two of us at my house because it was closer to the scene and asked me to drive Elaine home. He had taken off as if he were relieved.

I had made the usual comments to Elaine about being a cop's wife. She didn't respond. To cheer her up, I suggested we stop at a steakhouse for a drink. We both found that we were starving, so we had dinner, too. I asked how things were going between the two of them. She said fine, couldn't be better, I'm used to this.

But then she had added, "I know he thinks he loves me. But love's not an idea, it's a presence. And he's not there."

I had been unsure what she meant. When I dropped her, we kissed. We had kissed many times before, in a friendly way. This went beyond friendly.

I had been faced with a choice that day. But as I say, I live by rules. The wife of a friend? Still, I had caught a glimpse of a side of Elaine that I had not suspected. It made me realize that her life with Frank, the Elaine that I had known for those years, that was only a facet of her.

So now I was less surprised than I would have been, less surprised, maybe, than Frank had been when he found out.

"This is funny," Frank was saying. "Life is playing a little joke on me. Don't you get it? You put in your time, you do your duty, you give up things, you sacrifice—I sacrificed for her—you spend your nights worrying, you try and try and try, and what you end up with is the sole of a shoe in your teeth. That's funny. That's the cosmic joke, Ray."

Elaine and her teacher were driving away now. I put down the binoculars. "You talk to her?"

"I talked. She talked. She's leaving me." I could hear the finality in his words, as if he were announcing that somebody was dead.

Eye contact between cops—you stare at each other, you're both used to projecting the Look, so the contact doesn't really mean much. But Frank's eyes were different that evening. The pain opened him.

"She told you?"

"A couple of days ago."

"Maybe she needs some time."

"It's for good, Ray. Permanent."

"Have you tried seeing a counselor, the two of you?"

He forced his mouth into a little smile that put that question to rest.

"I'm sorry about this," I said. "It's hard. No way it's not going to be hard."

"I wanted you to see it. Believe me, it hurts, have somebody watch my wife go with another guy. But you were close to Elaine and I want you to know the truth, whatever she says. I want you to know whose fault it was."

"It's nobody's fault, Frank. Things happen, people change. There's no blame."

"No blame? Till death, am I right? How I remember it: Till death do us part. Death. She lied."

"When she said it, she meant it. Just like you did."

"Said it? She swore it. She took an oath. I told her that: 'Elaine, you took a goddamn oath. An oath is permanent. Sickness, health, richer, poorer.' She says to me, 'You wanted to have a wife, but you didn't want to be a husband.' Can you believe that shit?"

"She's playing word games," I said.

"Till death means you work it out. What's a marriage? Working things out."

"She talking divorce?"

"Her lawyer is already on top of it. Elaine with a lawyer, right? Papers will be filed."

"It's a tough one, Frank."

"She says she doesn't know me anymore."

"She knows you."

He crossed his arms. The rain continued to patter. We were enclosed in a space that felt too small.

Frank said, "You told me it was my imagination. 'She isn't cheating on your, Frank.' "

"I was wrong. I didn't think it was possible. Not Elaine."

"All this time, six months, she's been lying to me. That's what really gets me. If she had come out and said. She made a fool of me, Ray. Sneaking and lying, that stinks."

"It stinks, but it happens. You know that. She should have been honest with you. But it's hard."

"I know about divorce. I've seen it end in murder. I know about stalkers. I collared a guy, burned his wife's boyfriend's house down, the boyfriend in it. I've seen it, but I'll tell you, it happens to you and you find out you don't know shit about it."

"Time goes by," I said. "People take each other for granted."

Frank pounded on the dashboard. "I took her for granted? Of course I took her for granted. I thought she *was* for granted. You're married, isn't that the routine? You take each other for granted. That's the whole point."

Kaiser stared down the road where the car carrying his wife had disappeared.

"What's bad," he said, his voice suddenly softer, "is I need her. I love her, I guess—I don't know what the hell love is. But I know what need is. I need that woman. You know the feeling this job gives you, that alone feeling, that cold-world feeling? I need to know she's there. I need to know there is somebody in the world who's thinking of me. Somebody."

He blinked once. Not tears, but a glistening. He didn't look at me. He reached to start the car.

LANCE PHONED ME, the husband. The sound of his voice knotted my stomach. It had been about a month since his performance at their backyard bash. I hadn't seen him and I hadn't seen her. I hadn't seen her except for a shadowy form in a window and a glimpse of her in the yard. I hadn't seen her except for the image of her plunging into the pool that night, which I carried around in my mind like a dog-eared wallet photo.

Lance mentioned the party. "Don't remember much. I've heard stories, of course. Sheila filled me in." He chuckled. "I have to apologize. You know how it is. I hope I didn't spoil it for you."

"No."

He wanted to invite me over, get to know each other, a little dinner, chance to talk.

"We're neighbors, we should get to be friends. Sheila asked me to ask you."

I should bring a guest, he said. Meet some interesting people. It would be a good time, good food, a lot of laughs.

I almost begged off. I didn't want it to go any further. It was up to me, but choice is sometimes an illusion. I agreed to go.

I hadn't spoken to Leanne Corvino in the week and a half that had passed since the night of the hostage drama. Her voice was full of enthusiasm when I asked her to go with me. My hopes revived. It wasn't too late; we could connect, she could still be my salvation. Everything would come together for us. We would have a normal life in the sunshine. A normal marriage, a couple of normal children, and a normal drive out to the Grand Canyon in a Winnebago.

She kissed me lightly when I arrived at her apartment. A simple midnight blue dress bared her stylishly muscular shoulders. I kissed her lightly. She touched my arm, I touched her arm.

"I was beginning to wonder about you," she said.

"Wonder how?"

"I'm the one who made you famous, remember?" She gave me a hard look for just that instant. She wasn't used to being ignored, especially by an ordinary cop, somebody who should have been honored to have her look at him.

She instantly switched back to her pert, charming self. She slipped a leather jacket over her dress-up clothes. The weather had turned brisk.

While we were driving to the Travises', she asked me about the investigation into the death of Keshawn Pitts. She had heard that community groups were taking up the case, that they were talking cover-up and planned to put the torch to Mayor Catlett's feet.

"I don't know anything about it," I said.

"You did testify before the grand jury."

"You're right, I testified. I told what happened as I saw it and that's it."

I didn't explain how four different cops had approached me before I took the stand. They had suggested that I change the emphasis of my story. Campisi and Taggart were saying one thing, I was saying something different.

Campisi's eyes had filled with tears when he came to me. He begged. You of all people, he said. Please, he said.

I refused to go along with the charade. The boys in our division didn't like that. Even the black cops didn't understand why I was being such a hard-ass about it.

Lance welcomed us at the front door. He was glad we could come, sincerely glad. I didn't need to introduce Leanne, he said. He had admired her work ever since he and Sheila had moved to Mansfield.

"Your reporting is really top-notch. You should be on network. You bring an intelligence to your stories that's pretty rare in the media."

She beamed at him. A hired woman in a black uniform took our coats. My eyes searched for Sheila.

Lance led us into the living room where Peter and Christy were waiting. We remembered each other from the party. While Peter and Lance chatted up Leanne, Christy told me she was a fan of mine.

"You saved a life. It's incredible."

Sheila appeared and crossed the room toward us. "What's incredible?" she asked. "Hello, Ray."

"He's a hero," Christy said. "Didn't you see it? He saved a little girl's life. Her father was going to kill her. Leanne here covered it on Channel Ten. We have celebrities amongst us, Sheila."

Sheila's eyes quickly flashed toward Leanne. "I don't watch television," she said. "Not the news."

Christy brushed her breast against my arm. "He's the hero cop," she said. "I squealed when I saw it was you. It's amazing, you meet someone, the next minute, he's famous."

"We're glad you could come," Sheila said to me. "Glad you could fit us into your busy schedule." Her mouth formed a wry little smile, but her eyes turned toward me with a look of intimacy that almost made me lose my bearings.

She and I were playing a game here. Or was I only imagining it?

Leanne joined us and I made the introductions. Sheila was cordial. I was the only one who picked up on the glint of a knife blade that came into her eyes as she smiled at Leanne and told her she must have an exciting job.

She gave us a quick tour of the house. In one room, concentrated light made the pristine green felt of a pool table glow. In another, rich leather furniture waited in expectation before a wall of gleaming electronic equipment. She was proud of her possessions, of the solid money they represented. It made me think of my own house, left over from another era, drab, dark, and shabby.

Back in the living room the maid brought around a tray of shrimp-tasting fluff on bits of toast. Lance took drink orders.

"I'm pushing champagne," he announced. "Sheila's got a real passion for champagne. Costs me a fortune to keep her in Dom Perignon."

We all asked for champagne. Lance made a show of popping the cork and told us he was on the wagon.

"She laid down the law," he said, indicating Sheila. "Sober up or ship out. She can enforce it, too. Separate bedrooms—she says I snore. All she has to do is lock me out. Right, honey?"

Sheila smiled. "For your own good, darling."

It became clear we were waiting for a fourth couple.

Peter asked me about the bulletproof vest I wore on the job, the technical details. He began to explain how Kevlar had been developed out of the space program and what the molecular dynamics were that made it absorb energy.

"But a spider's web is actually stronger," he said. "Did you know that a single strand of spider silk can–"

The bell rang. Lance hurried to the door.

"It's Sandy LoPresti," Leanne whispered to me. "And the missus."

It was another social coup for the Travises. LoPresti was a real mover in Mansfield. The whispers about mob connections gave him an aura of glossy danger that was as irresistible as his wealth.

LoPresti, who was now pushing fifty, had made his money in construction. Some well-placed campaign contributions had won his company the contracts to put up the new Municipal Plaza downtown. It was one of the LoPresti companies that had bought my land, had built the development where we were now drinking fizzy wine. Lately he had purchased a chain of discount stores, the kind that sold closeouts and overstocked merchandise. He was always getting awards from the Kiwanis, the VFW, and the Muscular Dystrophy Association.

A Niagara of mink cascaded to his wife's ankles. When Lance complimented her, she spun around, making the coat flare and showing off its apricot satin lining. She touched a fire-engine fingernail to the tip of Sandy's nose. She was perpetually young and had the smile of an accountant.

She was one of the Kiffman clan. They had settled out here in the mud-hut days and had made a tidy fortune in dolomite mining and cement. Her wedding to Sandy had filled the society pages and cost, they said, over a hundred grand. It was an alliance of Mansfield power brokers. She was Tina, a name that didn't fit her rangy, up-holstered body.

One of the local papers had hung the "hero cop" label on me, and that was how Lance introduced me to the magnate and his consort. Sandy seemed to be trying to make himself taller by lifting his cleft chin in the air. When he smiled, he set the edges of his very white teeth together and crinkled the corners of his eyes.

LoPresti squeezed my hand and told me he was proud to meet me.

"The rest of us, we just don't ever have the opportunity," he said. "I mean, when do any of us get the chance to be a hero? That's the way life is these days. There are no more wild animals."

"After being married to you, Sandy," his wife said, "I have to disagree."

The line got a big laugh. Peter said he wished he had the *cajones* to be a cop.

"We have the death penalty now," Tina said to me. "Why don't they use it on that guy you arrested, with the little girl?"

"The man didn't kill anybody," Christy pointed out. "Thanks to Ray."

"Give it to him, anyway," Tina said gravely. "Fry him."

Leanne mentioned that the mayor was going to award me a medal and they all agreed that I deserved it.

"We need more cops like you," Lance said. "Thinking cops. Dedicated. You should get ten medals. Right, honey?"

"I'll pin a medal on you," Sheila said. She planted a hard, hot kiss on my lips.

The air was full of static and I wasn't breathing as I watched her grin at me and then at the others.

Then Tina said, "Me, too," and she kissed me, and that made

everyone laugh. I said the words that were called for and of course Christy had to kiss me, too.

I didn't like being the center of attention. I looked at Leanne, who smiled and slipped her arm around mine and gave it a possessive little squeeze.

Champagne is different from other types of booze, at least at first. It turns people tipsy in a slanting, bubbling way. Lance kept refilling glasses, making sure everyone took note of the label on the bottle. The stuff tasted like helium. We all became instant, giddy friends.

Peter produced a deck of cards and was showing Tina some parlor magic. The tricks made her foam over with laughter.

Lance drank soda water and talked earnestly with Leanne about a series of political exposés she had done on Channel Ten, something to do with the siting of a water treatment plant. I hadn't seen the programs but Lance assured us that it was some dynamite journalism, that it had helped put Catlett and the new administration in office. Leanne demurred but was obviously pleased.

Sheila sat across a long coffee table from me, taking it all in. I felt left out and was on the verge of speaking to her, but she had to go and check on the dinner. When she rejoined her guests, everyone was talking at once. She looked at me from across the room. Her eyes shined into me—that's the only way I can describe it. I couldn't stop staring at her.

She announced dinner.

Lance and Sheila sat at either end of the table. I was directed to a place on her left, Leanne sat beside Lance. The woman who had taken our coats and a teenage girl in an identical uniform served us in courses. I remember a mushroom soup, a heap of raw tuna with a translucent slice of lemon curled on top, crab ravioli, very succulent veal chops for the main course, sherbet, and a dessert heavy with cream. We washed the food down with several bottles of excellent wine. I'm sure it all would have delighted a gourmet.

LoPresti picked up the thread of the political gossip. He agreed with Lance that Mayor Catlett was a good boy, a boy with a lot of promise. He had to get the crime situation under control, was all.

He said, "Don't you agree there, Ray? An element coming up from New York, pushing dope to our local people, am I right? Causing lots of problems."

"That's what they say."

"Get a handle on the crime thing, bring in some industry, Catlett is unbeatable. No stopping the man."

Leanne glanced up the table at me and rolled her eyes.

At some point I touched Sheila's knee with mine. It was one of those casual contacts that can mean nothing. But she didn't pull away, and the pressure concentrated my attention. Above the table we continued to converse the way people do at dinner—I can't remember what about.

I could only focus on one part of her at a time—the buoyant flex of her mouth, the dimple that formed and vanished in her cheek, the hollow behind her collarbone, the curls of dark hair that framed her forehead. It was less a face than a mysterious puzzle that I needed to solve.

Several times I turned my gaze to Leanne, but she seemed not to notice my confused infatuation. The byzantine workings of our city government provided plenty of fodder for the conversation. Lance gave his opinions and continued to flatter Leanne, assuring everyone that her analysis was flawless and hardheaded.

I had little to add to the discussion. My opinions about politicians did not, to me, seem worth airing. I put on what I hoped was an amiable smile and waited in a kind of tense expectation—for what I wasn't sure.

The choker of diamonds around Tina's neck gathered the light into colorful pinpricks and fired it at my eyes. Lance made a comment about women's "survival strategies" being different from men's and called to Sheila, "Right, honey? Right, honey?" until she agreed with him. Peter described with relish how veal calves are raised, the short life of torture they had to endure. Tina didn't believe him at first, then actually shed a couple of tears for the oppressed bovines of the world and for the slender arc of bone that was all that remained of her chop. Sandy and Lance guffawed over her sentimentality.

Sandy announced that he was now going into the movie business. He had an investment company, he was acquiring properties. He was working with top producers, top directors, top writers.

"Family films, but sexy," he said. "That's Hollywood in a nutshell."

He talked about the actors he'd met. He called them "talent" and referred to them by nicknames like Bobby and Sly. Peter quizzed him about the technical details—options and subsidiary rights. Lance said it might be something he would want to throw some cash into himself. Sandy told him there were some great opportunities out there if you knew where to look.

When we reached the coffee and cognac stage, Lance brought out a box of what he said were genuine Cuban cigars. Sandy was interested in the source. I passed, but Leanne said she would try one. She made a production of lighting the stogie and blowing a perfect smoke ring. Sandy whistled at that.

When Lance discovered that Leanne was a serious billiard player, he was eager to show off his table. He made some jokes about playing a game for high stakes. LoPresti said he'd been something of a pool shark in his youth and wanted to join them. So did Christy. Before they left the room, Leanne gave me a reassuring pat on the arm.

The rest of us, worn out with eating, returned to the living room and sank into the soft furniture. The others engaged in furious small talk. No one seemed to notice my silence. Sheila supervised the serving of coffee and small, hard cookies. She joined in the general banter, occasionally turning to me with a casual look or an offhand remark. When I tried to question her with my eyes, she blithely turned away.

My growing discomfort fueled my instinct to retreat. I excused myself and went upstairs. In the bathroom I splashed cold water on my face. I looked at myself in the mirror. You know how you begin to study your face and it becomes somebody else's face, a stranger's?

I wandered down the hallway to the last room in back, her room. A creamy night-light glowed near the floor. Our coats were laid neatly across the bed.

I had stared into this room so intently from outside that seeing it close-up felt like a dream. There was the gauzy curtain. There was the chair beside the window where she had propped her foot. There was the bit of wallpaper I could see from my back porch.

I stepped to the window and looked out. They had turned on the underwater lamps in the pool, though it was past the season for swimming. The lights emitted a pastel glow that seemed out of place in the autumn darkness, almost otherworldly. I stood studying that odd, negative geometry—the perfect rectangle, the widening curve of the steps in the shallow end, the dark protrusion of the diving board.

Beyond, my house stood in stark contrast. Old-fashioned, ramshackle, gloomy—it almost looked haunted. The gables and corbels and cupola gave it the personality of a mad recluse that these new homes, so immaculate and elegant, could only turn their backs on.

I switched on the lamp by the bed to judge the effect. It was not a bright light, but it made the scene outside much less distinct. I could see my own face in the black window. I pulled the gauze curtain closed. That gave the impression of total privacy.

I decided that I had been wrong. She had not been showing herself for my benefit. She had never guessed that I was watching her. It had been pure coincidence, those times I had happened to be looking and she had happened to appear. Why had I assumed so much?

"Ray?"

Sheila stood in the doorway. Her face did not form any expression. For a long moment, we just stared at each other.

All of the looks and the touches now suddenly took flame. All of the words and all of the innuendoes. The image of her dancing through my sprinkler, the glimpse of her shadow against the curtain, the sensation of her lips on mine earlier that evening, it all went on fire.

Sometimes, in the middle of the most intense experience, a part of you breaks off and takes a step back and watches the action that is engulfing you, comments on it. Now a voice in my head said, This is love.

Love. I realized in that instant that I had never been in love before. I may have told myself I loved this one or that one, but I didn't know what I was talking about. This was what the word meant, this light.

Crossing the room was an expedition. Halfway there I sensed that she was about to turn and flee. She didn't. She closed the door.

I grabbed her upper arms tightly in my hands and kissed her. Her body tensed and pulled away, but she kissed back.

"No, Ray," she whispered. She strained against my grip.

I wrapped my arms around her and kissed her neck. She struggled, making small, desperate sounds in her throat. I would not let her go.

I led her to the window. I didn't know what I wanted to show her. I pulled the curtain aside and stood behind her and pressed against her. She held my arms around her, leaned back against me. We stood that way for a moment, an hour.

She turned and looked at me, a look of utter abandon. She moved across the room and threw the coats onto the floor, all but the mink. She spread that out across the bed, fur side up, a field of softness. She knelt on it, beckoned.

We kissed again. She fell back, flexed her knees. Her silky skirt bunched around her thighs. She kicked off her shoes. Her toes caressed the pelt.

"Hurry!" was all she said.

Hurry. The charge that had been building since that hot night weeks before now arced. It lit us up. She wrapped her legs around me and we rocked quickly, brightly into oblivion.

We both lay panting on the lush fur. We turned to look at each other. I was staring at the only person in my life who knew me as I knew myself. Who knew me, understood me, forgave me, and gloried in me. It was an intimacy like nothing I had ever known. I was home.

She laughed. I laughed.

I stood. She pulled the mink around her and kicked her legs. She waved me away.

I arranged my clothes and left the room. I was a cicada crawling out of a cracked, dry skin, unfolding iridescent wings in the sunshine. Does that sound poetic? I felt poetic. I felt damn poetic.

The future had always been a blank to me. Now it swarmed with possibilities. Survival had always been my watchword. Now my watchword was Sheila. Sheila was my salvation, the only salvation possible for me on this earth. The time that it took me to walk downstairs was that much time away from her. I felt a kind of panic at the separation.

I could not imagine how long we had been upstairs. I envisioned all the other guests engulfed in an embarrassed silence. I would find them staring at their watches and shaking their heads. Lance would be storming up and down the house, intent on revenge.

We weren't even missed. Lance and Sandy and Leanne and Christy were still shooting pool. Peter was still trading jokes with Tina, who had quite an inventory of raunchy knee-slappers herself, several of which he made her repeat for my benefit.

I felt as the astronauts must have felt when they came back from walking on the moon, when they finally got done with the quarantine and the tests and the debriefings and climbed into their cars and drove home. How ordinary, how pathetic it must have seemed.

Lance and the others returned from the billiard room. I noticed how fleshy his lips were, how small his eyes, how pink and plump his manicured hands. Separate bedrooms. I thought. At least they have separate bedrooms.

He and Sandy joked about how Leanne had buried them, emasculated them, won a box of the Cuban cigars. She had run a whole rack of balls without pausing, Lance told us. Leanne apologized, said she knew all about men's egos, and laughed and traded looks with Lance.

Sheila reappeared, cool, poised, aloof. She went about her duties as hostess, I drank a couple of brandies, and talk swirled.

My mood veered wildly from giddy amiability to murderous rage, hitting every emotion in between. One minute I was entertaining the house with a story about something that had happened on the job, the next I was glowering impatiently, filled with fantasies of clearing the room with a riot gun so that I could be alone with Sheila. In my saner moments, I made an effort to cover my erotic glee. I avoided looking at Sheila and addressed some private remarks to Leanne, even leaned over to touch her arm in a cozy sort of way.

Sheila was more bold. She shot me looks so flagrant they made my skin burn. They filled me with an urge to drag her out of this phony house with the hanks of pleated fabric above the windows, carry her across to my dim and dusty dwelling, and have my way with her. What was she thinking? Why didn't the others see? Why didn't her own husband?

Christy started telling about their neighbor, an engineer at Carborundum, who had—"Can you believe this?" she said—left his wife for a nineteen-year-old girl who was trying to make it as a country singer.

"He's going to back her in her so-called career and he's in his forties, I'll bet you anything," she said.

Peter remarked that there were sound sociobiological reasons why—not that he approved.

"The guy's Johnson rod is behind the wheel, is why," Lance said, laughing.

"I sat up all night with the man's wife," Christy said. "If you knew the kind of pain that woman was going through, you wouldn't laugh. Two kids on top of it."

"And only for love," Sheila said.

I didn't know what she meant any more than the rest of them, but somehow I interpreted her words as a secret message.

Peter announced that he had to fly to Denver in the morning for a broadband interconnect meeting, so he needed to get some shuteye. Tina, whose face had been suppressing yawns for half an hour, took the occasion to drag her husband off as well. The maid brought down her mink.

I wanted to go, but Lance insisted Leanne and I stay and have one for the road.

"I haven't swallowed a drop of booze all night," he said, refilling our glasses and pouring more soda for himself, "yet I feel almost drunk. I guess the delightful company just goes to my head."

He smiled at Leanne. He asked her to relate to Sheila and me what she had said about a couple of newscasters at Channel Ten and she told a funny story.

Sheila treated her with gracious warmth now. She waxed enthusiastic about how exciting a reporter's life must be. "Almost as exciting as a police officer's. I envy both of you."

I finished my drink and took advantage of the first lull in conversation to suggest we go. Leanne was ready.

I inhaled deeply of the cold, unreal air outside.

In the car I kept waiting for Leanne to make a comment, to call me on the electricity that had flowed between me and Sheila. Instead she said, "That Lance is a lout, but he can be fun. I hope you didn't think I was falling for his line of bull. He's a bit of a Don Juan."

"I could see he was attracted to you."

"Get out. You can bet he's that way with every woman he meets. At least he's more interesting than Sandy LoPresti. What a bore. And that wife of his."

She chattered on like that all the way over to her house. I really didn't know what to say to her. She was a sweet girl and I felt for her the kind of affection you feel for a child.

When we arrived, she invited me in. She didn't say for a night-cap or anything. I guess she figured we would pick up where we'd left off the last time.

I told her I was feeling under the weather, maybe it was the flu coming on. She gave me a curious look. This wasn't what she had in mind.

We exchanged a brother-sister kiss at her door and parted.

"Really, Ray, you're not jealous, are you?"

"I'm not jealous."

"You are a little bit, I can tell. Don't be, okay?"

"I'm really not. Another time."

"Make it soon."

I walked away from her door knowing there wouldn't be another time. The idea that she could be my salvation was an empty and alien notion now. I did not need or want to be saved, not by a long shot.

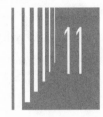

11

EVERY DAY, I USED to see people taking risks that didn't make any sense. An armed robbery nets a guy four crumpled twenties and a worn-out Seiko, and leaves him open for a five-year jolt in Dannemora. An eighth of an ounce of crack cocaine buys major league trouble, but the high only lasts ten minutes. Some fool climbs into a barrel and goes over Niagara Falls just for the hell of it. I could never understand the logic.

Now it was me taking the risks.

She called me. It was three days after the dinner party, three days of my beating my head against the wall and wondering what I should do next and if the incident in the bedroom was maybe just some kinky urge she had. She called me and the sound of her voice made my skin come alive.

We arranged to meet on my off day. She chose the place, the Satellite Motel way out on Culver. It was a joint left over from the early sixties, with little Sputnik flourishes on the sign and a space-age decor inside.

The day was dirty and gusty. The cold drizzle turned to a downpour and wet us as we ran from our separate cars toward the neon sign that said "Office." The desk clerk was a lanky, acne-necked kid who looked like he lived on a diet of Seven-Up and pencil erasers. He didn't look at us during the perfunctory registration and the payment of fifty-five dollars cash. Maybe he didn't think it was polite to look at a couple checking into a motel at two-thirty in the afternoon, no luggage.

I told her I wanted to take her to someplace else, a place with class.

"I like it here," she said, as we entered the musty room. "It's sleazy. That makes it sexy. Anyway, it won't matter in a minute. You'll see."

She was right. The tiles in the bathroom were cracked, the tub sloppily caulked, and the grout speckled with mildew. But once we had shed our damp clothes and were standing together under the steaming shower, we were in the Ritz.

The bathroom mirror reflected her shoulder blades as I dried her. The cool fluorescent bars down the sides of the medicine cabinet buzzed softly. The sheets were clean. At one point she was standing on the bed, bouncing and giggling like a child. I thought of her that Saturday morning playing under my sprinkler and I laughed so hard I could barely breathe. We both laughed. And plunged. And grappled. And clung.

At some point I drifted into sleep and awoke in a small panic and saw her beside me, her sleek hair the black of enamel paint against the white pillow, her eyes watching. We stared at each other, as time swung from moment to moment without us.

I was being cured of an illness that I had never known I was suffering from, an illness inside my cells, inside the nerves whose firings were the very thoughts that streamed into my head.

We talked. It was not a matter of getting to know each other. We already knew each other beyond what any words could say—or so I thought.

"My mother was beautiful," she said, "really beautiful, and it ruined her. Her beauty was her curse. She attracted men and didn't know how to control them, or attracted men she couldn't control. I think they were so turned on by her looks, their expectations were so high, that reality could never live up. She disappointed them and they were mean to her. They cursed her and abused her and shoved her around and hit her with their fists. Let me tell you, for a child, to see your mother get smacked by a man with arms like this, drunk and loud, that is an experience you don't forget."

"What about Lance?" I asked. "Is he somebody you can control?"

"I've learned some lessons. I'll only take so much shit, Ray, believe me."

"How did you hook up with him?"

"Young love. We were happy once, I guess. He was a real charmer—you've seen how he can be. He was the one who took me out of the tarpaper life and showed me how money can make the world wonderful. Later I learned things about him that I never wanted to learn. He screws around with women, he always has. But if he suspected me— He can be frightening, Ray."

"You mean violent?"

"He gets into these black moods and I don't know what the hell he's going to do. You've seen him. He's a stranger. I've been living with a goddamn stranger for years. He scares me."

"Don't worry about him." I held her and felt her shudder.

"You remember how you said, if I ever needed you. You meant it, didn't you?"

"You can count on it."

She said, "Because I'm taking a chance here. I don't mean about Lance finding out. I've never felt about anybody in my life the way I feel about you, Ray. I've never burned like this. It's wonderful and it's painful. It is painful, but I love it. I love the way it hurts. I love wanting you so badly that I can never ever have enough of you. Understand? I'm going way out on a limb."

"I understand." I wanted to say something else in reply, but no words would fit into my mouth. I've always expressed myself better in action. I pulled her to me and for a long while we didn't talk.

Then we both decided we were ravenous. We walked over to the diner connected to the motel. We sat next to the picture window in front. It was already dark. The rain washed down the glass and Sheila put some quarters in the table jukebox, but the waitress told us it was broken. We ordered chicken noodle soup and club sandwiches and french fries and coffee. It was the best food I had ever eaten. I reached over to wipe a dab of mayonnaise from Sheila's lip and she smiled at me and we were happy.

That fall we had a couple of weeks of nice weather, a fragrant Indian summer. The bees kept buzzing and the chrysanthemums and asters kept blooming, and every day was a day I saw her or so many days since I had seen her or so many days until I would see her again.

We met at the Satellite three times. We met at another place over on the north side, the Bayberry, that had a whirlpool bath in each room. That time, she fought me. She made me remove her clothes and tried to keep me from removing them. Then we soaked in the tub. Then she brought out some oil and she massaged me and I massaged her and we slipped and squirted over each other like a couple of eels. Then we drank tequila straight from plastic cups, licking salt and sucking on lime wedges. I guess we got drunk.

Those honeyed days went on and on. At first we were very careful. Then one Wednesday, while I was on duty, I stopped home for lunch. You get tired of fast food. I made a tuna fish sandwich. I was reading in the paper about a man who had slit the throats of his two daughters, six and eight, stabbed his wife five times, then jumped from an overpass onto a highway. The wife lived. The husband was paralyzed with a broken back. His lawyer was pleading insanity.

A noise at the back door—I was not surprised that it was Sheila. The whole thing was scripted and it was escalating. My chest tightened in anticipation.

She was holding my cat. I let her in.

"Cairo was in the road. A UPS truck almost ran him down. I saw your police car."

"Thanks," I said.

She put the cat down and squatted to pet it. "We had a kitty once," she said. "Tiger. I must have been six. He was running across the street to me. A car hit him."

She pinched the bridge of her nose and seemed to be sobbing. I touched her shoulder. She raised her head and laughed through her fingers.

"He got killed," she said, and laughed again.

"A shame," I said.

She touched the badge on my chest.

"Lance'll be back soon. He checks up on me."

"Don't worry."

"I know I shouldn't come over here like this."

"No, you shouldn't."

I ran my fingers down her neck. Her hand unfastened the strap over my service pistol. She eased it from its holster. The leather groaned. We both looked at the gun. She touched the barrel to her lip, smiled.

Upstairs I lay naked on my bed. Sheila knelt astride me, wearing my uniform shirt and my hat. She pointed the pistol at me.

"Show me how to shoot," she whispered.

I took the gun away and pulled her down on top of me.

Afterward, we went down to my basement. My mother used to put up peach preserves and strawberry jam and stewed tomatoes. The shelves were still labeled in Magic Marker. It was a large basement, damp. On the pegboard above my workbench I had painted an outline for each tool—micrometer, needlenose, ball-peen, vice grips. A place for everything, one of the rules.

Against the far wall I had hung a foot-square sheet of three-quarter-inch slab steel from two chains.

I switched the clip of copper-jacketed hollow points for a rack of plain lead soft-nosed. I slipped on my ear protectors and handed her a pair. I aimed at the plate and fired. The dull twang set it swinging gently back and forth. I shot four in quick succession. Each cartridge pounded the gun back into my hand. Each round banged home.

I handed her the pistol. She smiled. I showed her how to hold it with two hands. I told her to squeeze—let it happen, don't make it happen. She closed one eye and fired. She turned to me, a pout on her lips. I pointed at the target with my chin. She fired, missed again. The third time she hit it. Her face lit up.

She banged off the rest of the clip, scoring twice more. When she was done, she gave a shudder of pleasure and a little laugh. She looked at me, her eyes wild.

"When the bullets hit the steel," I told her, "the heat of the impact melts them."

I showed her where they lay on the floor in splatters, like snowflakes of lead, where they had accumulated by the hundreds. They formed a little drift on the dank concrete.

"You shoot a lot."

"I used to. Not so much lately."

"You've been busy lately."

"Marksmanship is something you need to work at every day. It has to be automatic. Pure reflex."

"Pure reflex," she said. She was eager for me to reload.

THEY WEREN'T MISSING a trick. They even invited a school group into the auditorium the day I received the award. Young kids, their excited popcorn voices bubbling over, carrying their world with them. Brought in not so much to see as to be seen. Public relations.

And the press. Three television cameras. Leanne Corvino, looking very smart in a blue suit, directed technicians while simultaneously talking on her cell phone.

Everyone was settling down now, dimming the house lights, getting ready. Midafternoon, plenty of time to get it on the evening news.

"If it's a slow enough day, it might even be the lead," Patrick Logan had told me. Logan was the deputy mayor who, two weeks earlier, had called me into his office at Municipal Plaza. He kept me waiting, but only five minutes.

He sat behind an aircraft carrier–size desk, with the mandatory picture of his wife and kids, crystal paperweight, and silver letter opener. My age, hungry-looking, you could see the plugs of his hair transplant. He slouched in his leather executive chair, perched his loafers on the desk, a man trying to convince himself he was a mover. I guess he was a mover.

"Catlett wanted me to talk to you, Ray," he said. "The word is, you're not enthusiastic about the award, the Mayor's Award, highest public service honor we have in this city."

"I don't want it. I don't think I deserve it."

He chuckled. "Maybe you should let others decide that."

"You pay me to do a job, I do it. I don't think it's right to make out that that's heroism. It's not."

"Fact is, you're not much of a team player, are you?" He picked up the letter opener and began to clean his manicured nails.

"I do my job."

"You're not very well liked by your fellow officers."

To him, that was a big deal, how well liked you were. To any politician, I guess.

"The department has protocols," he continued. "Procedures. Doing your job means going along with those protocols and procedures. The way you handled the situation that night, that was pure grandstand. You think we don't know that? That was not efficient police work, it was a circus. You should be up for a disciplinary hearing. So why are we giving you a medal?"

"Because nobody in the department cares about discipline or protocols. Because it's all public relations."

"Spoken like a true politician. You know, they have this saying, if you're going to do something good, do it in front of a television camera. When I saw the newscast that night, I said, this boy has instincts. You came off as a genuine hero. You put some real polish on the image of the department."

He swung his feet down from the desk and leaned toward me.

"Your father, Ray. Your father would have been proud."

I gave him the cold eye. He tried to match stares with me for a few seconds, then licked his lips and looked away.

"Let's talk like men," he said. "Catlett is up next year and he's vulnerable on this police issue. The Pitts case is killing him with the Mau Maus. They're a swing vote in the city now. Make or break. These groups, they're calling Catlett white."

"He is white."

"They're calling him white. And worse. But guys like you make everybody feel warm and fuzzy about cops. It would have been better if you had saved a black kid, but hey. We have to project a positive image. That's as important as any procedures."

He was up and around the desk now. He gripped my hand. "You'll be there," he said. "And you'll be smiling. Are we agreed on that?"

"Is that all?"

"Play ball, Ray. It'll pay off for you."

So there I was in my dress uniform, the lights on me, listening to Catlett stir the air. Everything about him said success—the way his head and firm shoulders formed a kind of bust, the sleek wavy hair, the white-on-white shirt, the ring of confidence in his voice.

Bravery, courage, he even used the word *valor*. Valor. An example. Our young people. Service to the people of this great city. Pride, honor, respect, esteem, high esteem.

The auditorium was stuffy; I was sweating. On the opposite side of the stage the woman from that night was fussing with her little girl. I barely recognized them; they could have been actors hired for the occasion. The woman's hands fluttered with the gestures of someone who wants a cigarette bad.

The kids in the audience were restless. I thought back to a field trip of my own. They took my fourth-grade class to the city jail.

They showed us the empty cafeteria, the barbed-wire yard. We filed into the cellblock and they opened a slot in a metal door. If you were tall enough you could peer in to see what a cell looked like. There were two black men inside. I remember them to this day, their faces, their attitudes, not looking at anything, not doing anything, just there, tense and unhappy.

It had struck me because I realized then that it was somehow connected with what my father did for a living, that his job involved more than just flashing lights and a shiny badge; this linked him to a world of darkness and mystery. I remembered that it had fascinated me and had made me glad he was a cop, glad he was on the right side.

I almost missed my cue. Now I was up receiving my plaque—walnut with engraved gold plate. Catlett was shaking my hand, tugging me toward the podium. I resisted, indicating I had nothing to say. He actually pulled the microphone from its holder and handed it to me.

"This isn't being a hero," I said. My words boomed. "Being a hero is an everyday thing. It's going to work and raising your kids and taking the blows that life brings without flinching. There are plenty of heroes riding patrol cars. There are plenty of heroes in any job. Any mother raising her child is a hero. Any father bringing home a paycheck."

That brought an explosion of applause. I don't know if anybody was listening. I thought I was telling the truth, but it sounded like more public relations, the modest servant of the people.

The mayor, beaming, brought over the mother. Her hands were trembling. She embraced me awkwardly. Her hair was stiff with spray and she smelled of flowery talcum.

Catlett was squatting, talking baby talk to the girl, grinning. He lifted her and presented her to me. She turned her head away. Finally they got her to reach out. I shook her little hand. A lot of cameras flashed and clicked and whirred.

Then the thing broke up. Frank Kaiser congratulated me. A couple of guys from the department. They were the only cops there, except for the brass. Leanne asked me to do an interview, an exclusive. She had me stand against the blue drapes at the back of the stage and asked me the usual questions.

When we were finished she said, "How about I buy you one?" I hesitated.

"We need to talk," she said. "And I have something for you."

I agreed to meet her for happy hour.

They had a weight room at the station house, but I liked to work out at Doyle's boxing gym on the west side. I liked the tools of the trade, the bolo bag and the speed bag and the heavy bag. I liked the idea of training your reflexes, not just bulking up your muscles. Reflexes are what get you through. It takes work to keep them sharp. I liked the intensity of the place, guys who knew that if they didn't do the right thing here, they could step into the ring and get hurt bad. It was no game.

I worked the heavy bag, pushing it away and then stepping and catching it swinging. I was practicing concentrating my force into the instant of impact. If I timed it just right I could feel the energy flow, feel the sweetness of the punch. You have to fight from inside yourself. Never overreach. Never extend all the way—one of the rules.

Pier Twelve was a posh, trendy joint that had opened when they rebuilt a section of riverfront downtown. It was dark and confidential inside, with lots of mahogany, thick carpets, and a man in the corner coaxing crystal melodies from a Steinway. City officials drank here, judges, lawyers, bankers—the crew that pulled the strings.

I was supposed to meet Leanne at six-thirty, but it was closer to seven when I got there. I spotted her in a far corner, speaking intently to a willowy blonde with porcelain features. Her companion said something that made Leanne emit an abrupt, slightly drunken peal of laughter. Leanne put a hand on her arm and leaned forward to whisper in her ear.

I joined them, apologized for being late. Leanne cursed me out in a lighthearted way. She introduced her friend, Yvonne.

The tablecloths were starched and white. The margaritas there were insane, she told me. I ordered a round. When the drinks came, Yvonne excused herself and went to talk with a knot of people at the bar.

"You goddamn bastard," Leanne said.

"Right, I'm a bastard."

"No, no you're not. I don't mean it. You just piss me off, is all. 'Cause I like you. I do like you."

"I like you."

"We like each other. How about that? Remember chemistry class? Huh? In high school? Put together the right chemicals, you get a reaction. Wrong chemicals, nothing happens. You and me, Ray, it was a chemistry experiment. So what did we get? Nothing. Nobody's fault. Just, chemistry."

"No hard feelings."

"No hard feelings. I thought some bad things about you that night after the dinner party, the night you walked away from me. Sicilian things. You don't want to know."

"Like you say, it's chemistry."

"But I still want us to be friends. You can say I need a connection in the department—wasn't I up front about that? More to it, though. We can be real friends."

"That's hard, a man and a woman."

"I know. But we've been through that, out the other side. Okay? We're both champs between the sheets, so leave it at that. Carry the ball, drop the baggage."

She reached across the table and we shook hands. She told me she had been digging into the Keshawn Pitts case. She said she was a bloodhound when it came to a story.

"Always sniffing. You have to go deep on these things. Look at the victim's background. Was it just chance that brought him to that place at that time? What about this guy Campisi? He has a history. This seems like a random event, but was it? What really happened that night?"

"Everybody's sorry about Pitts."

"I'm sure."

We endured an awkward silence. She was interested in Truth with a capital *T*.

I steered the conversation back toward nothing. I finished my drink and said some sincere things about keeping in touch. She punched my arm lightly.

"Almost forgot," she said. "I made you a tape of that night, an unedited version. I thought you might want to have it."

"I can show it to my grandchildren."

"You love to downplay it, but I really do think you're special, sweetheart." She kissed me quickly on the cheek. I got up to leave.

The air outside smelled like Halloween. I drove home, gave Cairo his dinner.

I slid the tape into my VCR and turned it on. I don't watch

much television. I don't need the ghost images of events when I have the real thing every day.

The tape was choppy, with some jerky camera movements and abrupt cuts.

Anything can happen at any time, my image was saying. *You have to remember that.*

Anything, anytime, Leanne's voice repeated. On the television I glanced at her and we both cracked up.

I fast forwarded.

Once you look with a cop's eyes, you never see things . . .

No, I didn't want to look at this. I didn't like watching it, yet it fascinated me.

A second later my attention was drawn by a tapping on my back window. Sheila. She was smiling at me from the porch. I switched off the tape and went to let her in.

"Brie's at her girlfriend's and he's gone to Cleveland overnight. Didn't you get my message?"

"I didn't check my machine."

"You should check, Ray. How many chances do we get?"

"You're telling me what to do?"

"You betcha. I'm going to tell you a lot of things to do. And you're going to do them, my friend."

I gripped her hair and pressed my mouth hard against hers.

"Yes, I'm going to order you around tonight. What are you watching?"

"It's me, the hero, the hostage thing. They gave me the medal today."

"I never saw that. Let's look at it."

"It's nothing. It was a grandstand play."

"I want to see."

She picked up the remote and switched it on.

"That's that darling girl you brought to my dinner party. What was her name? Lisa?"

How do you stay detached emotionally? Leanne was saying on the screen.

"Corvino, Leanne."

How do you keep the job from– The call for the hostage situation interrupted her.

" 'How do you stay detached emotionally, Ra-ay?' You're not seeing her anymore, are you?"

"Why would I?"

"Better not be." She grinned.

On the screen I was standing near the door of the apartment. The mother of the hostage was talking excitedly. Some of the others kept looking at the camera. One old lady smiled. I watched myself check my service pistol before stepping around the doorjamb.

Sure, it was a grandstand move. But now I didn't care. I was proud of it. I was a hero.

"Look at that," Sheila said. "You're not afraid of anything, are you? Are you, lover?"

We watched it until the end. It even contained the footage of me punching out the gunman after I had put him in the car.

"Police brutality," Sheila said, giggling.

The screen went blank for a moment, then a new image came on. It showed me naked, jutting.

I tried to grab the remote control but Sheila held it out of my reach.

"What's this? Ho ho!"

Leanne was undressing on the screen. I watched myself caress her cool skin.

"I knew you were doing it to that bitch," Sheila spat.

"She liked the uniform."

"Why is this on here?"

"Souvenir, I guess. Believe me, it was strictly a one-night stand."

"You had better be telling the truth about that one, chum. Look at the two of you go at it. God. Was she good?"

"The chemistry didn't work out."

"Did you fuck her that night you brought her to my place?"

On the television, Leanne and I were writhing across the bed. Sheila leaned forward, engrossed.

"Are you kidding?" I said.

"You didn't have anything left."

She couldn't leave it alone. She stared, taking it all in. She was breathing heavily.

It was embarrassing, seeing myself like that, seeing how the sublime act can be made comical and absurd just by taking a step back. It was embarrassing and painful and arousing. Sheila's jealousy annoyed me and comforted me. I guess I didn't want her to know how absolutely she dominated me.

The camera jerked and now only showed a corner of the bed, only the feet of the video lovers.

"It doesn't mean a thing," I said.

"It better not." She gave me a look that was pure vengeance.

But the show had aroused both of us. That night we were both heroic.

AT ROLL CALL before every tour the lieutenant goes over a list of lookouts. These are people we're after for one reason or another—suspected criminals, parole violators, a guy with an order of protection who's harassing the wife. He also mentions recently stolen cars.

I don't exactly memorize the plate numbers, but they stick somewhere in my head. Usually I pick out a couple of letters or digits as a cue. When I see a 27, for example, or a VM, I'll check it against a list on my visor.

Saturday night of the weekend after Thanksgiving I was rolling along Ballston Avenue, my eyes scanning. The night was mild for that time of year, full of the dark smells of late autumn.

I spotted a Cutlass with six people in it, teenagers. Something woke up in my brain. I pulled closer to check the plate. Whiskey-Sierra, WS, I remembered it. I glanced at my list. Stolen that same afternoon.

I switched on my light bar, reported it to dispatch. A face turned to peek from the backseat. I punched one note from my siren.

He tapped his brakes. Decision time. Don't make it tough on yourself, I was thinking. Don't be stupid.

I was good with kids. I had a rep for it. They would put me on a juvenile case that needed a light touch. I would talk to kids about vandalism, graffiti, gang stuff. If a parent felt a child was out of control, I would try to intervene. Kids trusted me.

I had done my share of screwing around as a teenager. As the son of a cop, I always needed to prove myself.

This kid decided to floor it.

Okay. In a second, your senses ratchet up six notches and the blood runs through your veins at ninety miles an hour. It's a dangerous, delicious feeling. I set my siren to whooping and reported a pursuit in progress.

An incident like this is the juicy part of police work. They do studies to prove that the high-speed chase is counterproductive. Too many accidents, innocent people hurt. And the perp is usually small-time, not worth the risk.

Granted. But during a chase all the bullshit falls away. It's just you and a lawbreaker. You're cranked up. Your mind is flying and you're on top of the world. A cop needs that once in a while.

What's funny is the calm that comes over you. You can feel that surge of exhilaration carrying you, but you're at the still point of utter concentration. No distractions. Your mind disconnects. It's a delightful sensation to ride that edge.

The Cutlass had a lot of speed. But I was driving a Caprice with the police package: Corvette engine, heavy-duty brakes and suspension. I could top a hundred forty without straining, so I had no problem keeping up with them. They tried to lose me in the maze of streets that wind through the older developments up on Kiffman

Hill. I was able to keep them in sight, all along reporting my location to dispatch and to the three other cars that were joining the chase.

We broke back onto the highway near the new cinema complex. You don't run right up on the bumper of a car you're chasing. If he's going to wipe out, you want room to maneuver.

This guy made a hard sliding turn onto another side road. By the time I made the same turn he was out of sight. Three roads intersected in front of me.

I radioed the patrol behind me to keep straight. I turned onto one of the side roads—the one I would have taken if I'd been running from the cops, I suppose. Just a guess.

Like any city, Mansfield is easy to get lost in if you know where to go. They could have pulled down an alley, ditched the car, and gone home. But just as the chase is an instinct, running is a natural reaction, a high.

My hunch paid off. Two miles ahead I caught up with him. He had slowed some, relieved, I guess, at having outrun the cops. He would have something to talk about for a long time, this wild night.

I had killed the light bar. I was on the radio again. I drifted up behind him.

Just as I was ready to hit the lights and siren he saw me and gave it the gas. The road continued straight for about a mile. I knew that it ended in a tee intersection. You don't see the stop sign until you come over a little rise.

When he reached the crossroads he stood on his brakes, spun, went sideways into a field, crashing into a thicket of brush and small trees. A cloud of steam rose from his cracked radiator.

I reported my location, hit them with the spotlight. I unbolted the short-barrel Remington from the dash. I leaned over the hot hood of my car and shouted for them to get out. These days, even kids can be deadly. You play it by the book, get the situation under control. Complacency kills—one of the rules.

The driver had the slicked hair of a Mexican gangbanger, but I recognized him as the son of a Braniff Lake stockbroker. Six months earlier I had held a powwow with him and his parents after I busted him for burglary. We sat in their golden living room drinking coffee and talked about his future. They were surprised that a son of theirs could go wrong—they had given him so much.

He started walking toward me now, a cigarette dangling from his lip.

"Halt!" I ordered. "Put your hands on the roof of the car."

He kept coming, his hands spread in an explanatory gesture. I racked a shell into the breech. A pump shotgun makes a distinct, unmistakable sound when you cock it. The sound stopped him cold.

The dude who climbed from the passenger side was a square-jawed kid, his face covered with blood from a cut on his forehead. He had forgotten about the beer can that he still held in his hand. Or maybe he just didn't give a shit. He continued to hold on to it as he assumed the position.

More officers arrived. I shined my light into the backseat. Four juveniles crammed in together, three girls and a guy. One of them was Brie.

I ordered them out, took their names. Brie and I both played it straight. At first I didn't let on that I knew her. She stood there sheepishly with the other girls.

The driver was throwing her goo-goo eyes the whole time.

"This your car?" I asked him. I was giving him a chance to be honest.

"Yeah, I just bought it." He glanced again at Brie.

"You're not connecting to reality, son," I said. "People can get hurt out here."

"Who's hurt?"

"Nobody's wearing seat belts. That's dangerous. You were lucky."

"So? Live fast, die young." He played a riff on his air guitar. He was very hip.

"And leave a beautiful memo-ree," his pal sang. They both broke up. They were cool.

"These girls are underage. Did you know that?"

"If they're big enough, they're old enough," he said. "That's my philosophy. Am I right, Chad?"

He looked at his pal with a smug grin.

"Elementary school, Doctor Watson," the pal said.

"Come here, let me talk to you a minute." I led the driver around to the other side of my car while the officers took information from the rest of the passengers.

"I'm sorry," I said, "about the way you got banged up in your accident. But it goes to show. I hope it teaches you something."

"Banged up?" He spread his hands and looked down himself shaking his head. "I'm fine."

I slammed my nightstick across his shin. When he reached down, I snapped it into his nose. I heard the bone crunch. He grabbed at the blood. Tears came to his eyes.

"I told you, people get hurt. You aren't in your playpen, buddy."

Whatever he said came out all liquid and garbled.

"What? Come on." I beckoned him. "You're big enough. Aren't you? Aren't you old enough?"

I turned him over to one of the officers on the scene. The ambulance came. One of the girls puked. I took Brie in my car.

"I know the family," I told Matt Lorry, the sergeant who had shown up to supervise. "I'll drop her around home, write up my report later."

I called out of service and drove off. Brie gave me a couple of looks but didn't say anything.

I stopped at the Tonawanda Diner, an all-night stainless-steel lunch wagon on Oregon Street. I ordered coffees and a couple of slices of lemon meringue pie.

"I saw what you did," she said.

"He disrespected me. I disrespected him. This is the world you're living in now—it's not a television show. I did him a favor. His parents will go his bail, hire a lawyer, buy him another chance. What I did was a little wake-up call."

"So you can just go around hitting people?"

"I'm human. That's about all I can say."

"The hero cop," she sneered.

"You're right. There's no excuse. You can't beat respect out of anyone. We all make mistakes."

"At least you admit it."

"You could, too."

"What's my mistake?"

"You had a choice. You chose to go for a joy ride in a stolen car. You chose to spend your time with guys who are losers. That's not smart."

"My friends are my business."

"Exactly."

She ate some of her pie. "Okay, so we have something in common. We both make mistakes."

She looked at me very intently. I wondered if she knew that I was having an affair with her mother. We had been discreet, I thought. But you never know. When you're hot for it, you don't always stop to consider.

"Do you know what it means to be psychic?" she asked me.

"No."

"You sense other dimensions."

"Are you psychic?"

"Sometimes I think so. Like, there are worlds behind the world we see. I know that. And I get funny feelings about people."

"Including me?"

"Yes. But not bad. Not necessarily bad." She surprised me with a smile.

I took her home.

"You won't tell him, will you?" she said to her mother.

"We'll talk about this later," Sheila said. "No, I won't tell him."

Brie went to her room. Sheila took me into the den and spoke in a low voice. "Thanks," she said. "She's getting more and more out of control. I knew something like this would happen."

"Most teenagers go through it."

"There's more to it with Brie. I'm afraid for her. Maybe I shouldn't tell you this. Lance . . . a few years ago, when Brie was thirteen, something happened. God, I've never said this out loud to anyone."

"What? What was it?"

"They always used to play around, he would tickle her, whatever. Brie's a needy child and he went out of his way to charm her— he can be very charming. One night—I had just gotten home, he didn't know I was in the house—he'd been drinking, as usual. Apparently he started roughhousing, all in fun. I heard the noise and went upstairs to see. I saw."

I could feel my stomach tighten.

She bit on her knuckle. "This is hard," she said. "Brie had been in the shower. She had on a robe. When I came into the room, he had her on the bed, the robe was open. His own daughter. God, do you know how that made me feel? Can you imagine . . . seeing that?"

"What did he say?"

"Didn't faze him a bit. He made a joke. Brie was so confused, so embarrassed, she just ran out of the room. When you're thirteen, you don't know anything."

"You didn't report it? You're talking about a crime."

"Crime? Do you know what it did to me, knowing? I didn't want to believe it. He said I had a dirty mind, what he was doing was all in fun. I wanted to think that was true."

"What did she say?"

"She closed up. She and I weren't getting along too well at the time. I was afraid to press her, afraid of what I might find out, I guess."

"The son of a bitch. And you just—"

"I know. I know what you're thinking. How could a mother? Isn't that it? How could I put up with even the possibility? How could I let my daughter live in the same house as a monster?"

"You did what you thought was right."

At that moment, a hot spasm of anger was gripping me by the throat. I knew about crimes against children. A guy robs a bank, peddles dope, even shoots his wife, it's one thing. Molest a child, that's evil of a higher order.

"I told him he had to get counseling. He said if I turned him in over this misunderstanding, as he called it, he would make my life hell. I knew he wasn't kidding."

"You really are afraid of him, aren't you?" Everything I learned about this man confirmed my impression of him. I could taste hate like metal on my tongue.

"He's a dangerous man."

"But you won't leave him?"

"Shh." She put a finger on my lips. That was the future. She didn't want to talk about it. Talk about the future and you jinx it, she said. Something will work out.

We had never discussed where the thing between us might be going. I imagined, I suppose, that it would end, the way all my relationships ended, sooner or later. And yet I couldn't conceive of it ever ending, not with her.

She let her finger slip between my lips now. She kissed me.

THE FIRST BIG SNOW that year hit two weeks before Christmas. The sun never rose in the morning. The sky was a blank gray-white sheet. The world trembled with quiet.

Canadian air rolls over Lake Erie, picking up moisture. On the lee side it drops snow onto Mansfield by the ton. We measure blizzards in feet. The ground is white from December until early April. We're proud of the brutality of winter. Every spring, we feel we've survived a war.

A few flakes came scouting soon after nine that morning. They didn't light, only danced into corners, tiptoed across macadam parking lots, tapped lightly at windows, leaped back into the sky. By eleven, cars were driving with their lights on.

They sent the schoolkids home early. Everyone started to get that giddy feeling that comes just before the deluge. Gonna be a big one? What are they saying? How many feet? You could feel the answer in the air, see it in the heaviness of the sky.

After lunch the invasion began. The clouds let loose, the air filled with thick flakes. They sifted down gently at first, quickly covered the ground. Then the wind picked up and the air went wild.

All afternoon the blizzard built in intensity. During periods of whiteout the headlights of a car turned into yellow smudges you couldn't see from ten feet away. It seemed as if the sky would empty itself, but if you're a Mansfield native you don't expect that. These storms have no end. It snows and snows, then snows some more.

Naturally, it keeps the department busy. Fender benders in every direction. In a snow emergency we have to work with the highway department to get parked cars off the streets so they can plow. We have to help people heave their cars out of snowbanks, and hook jumper cables to batteries, and control traffic when power lines come down.

I worked all day and stayed on into the evening. When I went off duty after fourteen hours, more than two and a half feet had fallen. I crept home at twenty miles an hour. Spiderwebs of snow came flying at the headlights. I drove a Jeep Cherokee, but even with the four-by-four I had to shovel what the plow had piled in front of my driveway before I could get off the road. It was still coming down.

I rarely kept my house much above sixty in the winter. My fuel bills were sky high as it was—something my father always complained about. But that night I cranked the oil burner up high. I needed the heat. I turned on more lights that usual.

I felt restless, antsy. I had been thinking about Sheila, about Lance, and about myself and my future. My throat felt full. I clicked on the television. Too many Christmas specials. I didn't want to think about Christmas.

I climbed the stairs. The wind had let up, but snow continued to filter down from the top of the sky. Sheila's window was dark, blank.

I descended into the basement and fired at my target for half an hour. Usually that relaxed me, but not tonight. I cleaned my gun.

When I finished, I sat in the kitchen under the humming fluorescent light for a long time, lost in thought. Time passed. Ten minutes? An hour? Inertia held me fixed to that spot, the lowest point in my geography.

A shout roused me. A shout or a scream, it was impossible to say. The wind shaped the sound. Maybe it was the wind itself that screeched as it tore around the angles of the old house, tore through the gingerbread trim I had never finished painting. I froze and waited. Nothing more.

I thought about how snow obliterates, softens and obliterates. For that we can be thankful.

Then another sound. Was it my name?

I switched on the back porch light, looked out the window. I couldn't see beyond the swirling snow.

I slipped on my jacket, took a flashlight. When I opened the door, the snow piled against it spilled inside. I waded down the steps into a drift three feet high. The wet cold seeped up my pant legs. The lights from the houses of the development were dim stains in the blackness.

Crossing the yard, I spotted footprints. Snow was already softening the cavities. The beam of my light caught a speck of crimson.

The quiet was intense. I followed the trail as it wavered across the yard.

I came upon her, shined the flashlight. Sheila was lying on her back. She wore only a thin dress. She was barefoot.

She spread her outstretched legs and closed them, spread them and closed them. Blood from her nose trickled down to her chin and the corner of her jaw. The spots of red beside her hair made the snow look very white.

She slid her arms from her sides up toward her ears, lowered them.

"Ray?" she said into the light.

"Let me help you up."

I pulled her to a sitting position. She spat blood. I lifted her. Her arms went around my neck.

"Ray, look." She pointed at the image she'd formed in the snow. "Angel. I made an angel."

I carried her inside and set her down on a chair in the kitchen.

"You'll have to get these wet clothes off."

"Hold me."

I wrapped my arms around her and hugged her. I could feel her shivering through the damp fabric. She pressed her mouth to mine. I tasted her blood, smelled whiskey.

I pulled the dress over her head. Angry bruises showed on her side and arm, one in the pattern of four gripping fingers. I brought her a flannel shirt and a pair of sweatpants, helped her to put them on.

"Tell me," I said as I buttoned the shirt.

"You know. Arguing. Same old shit. Bastard starts, 'Going to teach you good.' Bam. Just out of the blue, bam. 'Teach you.' "

I ground my teeth so hard that my jaw ached. I put a kettle of water on the stove. Her left eye was swelling closed. Her lips were puffed out on that side.

"He has a gun," she said, quite casually.

"He threaten you?"

"Oh, yeah. He told me what he was going to do with it, where he was going to put it, how many times he was going to pull the trigger. He's not joking."

"Son of a bitch." My blood was catching fire, making me feel wild. I could picture myself confronting him. Let him pull his little pistol on me.

"I'm afraid of him, Ray. Oh, God!" She buried her face in her hands and sobbed.

I hugged her, rubbed her back. The kettle whistled.

My hand shook as I poured the boiling water, added a spoon of instant coffee. She wrapped her hands around the cup and breathed the warmth.

"What about Brie?"

"She's sleeping overnight with friends. She stays out as much as she can. I don't blame her."

I found a pair of woolen socks and pulled them over her icy toes.

"I'm going over there," I said.

"No! Don't do it. He'll shoot you."

"It's my job, remember? He's a danger to himself and others."

I dialed 911 and got a couple of squad cars rolling.

I pulled on my coat and dropped my service pistol in the pocket. Sheila was breathing into her folded hands. I kissed her on the forehead and told her to sit tight.

"Don't leave me alone," she said. "Please!"

"Okay, but you'll have to stay in the car."

I drove around the block and parked in front of their house. I waded through the snow to the door, removed the gun from my pocket, cocked it, stepped inside. The place was filled with an oppressive quiet.

I moved from room to room, cautiously glancing in before sliding around the doorjamb. Lance lay passed out on the couch in the family room.

I waited, watching the big man breathe. I wanted very much to hurt him, but my police instincts kicked in. I would be able to control myself. I didn't see a gun near him.

I moved close to him. "Lance!"

He rolled over. "What time's it? What the hell? Whaddaya want?"

"You've had a fight with your wife." I put on my cop personality, the voice of reason.

"What? Is that business of yours? Whaddaya doing here?"

"Where's the gun?"

"What you talking? What gun? Get the hell out of my house."

"Buddy, you're under arrest. You're going to have to answer in court this time."

"What the fuck?"

"You'll be arraigned on assault charges."

A drunk is a slippery personality. One minute they're pleasantly perplexed, the next they're in a holy rage. You don't aggravate them, you don't take any shit. Everything straight ahead. You don't humor them. You don't play games.

"You going to tell me where the gun is?"

"Fuck you, gun. I'm sick of cops. Get the hell out."

"I'm not going anywhere."

"My fucking house!"

He was on his feet now. He took a couple of steps, pointing his finger at me.

I grabbed his wrist and bent it. It's a hold that can deliver a lot of pain if the person doesn't submit right away. His bulk and the booze he'd consumed made him slow to go down. He inhaled sharply as he finally dropped to his knees.

He closed his eyes and vomited onto the carpet.

I saw lights flashing outside. The two patrol cars arrived simultaneously.

One of the officers was Jane Briggs. She's good on a domestic call. It reassures a female to have another woman handling the situation. Teddy Leenhouts came in after her. He was a big guy with a dry sense of humor.

I told Jane to bring Sheila in. I borrowed Teddy's cuffs to put on Lance, who was snoring again, lying in his own puke. Teddy went to see if he could spot a weapon.

Jane came back with Sheila, took her into another room to get a statement. She carried a Polaroid camera to document the injuries. She also photographed the kitchen where the fight had taken place. Teddy had found the pistol on the counter there.

When she returned, I told Jane it was her arrest. She recited Lance his rights.

"Arrest for what?" he demanded.

"Assaulting your wife. You have a license for the pistol?"

"Leave us the hell alone, we'll sort our own problems," Lance bawled. "Fight all the time, right, honey? Heavyweight champion of the world. Always end up kissy-poo. Don't we, honey?"

An ambulance arrived to take Sheila to the hospital. She resisted that idea at first, then agreed to go and be checked over. I helped Jane put Lance into the backseat of the patrol car.

"This is crap," Lance said. "Fucking cops. I'll fuck you up, all of you. My wife, for Christ's sake."

I drove down to the hospital and waited a couple of hours while

Sheila had X-rays taken of her ribs and arm. Nothing broken. They put a couple of stitches in the cut by her lip.

I gave her a lift home. The snow had stopped. The plows were busy clearing the streets, their yellow lights bright in the tepid dawn.

Brie was home when we arrived back at the house. She got nervous when she saw her mother. Sheila was numb with fatigue. I explained to Brie briefly what had happened and told her to put Sheila to bed.

I went home, drank a couple of cups of coffee, and got ready to go to work.

IN THE WEEK FOLLOWING the snowstorm Sheila and I were to-gether a lot. She came to my house and we climbed in under the covers and I held her. I had to be gentle because of her bruises. We breathed together and told silly jokes to each other and whispered secrets and talked and talked.

The judge kept Lance in jail for three days. The state had been cracking down on domestic violence, finally taking it seriously.

Then they let him out with an order of protection that would keep him away from his home for three months. Later, he pleaded to simple assault and the judge gave him a couple of years' proba-tion. He had to agree to go for substance-abuse counseling. He was living in the Sheraton downtown.

"Leave him," I told her.

"It's not that simple."

"Why? Leaving is always simple."

"You think so? Where do I go? What do I do with myself? I've got a kid to think about."

"Move in with me."

"Live on a cop's salary?" It was the first time her laugh hurt me. She saw that and kissed me to make up for it. "You can barely get by on what you make. I have expensive tastes, Ray. I don't mind admitting it. And I know what being poor is all about, remember. Sooner or later, I'm going to have to let him come back."

"So where do we go, you and I?"

"I don't know. I don't know any more than today."

And that's the way we went, speeding through the present. It was like driving a hundred miles an hour in a dense fog. I guess we were bound to crash into something sooner or later.

All my life, Christmas had been a sad day. Even when I was a kid, when the day meant footballs and BB guns, it also meant a letdown from the weeks of anticipation. It was a time when you learned that reality never measures up to your dreams. That sense of disappointment remained attached to the day even when I stopped receiving gifts, stopped giving them.

I worked a double tour that Christmas Eve, as I always did, to give the guys with families some time off. For a night that's supposed to be about tranquillity, Christmas Eve always means trouble. You'd be surprised at the way people drink, lash out. Relatives get together who haven't seen each other and suddenly they're neck-deep in old feuds. They shout and fight. They drive into telephone poles. A lot of anguish comes to the surface Christmas Eve.

I had only been asleep two hours when the phone rang Christmas morning. Sheila wanted me to come over to dinner. She didn't want it to be just her and Brie. She wanted us to be together.

I couldn't get back to sleep. I took a long shower, shaved, drank some coffee. I remembered to plug in the lights on my Christmas tree. For a long time I sat staring at the decorations, the chipped green and blue ornaments my mother had bought thirty years ago.

In the quiet house, the tree began to strike me as grotesque. I don't know why. Too many memories. I've always had the bad habit of picking at my past the way you pick at a scab.

I cut through the backyard to Sheila's, knocked the snow off my boots. She kissed me. The house was pregnant with the smell of roast turkey and cinnamon and sweet baked things, the aromas of Christmas.

The gifts under the tree were still neatly wrapped. They were, I realized, only for show, empty boxes to complete the greeting-card scene. Sheila showed me an elaborate turquoise and silver necklace that Brie had given her.

"Made by Native Americans," Sheila said, "with their own little hands."

I said it was striking. She held up an expensive-looking blouse and two dresses she'd gotten for Brie.

"All grays and blacks, that's what she likes. I think she could use some color, some peach."

Brie groaned and wished me a merry Christmas.

"Here." She thrust a small package into my hand.

I tore off the neat blue wrapping paper. Inside was a carved figure in black wood. He was squatting, his face a mask, his slender penis jutting to the level of his chest.

Sheila laughed.

"It's African," Brie said. "For courage."

"It's great. I'm sorry I don't have gifts for either of you. I'm not much on that."

"Being here is your gift," Sheila said. She handed me a package that contained a flannel shirt.

"Just what I needed."

"I got blood on yours," she said.

I squeezed her hand. I could still see the yellowish-purple bruise behind her eye makeup.

"Come on," she said. "You can help me in the kitchen."

She handed me an apron and set me to chopping apples for a Waldorf salad. She fixed us both whiskey sours.

"You get two cherries," she said.

The front door chimed. Sheila went to answer it. A minute later I heard Lance's voice. I stepped into the foyer.

Lance stood with the door half open behind him. He was holding an armful of packages. He was wiping tears from his eyes.

"Please," he kept saying to Sheila. "Please. I want to give Brie her presents. Please."

"The rules are—"

"I know the rules, Sheila. I respect the rules. It's Christmas, though. It's goddamn Christmas."

His small eyes were full of ache and vulnerability. I thought he was going to sob. Sheila looked away.

"This means everything to me," he said.

He took a couple of deep breaths. He glanced at me. I realized I was still wearing the apron. I untied and folded it.

They continued to talk. I moved back to the kitchen. I could hear his salesman's voice prevailing.

Sheila went to fetch Brie, who had gone upstairs. Lance came into the kitchen.

"Glad you could come over," he said. His eyes were dry now. "Hell to be alone on Christmas. Anything I said there the other night, it was the juice talking. You understand."

He held out his hand. I shook it—it would have been silly to refuse. His mouth twitched, almost a smirk.

Brie and Sheila opened the presents Lance had brought. Brie smiled at her new portable CD player.

"Oh, Christ!" Sheila said as she opened the velvet box. Gold and diamonds sparkled from inside.

"Put it on," Lance said.

"No." She snapped the box shut. "Is this my price? You already decorated me."

"Okay. Okay, I deserve that. Just keep it for later. Put me to the test. Later you'll love it."

She gave him a hard look. "I have to check the turkey."

Pulling me aside, she said, "Don't leave until he goes. He scares me. I shouldn't have let him in."

Lance poured himself a club soda. He and I settled on facing couches in the living room. Out the picture window we could see the other fine houses, the snow, the perfect Christmas day. Self-conscious, I sipped my whiskey sour.

"You a backdoor man, Ray?" he said. "Huh? You see an opportunity here?"

"You want to start something?"

He laughed. "No way. I just see you in my house, I ask a legitimate question."

"Sheila invited me for dinner."

"Sure. She's a good cook."

Silence thickened the air. I didn't mind. I was happy with silence, happy to let him talk.

"I've been through this before," he said. "Judge puts you on probation. One of the conditions, get counseling, kick the sauce. I need help, Your Honor. See, I know the drill. First step, admit you're powerless."

"To you it's a game."

"Isn't it? I'm helpless? The booze made me do it? I can't control myself? There's a higher power? What does that mean?"

"It means what you make it mean."

"In Sunday school. Domestic violence workshop. Every Wednesday night we get together, the wife beaters' club. We sit on folding chairs, shoot the bull. Every guy's got a story more horrendous than the one before. Hey, I broke her arm. Well, I busted her spleen, they had to operate. That's nothing, you should have seen my wife's face—I couldn't fucking recognize her. Oh, we have a lot of laughs. Conflict management. Constructive ways to vent your anger. Role playing. Self-esteem. Do you lack self-esteem, Ray? Is that the real world to you? It's not so fucking simple."

"The tools are simple."

"Nothing's simple. Am I a monster? Is she a victim? That can't be all of it. It takes two to tango, doesn't it?"

"A tango's a dance. Assault somebody, it's not a dance."

"Marriage is a dance. Very complicated steps. Action and reaction. You might see the reaction, think it's the action. Depends on when you come in."

"I know what I see."

"That's cop talk. Just the facts, ma'am. Black, white. Guilty, innocent. You're looking at the tip of an iceberg. I pop her one—okay, I'm wrong. Maybe. But there are reasons for everything. That's logical, isn't it? Something's motivating me to do what I do. Maybe she hurt me very very deeply. Maybe she kicked me in my spiritual balls. That can do a lot more damage than a couple of love taps, you're both drunk. Understand?"

"You're a sensitive guy, is that it?"

He snickered. "You think you've seen it all, know it all, right? Let me tell you something, pal. If you had ever tangled with that one"—he nodded toward the kitchen—"you would have found out you don't know jack-shit. You don't have any idea."

We locked eyes. A grin slowly spread across his mouth. He turned to look at a crystal ashtray on the coffee table, examined it as if he'd never seen it before.

Sheila announced dinner. The house felt overheated. I glanced at the shadows creeping across the snow outside. I wished I was out there breathing the cold air.

The four of us sat around the table draped in green linen. Lance announced he was going to say grace. Brie snorted. I kept watching the way she reacted to him, imagining the things he might have done to her.

"Bless this food, O Lord, and make room for love to enter this house, amen."

It was a hell of a dinner. We all pretended. We all avoided each other's eyes. I chewed my turkey and roast potatoes and cranberry sauce, aware of each bite. I wanted out of there.

Lance had a salesman's ability to keep a conversation afloat. Ordinary gossip and opinion got us through it. Brie asked me questions about being a cop. She seemed interested.

Afterward, she moved into the living room with me. She wanted to read my palm.

"I told you, I'm psychic," she said.

She perched on an ottoman and laid both my hands in her lap.

She traced the lines and mounds, described me as a man of courage and honor. My heart line, it seemed, was phenomenal. My head line, though, forked in a disturbing way. My mountain of Mars pointed toward rashness.

"See this cross here? I'm worried about that." She caressed the spot with her fingertips.

"Am I going to be struck by lightning?"

She looked at me with serious, disarming eyes.

"You're weak," she said. She wasn't joking. "You think you're strong, but you're weak."

"You really read it the way it's written, huh?"

"No, I see a bright future for you. How's that? Great wealth."

"Sounds better. You should get a turban. Madam Brie, the All-Knowing."

She smiled.

"Really," I said. "I'll be your manager. Get you on Jay Leno. This can be a very lucrative racket. You have the knack."

"You think it's a joke."

"I don't know if it's a joke or not," I said. "It's my nature to look at everything as a scam. But maybe certain people have faculties the rest of us can't grasp. I wouldn't be surprised if you were one of them. No, I wouldn't be surprised at all. I mean, you look into space, you know the possibilities have to be infinite, there's so much out there. . . ."

I was talking too much and I couldn't stop talking because Lance and Sheila had disappeared. Now, after a long silence, an occasional sound came from upstairs, very low, the sound of a bed. I was sweating.

"I have to go." I told her to thank her mother for me. I headed for the door. Brie came running after me to hand me my shirt and the carved figure. I kissed her on the cheek.

In the driveway I inhaled the sweet, living air of winter evening. I drove to a bar out on the highway. I didn't know a soul in the place. "Silent Night" was seeping from hidden speakers.

I drank three quick boilermakers, left a five-buck tip. The bartender wished me a merry Christmas. Back home I resisted the urge to look for a light in Sheila's window.

NEW YEAR'S EVE CAME and went. I had planned to spend it with Sheila. I had laid in a few bottles of champagne, the good French stuff she liked. I had imagined us getting drunk on it and seeing colors and having sex as the clock turned over the year and fire-crackers went off far away.

But we hadn't spoken since Christmas. I knew Lance was back, that she had let him come back, that they were living as man and wife. So what? They were married. They were a couple of juice-heads. They deserved each other.

She was a bitch. She had never loved me. We had no future together. She was no different from any of the other women I had known, except this time I had lost the end game.

Don't mess with married women. Go back and follow the rules. New Year's resolution.

The sixth of January I was working a night tour. The air was cold enough to freeze a cannonball. Black cold. Brittle. Mounds of dirty snow lined the streets.

At seven thirty-six I responded to a house on South Lewiston

Drive. A drunk had gotten into an argument with his own dog. He had decided to drown the animal in his aquarium. In the process, the glass had shattered and the man had cut his arm to the bone and passed out. His wife had called for an ambulance. Then the drunk had come around enough to take a swing at the paramedic patching him up. We tied him to the stretcher and another officer rode to the hospital with him. Cabin fever runs deep during Mansfield January.

Later it began to snow lightly, looking exactly like one of those paperweights full of water you can make a snowstorm in. I got a call for a motor vehicle accident up on the Chester Albright Expressway. When I arrived, I saw a semi jackknifed across most of the roadway. I parked my cruiser with the lights flashing, set out road flares to route cars into the open lane.

Somebody who had stopped to help came running back to me.

"A woman is trapped!" he shouted.

I pulled my car in front of the rig and aimed my spotlight. Part of the guardrail was twisted. Down in the embankment, a small sedan, a slate-blue Toyota Corolla, had its front end jammed into a drift. The driver's door and the roof on that side were both beaten in pretty badly.

I slipped several times getting down to it. I tried to dig my heels into the crusted snow. I circled to the passenger door. Snow had already built up on the window. I brushed it off. The driver lay slumped across the seat.

When I opened the door, packages piled on the passenger seat spilled out. Through a cellophane window I saw a collection of plastic farm animals. A yellow bat and ball were attached to cardboard backing.

It was quiet inside the car. I caught a whiff of perfume, orange blossom.

The caved-in door had pushed the woman toward the center console. Her head hung at an unearthly angle. I tucked two fingers under her chin. Her skin was still warm. No pulse. Her small hands were fragile and limp. I lifted one, let it drop. Leaning farther in, I could see her eyes: dilated, staring at nothing. I reached instinctively to close them.

A dozen gawkers had gathered on the roadway, people who had stopped to see, who had been attracted to the flashing lights and action. They congregate at every accident, every shooting, every scene of violence. They look and look. They want to see something, somebody else's blood, somebody else's pain. Their own lives are plain vanilla, and they're hungry for anything that tastes exotic.

The driver of the rig was squinting like he had to sneeze. I didn't need to tell him she was dead.

We sat in my car. I took down his account, how the Corolla had gotten a wheel off the pavement and had just gone sideways. Nothing I could do, he said. Nothing. I ran his license, checked his log. The fire department took the car apart getting her out. They used a blue tarp to conceal the body from the onlookers. A tow truck winched the Corolla up the embankment. We waited for a big wrecker to come for the truck.

I had seen accidents a lot worse than this one. But the woman's hands stuck in my brain and knocked me a little off balance. Smooth, pretty hands, the nails coated with transparent polish. A mother's hands.

The truck was gone, my paperwork was done, the fire department was ready to open the road. I went on my way.

I wasn't hungry, but I called out of service and stopped at a diner out on Crompton Boulevard. They served me a burger, a slice of fleshy pink tomato, a couple of serrated pickles, a pile of fries. The coffee came in a thick porcelain mug. The place was always busy, always full of living, breathing people. I needed that.

My beeper sounded. The number that came up was one I didn't know. I dropped a quarter in the phone by the cigarette machine and dialed.

"Ray?" It was Sheila.

"What is it?"

"Lance. Come over quick. Please." The desperation in her voice instantly dissolved the hostility I had been feeling toward her.

"Are you in trouble? Where are you?"

"I have to see you right away. Hurry. I'll be at the house. Please, hurry."

"I can be there in ten minutes."

"I need you."

"Did he—" The line clicked dead.

I left my food, dropped some money on the counter, and hurried out to my cruiser. I imagined scenarios. I imagined that Lance had beaten her, threatened her. He had molested his daughter again, was holding Brie hostage. Threatening suicide. He was, this very moment, stalking Sheila, tracking her through the house with a gun.

Or did she just need to see me very badly? Did she realize all of a sudden that she couldn't live without me? That she and I were meant to be together, no matter what?

It was quicker to stop at my house and cut through the yard than to go around the block. Plus, I didn't want to pull the patrol car into their driveway without knowing what the situation was. The crust of snow out back was so hard I could walk on it without breaking through. I tapped on their patio door.

Sheila's eyes looked at me wildly through the glass. She yanked the door open. Heat poured out. She flowed into my arms.

"Do you love me, Ray?"

"Oh, baby."

"No matter what?"

"Is something wrong?"

"You said I could count on you. You promised, didn't you? Anytime. You said it."

I nodded. She pulled me inside. A single fluorescent bulb over the stove filled the kitchen with a cool glow. Lance lay on the floor. I could see blood. I just barely caught a whiff of smokeless powder.

"What happened?"

"I don't know," she said. "I just— The idea of him touching me, threatening me. All those years. I couldn't take it. I had to . . . erase him."

I squatted beside him, careful not to step in the dark pool. I touched his throat, the second time that evening I had searched in vain for a pulse.

"Why?" I said. "Why now?"

"It had to happen, Ray. Didn't it? It was in the stars. You know it was."

I stood and looked at her.

"You were afraid for your life," I said.

"I just wanted to get rid of him."

"Okay, but when the police come, you were afraid for your life. Stick to that. The abused woman, it's your best defense."

"No! No, I don't want that. I don't want to go to prison, Ray."

"Plenty have gotten off on it. Juries are sympathetic. They'll believe you. Brie will testify. Molesting his own daughter—the man was a monster."

"But I shot him in the back. I emptied the gun. I wanted to kill him and I did. Nobody's going to swallow self-defense."

"You have no choice."

"Ray, don't!" She clutched my hand. "You told me to call you. You're the only one in the world for me. We're together. Please! Don't turn on me now."

"How do you get around it?"

"I was in bed. Somebody came to see Lance. A drug deal. Lance takes drugs. Did you know that? I heard shots. I panicked, I froze. A man appeared in my bedroom, fired at me, ran out. So I was shot, too."

"You?"

"I'm shot, too. I'm a victim. I'm left for dead. See? Then we're home free. Then it'll be just us, you and me, forever."

"It won't work."

"It will. It's the only way. You don't want me to go to prison. It's the only way. I did this for us, Ray. You have to believe that. I did it because you said to trust you."

Decide? You don't decide. Something like this, it just happens.

I don't remember climbing the stairs to her bedroom. We were just there all of a sudden. She handed me a revolver and began to undress. Events were rushing forward.

"I reloaded it," she said. "Here are the shells. I wore gloves while I did it. I made sure none of his blood got on me. Brie is at her girlfriend's. I called your beeper from a pay phone. I thought of everything."

"You've been planning this."

"I've dreamed about it. Tonight, it happened the way I dreamed. I didn't make it happen. It just happened. Understand? He brought it on himself. It was the right thing. You know it was."

She had her clothes off. Her skin glowed.

"Okay, listen to me," I said. "Wait ten minutes, no more. If you pass out, you're in bad trouble. You heard a noise."

She climbed into bed. "I heard a noise?"

"A man appeared at the door. He was wearing a ski mask. You were terrified."

"Yes, terrified."

"Keep it simple. Don't play games. You're distraught over your husband."

"Lance, my poor husband."

There are moments when the world cracks open and you see that the only limits are the limits to what you dare. Risk it all, it all falls at your feet. Everything is possible.

"Come here," she said.

"No time."

"Come here."

She sat up. The sheet slipped. Her breasts were alive, her eyes eager. She was panting.

I sat on the edge of the bed, laid the gun on the mattress. We kissed. Her fingernails dug into my scalp.

"It's now, Ray."

"I can't." I heard myself say it. I didn't know at that moment who she was, who I was. I was living a dream.

"You have to. I want you to."

"You could say—"

"No. Do it. Do it to me."

She flung the sheet away. She stretched out on the bed, utterly naked, her legs crossed, toes pointed.

"Do it."

I picked up the gun and shot her.

IF I BROKE THROUGH the crust, I would engrave a trail directly toward my house. There would be no way to cover it up.

But with snow like that you never know. It can seem firm and the next minute it shatters and bites at your ankles. I was holding my breath, crouching, hurrying.

I was stepping easily, easily. I made it past the pool, halfway across their lawn. Should I look around? Somebody could be watching from one of the other houses in the development.

I took time to glance upward. Patches of clear sky were showing through. Stars appeared and disappeared.

I took a step and broke through. The crunching reverberated in the stillness. My next step, though, I was back on the solid rind of snow. I stooped over to claw at the print my shoe had left in the hole. Would it mean anything, a single depression?

I continued on. Easily, quickly. Time was a torrent now, tearing ahead, the last mad dash of current rushing toward a waterfall.

I was at my house. I reached the path I had shoveled so the oil delivery man could reach the fill pipe. I climbed into my cruiser and drove half a block before turning on my headlights. I called dispatch and reported that I was back in service after my dinner break.

Ten minutes. I had received enough first-aid training to know that the lower left abdomen contains no vital organs, no major blood vessels.

I took the gun out of my pocket and examined it closely for the first time. A snubbed .32, banker's special. Good. Most of the damage of a gunshot wound doesn't come from the bullet itself. It's the shock wave that hurls tissue into other tissue, that magnifies the injury. Momentum is the key factor. Momentum is velocity times mass. A small-caliber bullet, low mass. A short-barreled gun, not much muzzle velocity. Good. Good.

Oh, yeah, everything was okay. Velocity times mass, only it was Sheila's body I was thinking about, the soft belly I had kissed a hundred times. That was the flesh I had fired a bullet into.

Trauma results in bleeding. Bleeding can lead to shock. In shock the body starts to close itself down. The body tries to preserve a flow of oxygen to the brain. The brain. The patient becomes thirsty, pants for air. The extremities go numb. The skin turns clammy. The heart races, spinning its wheels.

But ten minutes was safe, a wound like that. Wasn't it? During the first ten minutes, first half hour, the body compensates. Yes, ten minutes would give me plenty of time to leave the vicinity before the call came in.

A murder weapon is radioactive. The longer you're exposed to it, the more vulnerable you feel. You want to chuck it as soon as possible. But not near the scene. No, not where they'll search. You have to be patient.

I reached Tonawanda Boulevard and turned toward downtown. I made myself keep going, a mile, two miles. I pulled onto Seneca, a main shopping drag. I drove three blocks to a deserted stretch near a Chevy dealer. I made a turn so that my door was near the curb. I leaned out and dropped the gun down a storm sewer. It made a hollow splash. I poured the empty shells after it. The cold stench from the sewer smelled like death.

I remembered what I learned in the academy about criminal investigation. A scene cools. Every moment that passes, more evidence is gone. Speed is essential. You have to get there and investigate. If you don't solve a crime right away your chances go downhill quickly. I could feel the heat of this crime already beginning to chill. It was a comforting thought.

But what was going on? I checked my watch. The ten minutes were up. No, twelve, almost thirteen. She hadn't called. Why was she waiting?

I swung back onto Seneca. I was moving farther from her house. I thought about her bleeding, lying there unconscious and bleeding. Bleeding. I considered the alternatives. If she passed out. If she couldn't call for help. What would I do? If I went back. If I called an ambulance myself. Any move I made would be suspicious. It would be enough to tip them. How could I explain?

I saw a car, engine running, parked down behind a shopping strip. It was a car I should have checked on. Suspicious activity. Question the driver. License and registration, please.

I kept going.

Why wasn't she calling? Nearly twenty minutes now. I should have told her, call right away if you feel light-headed. Don't wait. Disorientation and confusion are the first signs of shock. She had to keep alert. She had to keep her head clear to keep her story clear.

I should have drilled that story into her, the noise, the ski mask. I should have told her to deny that Lance took drugs. She should say she knew nothing about that. Nothing about him buying cocaine. Later she could admit it. She would say she was trying to protect his reputation. Yes, he did take drugs. He had a substance-abuse problem, a serious substance-abuse problem.

Something had gone gravely wrong. I knew that now. More than twenty-five minutes had rushed past. Sheila was lying naked on that bed, a red stain blooming and blooming around her. I saw it. I had to go back.

I continued on.

I don't know how long I drove—time yawned. Without thinking, I turned the car around and gunned the engine.

I grasped at explanations. Why would I be at the house? Routine patrol, I saw a broken window in a residence. Stopped to investigate. Heard a moan. Forced entry. Found body.

It meant I would have to break a window myself. It would pull me in, involve me. But I had no choice. The alternative was to let her die.

I passed my own house and turned into Maple. At that moment, my radio came alive.

"All available cars respond to a shooting at 33 Maple Drive. Caller is reporting one down, one wounded at that location."

I almost ignored it, intent on getting back to Sheila. I stopped, backed into a driveway, headed out of the development. As I was hitting Tonawanda I radioed in.

"This is patrol one seven. I'm approximately one and one half miles from that location. My E. T. A. is two minutes."

I heard several other units responding. I drove a half mile up the highway and turned around in a dark gas station. Now I switched on my flashers, set my siren wailing. I sped back the way I had come.

I skidded to a stop in front of the Travises'. I hit the house with my spotlight. Everything dead still.

I climbed out of the car, drew my pistol, waited for backup. Standard operating procedure. No heroics tonight. Everything by the book.

Jimmy Taggart was next to arrive. He was patrolling by himself now. He parked his cruiser behind mine, joined me squatting at the fender. I hadn't worked with him, hadn't spoken to him since the summer night I collared the young man, Keshawn Pitts, the one who had reached the station house with mortal injuries. Tonight the awkwardness was forgotten. He was more wired than I was. His eyes were wide and frantic.

"I'm going inside," I said.

He didn't answer. He had his gun out and now he was pointing it.

"Don't move!" he shouted. "Put your hands in the air!"

I ducked quickly around the front of the car and put myself in his line of fire.

Sheila stood on the walkway. Her robe showed a dark stain near the waist.

I ran to her. She was pale, glassy-eyed. I led her quickly back to my car.

"I want you to lie down," I said. "Can you tell me if the gunman is in the house now? Is anybody else hurt?"

"I love you, baby."

"Mrs. Travis? Can you tell me what happened?"

Taggart was waddling over toward us, keeping behind the cover of the cars.

"No matter what happens," Sheila whispered, "even if I die, I still love you."

"Is it your husband?"

"We did it, lover." She took a sharp breath, folded her face in pain. Taggart arrived and helped me get her onto the backseat. She groaned.

"She says the perps have gone," I told Taggart. "Cover me, I'm going to secure the house."

I headed toward the front door. Another patrol car pulled up. I could see an ambulance turning into the street.

It was not the same place I had left a half hour earlier—could it be only a half hour? It was not any place I had been in before. It was a crime scene now, full of menace, but also fragile, every object a potential piece of evidence.

My training kicked in. My first objective was to clear the scene, make sure no gunmen remained inside. I glanced at Lance's body in the kitchen. I should have felt for a pulse. I didn't want to touch it again. I hugged the walls as I moved through the first floor.

In each room I shined my flashlight around, took a quick look. I exposed myself as little as possible. If a room appeared empty, I moved through it, checking closets and other hiding places.

The idea was to search thoroughly as you go. You never want to leave open the possibility of someone taking you from behind.

I could hear more units arriving outside.

I went up the carpeted stairs. I wasn't acting. I expected an armed man to jump out at any moment.

In Brie's room I was surprised to find my picture tacked above her bed, "Hero Cop." It stopped me for a second, caught my eyes.

I made myself keep moving, into Sheila's bedroom, the room where I had first glimpsed her. A clotted puddle of blood, not very big, pooled in the center of the mattress. I thought about the mink coat spread there. I thought about the way Sheila had looked as I aimed the gun at her, how her body had seemed to shimmer.

I checked the other rooms. A night-light glowed in the bathroom. Better watch it, he'll bust your ass. I heard Lance's laugh.

In his bedroom, on the dresser, in a silver frame, he kept a nude photo of his wife. She was wrapped in her own arms, smiling at the camera in a way that bothered me. I was glad then, in the instant that I took to think about it, that he was dead. I was glad that he would never look at this picture again. He was a man who deserved to be erased. I was glad she had done what she did. I was glad she had counted on me. She was going to get away with it. I would make sure of that.

I went downstairs, the beam of my light jumping. I approached the kitchen.

Something was different. Something had shifted. I studied the scene in front of me. What's wrong with this picture?

Then Lance took a shallow, wheezy breath and moved his left hand convulsively.

COLD. CHRIST, I WAS COLD. We put tape around the scene and I stood talking to the other officers. The stars were blazing, sucking heat from the earth the way they do in winter.

The ambulances were gone. I had watched the paramedics take Lance out, head bandaged, an oxygen mask cupping his face, his shirt torn away to reveal his large white torso. They were hurrying, hurrying to get him help, to restore him to the land of the living.

It was the most exciting thing that had happened to Jimmy Taggart since he'd been on the force, and he couldn't stop talking about it. This was what it meant to be a cop—first on the scene of a shooting, catching the taste of fresh violence, helping a victim, establishing law and order where there had been mayhem. This was something he could tell and tell, long after he had put in his twenty and was looking in his mailbox for the pension check.

He had to relate the story to every new man who showed up. How he had covered me with his pistol while I rushed the house. I was always trying to be the hero, he joked. I couldn't get enough of it. And Sheila—she had lost so much blood he was pretty sure she wouldn't make it. Good-looking broad, he noted. A shame.

I began to shake. I couldn't get warm. My toes and fingers had gone numb. My ears were ringing.

It was more than the cold. I was falling apart. Pieces of my mind were flying in all directions. I had to bear down. I had to pull myself together. How? I had no center. Each of my thoughts was a piece of shrapnel.

Sheila. Lance still alive. The hole out back in the crust of snow. The gun glowing, I imagined, from the icy black of the storm sewer. All the eyes that might have seen me leaving the Travis house. My picture over Brie's bed. Hero. Love. No matter what. Do it.

I told the others I was going to sit in my car. I turned up the heat, blew on my hands. I tensed my muscles, let them go all at once. I took some deep breaths. Nothing helped. The chill went into my soul.

The police brass were starting to show up. I had to climb out and give Captain Barnes the lowdown. He said Chief Preston was on the way. Two detectives arrived. Frank Kaiser would lead the investigation. He was coming later.

Nobody was going inside yet. The detectives walked the perimeter of the property, looking and pointing. It didn't make me feel good.

Again, I began to run through scenarios. Lance would come to and point the finger at his wife. My involvement would be obvious. I would be sentenced to prison. My career would be ruined. My house sold to cover the legal expenses. My picture in the paper. On the evening news. Accessory to murder. Disgrace. Some sleazeball true crime writer would do a book about the whole thing, turn it into a soap opera.

I couldn't sit still. I climbed out and walked, beating my feet against the hard macadam, breathing plumes of vapor. I walked up to the corner and down the next street, passing one smug house after another, houses filled with comfortable, sleeping innocents. They had no idea how dark the corners of the world were. Walking back, approaching the throbbing lights and bustle of activity, I could see, between houses, my back porch. The solution to this crime was geometric, I thought—a line of sight.

Half an hour later I watched a black Camaro turn the corner, approach slowly, and glide to a halt three doors up the street. It sat there humming for maybe five minutes. Somebody had painted flames flaring behind the wheels, but rust was eating the fire. Finally the door opened, Brie climbed out. She stared at the commotion in front of her house, walked around to say something to the car's driver. She leaned in to kiss him. The Camaro backed into a driveway, then took off in the other direction, its tires emitting an angry little chirp.

Brie lit a cigarette and walked toward me along the street. I moved forward to meet her before any of the other officers.

"What happened?" she said. "What's going on?"

"There's been an accident."

"A car accident?"

"A shooting. We think someone broke into your house. Your parents have been shot. I'm sorry."

She dragged on her smoke, acting tough. "Are they dead?"

"No. They've been taken to the hospital. Your mother walked out, your father was unconscious. Doctors are doing all they can."

"Are they hurt bad?" She was clenching herself to keep from reacting.

"We don't know yet. We know they're both alive. You can go down and see them right away."

"Who did it?"

I shook my head.

"Who did it?!" she screamed. Her face demanded an answer.

"The detectives will want to talk to you, ask about any enemies they might have had."

"Enemies?"

I nodded. "Enemies or strangers who might have been hanging around, anybody who could have wanted to hurt them."

She stared at me. Every gesture seemed an accusation. "How should I know who? All those people they had over, you saw them. I don't know who their enemies were. That's absurd."

"Any scrap of information you can give will be helpful."

"I don't know anything. I don't want this to be happening." She pressed her fist against her mouth.

"I'm very sorry."

"Why are you sorry? You didn't make it happen. Why is this— I can't deal with this."

Her face became that of a frightened child. I reached my hands out to her shoulders. She pulled away. She turned and ran a few steps up the street toward where the Camaro had vanished. She stopped and turned again, dropped her cigarette and held both her hands out toward me. I walked over, embraced her. She sobbed against my chest.

I had not thought about this part of it. I had made myself think about what Lance had done to her. She would be better off, I told myself. After the shock passed, her life would clear. I had done her a favor by keeping her mother out of prison.

I walked her toward the house and put her in a warm police car with a female officer. I felt better when she was on her way to the hospital.

It was still pitch dark. Barnes asked me to stand on the road and question any neighbors who rolled by on their way to work. Had they seen anything? Heard anything? Did they know the Travis family? Anybody with information, I was to give the detectives a yell.

A few commuters drifted past over the next hour or so. Nobody had anything to tell me. I kept expecting them to say, You. I saw *you* go in there. I watched *you* sneak out.

Instead they asked me questions. What's going on? Anybody hurt? What is it? Why this invasion of my neighborhood? They were nervous. Maybe they were thinking of their property values. I gave them no information.

I had seen dawn break in that sky many times working the last-out tour. Never had the brightening in the east been as welcome as it was to me that morning. The earth took shape around me and reassured me.

The newspeople started showing up just as it was getting light. A TV crew set up a dish antenna and had a newsman broadcast live from in front of the house. A reporter I knew from a paper in Buffalo tried to get me to describe the scene inside. I told him all the information had to come from the investigators.

The detectives liked to keep strict control of what went out. They always held back some of the details of the crime. They hoped a suspect would mention facts that hadn't been in the press. It made for a tighter noose.

I was stamping my feet and wondering if the lowering sky meant more snow when a voice said, "Black, right?"

I turned to see Frank Kaiser standing behind me. My jaw was clenched too tight to say anything.

"At least it's hot." He handed me a large Styrofoam cup. I pried off the lid and sipped at the metallic coffee.

"You're a life saver," I managed.

"Funny thing," he said. "I couldn't sleep. I can't sleep anymore, since this thing with Elaine. All night the big eye. I could almost feel something was going to come down. I kept looking at the phone. When it finally rang, I wasn't surprised. When I heard what it was, I thought. This is what I've been waiting for."

"Hooked a big one, huh?"

"Big. Reel it in, it could make quite a trophy. I've already talked to Catlett. Apparently he knew them. This one is going to make people sit up and pay attention. Crime in the streets is one thing, crime in the living room, you get a whole city full of nervous citizens. You first on the scene?"

"Yeah. Me and Taggart. We got here, she came out, the wife. I found him on the floor in the kitchen. Looked like a goner."

"Get any sense of it?"

"I didn't question her and he wasn't talking."

"This is close to your place, isn't it?"

I sipped the coffee. The warmth did me good. "You can see my house through there."

"Practically neighbors. You knew them?"

"I saw them around, went to parties here a couple of times."

"What are they like?"

"She's a looker, he's a juicehead. They moved in last summer."

"Notice anything wrong about them? Who did they hang with?"

"CPA-types. Lawyers. Like you say, Mayor Catlett. I met Sandy LoPresti over there once."

"Yeah?" Frank smiled for no reason. "They get along, this couple?"

I shook my head. "They fought, yelled a lot. He beat her up before Christmas. Order of protection, but apparently she let him come back. I had seen him over there lately."

"Any indication of dope?"

I pretended to think. "Once I did catch him doing some lines. Seemed recreational, though. Naughty-boy stuff."

How curious should I be? I was trying to strike just the right tone, put on the face I would wear if I were not involved. But what did that mask look like? I knew them, I should be curious.

"You talked to the wife?" I asked him.

He nodded.

"How is she?"

"Serious, but she'll live. The husband's circling the drain. He was still on the table when I left."

Another news crew arrived and hauled their cameras out. I was starting to feel the cold come to the surface again in spite of the coffee.

"Yeah, this is going to be a very high visibility case," Kaiser said. "Very high priority."

"I figured."

"Fortunately, the guy who did it made a big mistake."

"What's that?"

"He should have made sure of them both. I mean, wouldn't you, if you were doing it? Would you leave them alive? What's he think, they're not going to ID him?"

"She saw who did it?"

"You cold, Ray?"

"It goes right through you when you're standing around."

"It is chilly." He clapped his gloved hands together. "Here's the lab boys. I've got to get to work."

"She saw him?" I didn't want to repeat it, but I did.

He nodded. "Oh, yeah. Detailed description. This case is going down, Ray. I can feel it. I can taste it."

WHAT I DON'T LIKE about hospitals is the stares of the patients. You walk past a room and a woman turns her head toward you, her eyes scared, lost. Every illness is an accusation.

The day after the shooting I carried a bundle of yellow tea roses into Lansing Brothers Memorial and took the elevator to the third floor. I was surprised to see Stu Holmes, a city patrolman, sitting in a white plastic chair outside the room I wanted.

"Ray, for me?"

"What's the deal, Stu?"

"Security. She ID'd the shooter, I guess Kaiser figures, take no chances. The guy could walk in here, wipe out a witness. For me, some easy overtime. You know her?"

"We're neighbors."

"They into some heavy shit, or was it just a random thing?"

"I don't know."

"The papers are full of theories."

"They always are."

"She's decent." His eyebrows danced a little jig. "You looking to see her?"

"I thought I would. They live practically next door."

"You said. Only Kaiser told me, nobody. The daughter—she's in there now—otherwise nobody."

"Press, you mean?"

"They've already tried. Television, newspaper reporters—everybody wants in, nobody gets in. Except Mayor Catlett, he was here. I got to shake his hand. Nobody else. Strict orders."

Okay, now you walk away. You don't press the issue. Don't call attention. You're a neighbor. You're only making a friendly gesture.

So I said, "Actually, I saw Frank yesterday morning, at the scene. He said it would be okay. She doesn't have many people here, they're new in the area."

"He didn't tell me."

"He has a lot on his mind. I'll let him know you did your job, Stu." I was pushing the door open. Holmes reached his hand out, but he wasn't about to grab me. He knew I was friendly with Kaiser. He looked away and shrugged.

As I walked into the room, Brie stood up. She stared at me, bit her lower lip. The haircut and piercings and tattoos that had seemed so defiant now all made her vulnerable, fragile. She was out of her depth.

"You're going to be tough, Brie," I said. "You're going to be strong."

She shrugged, nodded, tried to smile.

The small private room was crowded with medical equipment and flowers. Sheila lay propped on the hospital bed. An IV line ran into her arm. A tangle of wires connected her to a machine that traced a ragged green line across a monitor.

She was dead pale, but even that made her look good. Her translucent skin emphasized a delicacy in her features that was new to me. Though obviously tired and drained, she seemed younger. A feverish brightness lit up her eyes. She smiled at me.

"My favorites." She closed her eyes and breathed the roses.

I asked the usual questions. The pain was easing, she said. A little. She didn't want to be loaded up with painkillers. The doctors said no permanent damage.

"I was lucky," she said.

"How about Lance?"

"They won't say what his chances are outright, but I know it's bad. I know he's on a ventilator. They're waiting to see how much damage there might be to his brain. But we're not giving up hope. Are we, Brie? We're going to be there for him."

"Sometimes people pull through some pretty bad injuries," I said. "They recover. It happens a lot. The experts don't always know."

"They don't know anything," Sheila said. "I still have hope. I just wish I could be with him. That's important. It kills me to think of him alone."

"I'll go back down," Brie said.

"You've been so good, sweetheart."

"Did you catch the one who did it?" Brie asked me.

"Not yet."

"You're going to, right?"

"We'll catch him."

"Because, he could come back anytime. You know?"

"You don't have to be afraid. He's a lot more scared now than you are, believe me."

She kissed her mother and went out.

Sheila looked at me. Her eyes took everything in and told me everything. She motioned me closer. I reached to take her hand, but she extended her arms and wrapped them around my neck and pulled me down and kissed me.

The quick electronic throb of an alarm sounded. A light was flashing. A second later the door swung open.

Two nurses hurried in. They examined Sheila's wires and replaced the ones that had come loose. They told her not to move around so much. She thanked them.

"The doctors opened me up pretty good," she told me. "I have a scar from here to here."

"You'll be fine. Everything's going to be fine."

"We did it, Ray," she whispered. "We did it. If only he would die. Jesus, I wish he would die."

I touched my finger to her lips. We exchanged a glance. She shouldn't be saying that.

"Why didn't he die?" she whispered. "You said he was dead. I believed you."

"It doesn't matter now. Keep your eyes on the road."

"What if he wakes up?"

"Don't worry about that. Don't think about it."

"I have to think about it. What am I going to think about?"

"I told you to wait ten minutes. What happened?"

"I don't know. I lost track of time. It all seemed so unreal. I drifted off. I dreamed, Ray. I dreamed about us."

"What about the ski mask?" My whispering voice hissed. It sounded harsher than I intended. "That was clear enough, wasn't it? A goddamn ski mask."

"That detective—what's his name, Kaiser?—the one you said was your friend? He's a monster. He came in to question me as soon as they got done stitching me up. I was still groggy."

"What happened?"

"He was suspicious, Ray. He didn't believe anything I said. He looked at me like he knew everything. I had to put him off the track."

"He's a cop. He's going to do what he can to get you to say more than you want to. Hell, if he really suspected you, you would never know it. He's a professional. You don't play games with a professional."

"You don't know what it's like. You're lying there, you're weak, and he's throwing insinuations, suggestions. That bastard! I had to give him something definite, not a ski mask. Now they're chasing somebody who doesn't exist. That's what we want." We were so close I could feel her breath as she spoke.

"Every detail you give them they can trip you up with later."

"I was trying to help. I was afraid. I was alone and afraid. All I could think was, you shot me. I kept asking myself, 'How could he do that? How could he shoot me?' "

"You think I enjoyed it? It was your idea."

"I'm not saying– I just didn't know it would hurt so much. The pain made me crazy, to think something like that. It made me weak."

"We can't afford weak," I said into her ear.

"I can't do it alone."

"I'm with you, babe. I'm with you all the time. We won't be able to see each other for a while. But I'm always with you."

She was sliding her hand along my neck when we heard a noise. I straightened. The door opened. Frank Kaiser entered.

When Kaiser was on a case, his eyes went to work. I had noticed it before. They didn't become judgmental or suspicious. They just opened a little wider, looked at things a little more the way a child does, with wonder, with absorbed interest. They didn't miss a thing.

He walked right up to me and pointed an accusing finger in my face. "You shouldn't be here," he said. I was about to make an excuse when his face softened into that little sideways smile he had. "Gotta be careful on this one, Ray."

I didn't say anything.

"So you two are . . . friends?"

"I told you," I said. "Neighbors."

"Sure. How are you feeling, Mrs. Travis?"

"Better, thanks. Tired."

I knew, at that moment, that he was thinking. He was adding it up. Ray Dolan. Sheila Travis. Maybe it meant nothing, my visiting her. My living so near. My being first on the scene. But I knew it wouldn't go past him. It was another figure in the complicated calculus that was working itself out in his brain. His eyes were taking it all in.

Don't explain anything, I told myself. Keep it simple.

"I want to know about my husband, Detective," Sheila said. Good, just what she should say. "I want to see him."

"That's not my department," Frank said. "I'm sure the doctors will let you see him as soon as it's possible."

Frank explained that he had a man waiting outside, a sketch artist. He would turn her description of the suspect into a drawing.

"We don't want to tax your strength, but the sooner we get the sketch on the street, the better the chance of apprehending the shooter."

Sheila's eyes glided past me. She said she would try.

Frank stuck his head out the door. He introduced the man who entered, Chuck Warburg. I had met him a couple of times.

"Did you see our man?" he asked me.

"No, this is the witness."

"I only saw him for an instant," Sheila said. "I'm not sure if . . ."

"That's Chuck's specialty," Frank said. "He'll help you to pull it back into focus. You'd be surprised the details he can get you to remember."

Warburg took a sketch pad out of a thick accordion briefcase.

"We want to start with the general shape of the man's face, Mrs. Travis. Oval, square, round . . ."

I announced that I was leaving.

"Oh, Ray," Sheila said. "Please stop down and see Lance. I know he'll sense your presence even if he's . . ."

"Of course. See you, Frank."

Kaiser said nothing. He followed me out of the room. In the corridor he said, "Ray, I haven't gotten you in for a formal interview yet."

"They gave you my report, didn't they?"

"Your scene report, yes. I want to talk about before, about her, the husband—you know, the vibes."

"Whenever you need me."

"I'll be in touch. There are a few odd angles to this one, angles you might be able to help me with."

"Really?"

"Oh, yeah. Very odd."

NARROW EYES AND high cheekbones, a Chinese look almost. Short hair. Unassertive chin. Wisp of a goatee.

They got the sketch out quickly. Soon his face—the mute, sinister expression you see on all composites—was taped to the dashboard of every patrol car, the cash register of every convenience store in the city. He stared, cold-eyed and defiant, from the front page of every newspaper. You could see him on telephone poles and in bars and Laundromats.

Male black. Twenty to twenty-five. Five-foot-nine. One hundred and fifty pounds. Medium-dark skin. Wearing dark pants, navy hooded sweatshirt.

Monica Hargrove, the Mansfield County district attorney, had appeared on the news promising to have the guy locked up within a week. Promising. It was a great occasion for the politicians to make noise. Mayor Catlett got into the act. He played up his visit to Sheila. He railed against crime. He praised the police department to high heaven.

We set up roadblocks. The Oak Hill area, the part of Mansfield that you would call a ghetto, lies between where I live, out on the far east side, and downtown. The whole section got sliced to pieces when they put in the expressways. People could drive downtown without seeing *them*, without worrying about what was happening in that forgotten chunk of the city.

The roadblocks were intended to catch people coming and going from Oak Hill. We would check registration, inspection, license. The tiniest violation, you were supposed to write them up. We asked some to get out of their cars and submit to a search. A few refused. Most did as requested. We shined our flashlights into their cars, always looking.

We busted crack houses that had been let alone for one reason or another. We busted hookers. We busted men with loads of dread-locks under their knit hats who were selling sticks of sinsemilla. We busted winos. Everybody sat out his time in a very crowded holding pen. Everybody's name made its trip along the electronic nerves of the computer. Everybody got asked a few pointed questions.

Who did it? Give this guy up. If you know something, don't hold back. It's not worth it.

I played along with it myself. I took the hunt seriously. I studied faces on the street, looking for the elusive suspect. What was I going to do? You're a cop, you play your part.

When I came in from my tour, I was hoping Frank Kaiser would be too busy or would have forgotten what he'd said at the hospital about getting together, questioning me about the case. I didn't want to face him. Lying to Frank was hard for anybody.

I knew he would be putting in sixteen-hour days on the case, that some nights he would never go home at all. So I wasn't sur-prised to see him strolling into the locker room at twenty after mid-night, wearing a brown suit and crisp white shirt and looking as fresh as if he had just returned from a vacation. That was Frank on a case. The smile he wore, a rarity for him, didn't quite fit his features.

"I want you to go for a ride, boy. Take your own car and follow me."

"Where are we headed?"

"You'll see."

I followed his taillights. He drove fast, as he always did. The night was very quiet. A faint mist hung above the snow.

We mounted the Albright Expressway and looped around to the Logan Avenue exit. Out Logan to Seneca. Then down Seneca toward the low glacial hills of the east side. It was a route I knew by heart. We were headed straight toward my house.

We didn't stop there, though. We turned into Maple Drive and wound around to the Travis house.

"They have special cleaning companies now," he said as we walked to the front door. "Crime scene cleaners. Blood, of course, is a biohazard—you need a permit. These people know how to handle it. They're coming in tomorrow before the wife and daughter move back. It won't be a crime scene after that."

He unlocked the front door. Did I immediately pick up her perfume in the air, her smell? Maybe not. The house had the dull odor of a closed space. Nobody had lowered the heat.

"I've been over here quite a few times," Frank told me. "I need to soak up a scene, get the feel of it. I need to know it this time of night, the time the crime happened. I need to imagine how it went down. Feed my imagination."

"I can see that makes sense." I waited. I wasn't going to offer anything. He sat on the couch in the living room, I let myself down into an easy chair. It felt strange, like trying out furniture in a showroom. I thought about Christmas, about me and Lance in almost the same positions. You a backdoor man, Ray?

"This I had figured as a drug case all the way. Who does this kind of thing? It wasn't robbery. There were plenty of goodies to take. We found his stash, half an ounce of snow and some meth. But the guns don't come out over half an ounce. Not in the suburbs. So what's it all mean?"

"You're the detective."

"What were your impressions when you came in?"

"I don't know—danger, I guess. I was focused on clearing the scene. I thought the shooter might still be in the house."

"How did the place strike you? Had it been invaded?"

"No sign of it."

"Smell anything?"

"Powder."

"Still? Doctors figured the wife passed out, maybe half an hour between the shootings and when she called it. She can't remember."

"I smelled it. I know the smell of powder."

"You saw the husband?"

"In the kitchen. There was a lot of blood."

"Did you examine him?"

"I thought he was dead. He didn't seem to be breathing. I have to admit something, Frank. I said I tried for a carotid pulse, but I never did. He looked dead to me. I never checked."

"That's understandable."

He got up and motioned me to follow him. We strolled into the kitchen.

Nobody had moved a thing. Still the black pool of blood, the plastic syringe and bandage wrappers that the paramedics had left. A chalk line now surrounded each item.

"He got violent with her?" Frank asked abruptly.

"A couple of times that I saw."

"Tell me."

"At a party back in September he got juiced, wrestled her around, poured booze over her. He was totally shitfaced, passed out, everybody left."

"Including you?" He looked at me. I couldn't see his eyes in the dim light. A smile flitted around his lips but never lit on them.

"I don't like domestic disputes," I said.

"Who does? Always nasty. And who knows where they'll end? Anything else?"

"They were both into the grape. One night I found her outside, banged up. He was charged, order of protection. After Christmas she let him come back."

"Then he got dead."

He stepped over the blood and opened the refrigerator. The light from inside was unnaturally bright. I could see there was still plenty of food inside.

"You hungry?" Frank asked. "How about an apple? I'm having an apple. They won't miss it. I forgot to eat dinner, can you believe it? I'm so into this, I forget to eat—and you know how I love to eat."

He bit into a red delicious. He stepped back over the blood, set the apple on the counter.

"Say I'm him," he said. "Come on. It's the middle of the night. You're there—male black, five-nine, one-fifty, a little guy, but with a gun. We're in the kitchen. Why? I turn my back on you. Why? We know the first one was in the back. Did you shove him, spin him around? Try it."

"Like this?" I pushed against his hard bulk.

"Is that how it went down? Or did he know you and he was

headed for the fridge to offer you a beer? Or an apple? Get some ice to mix drinks? What was it?"

His patter was making me jittery. Was that the idea? Did he already have it figured? Was he playing with me? Trying to crack my nerves?

"I haven't a clue, Frank."

"Or maybe it happened like this. Maybe he got in your face. You didn't intend to do it. But he pressed you." He moved very close to me. A drop of his spittle landed on my chin. I didn't wipe it. "He put it to you. Grabbed you. Like this. You weren't about to back down, this asshole. You grappled with him. Like this."

He leaned his heavy forearms on my shoulders, clasped his hands behind my neck. I pushed against his chest. He twisted me. Frank was a strong man. He started to slip on a half nelson. I struggled against his grip. We danced around the dark kitchen. I thought I heard him say, right in my ear, "I know you did it." But maybe it was something else he said. Maybe he was just breathing hard. My mind contorted the sound. I managed some leverage and broke his hold. I pushed him away.

He laughed. "Maybe that's not how it went down at all. Maybe you just blew the sucker away. Just one cool motion. Maybe, huh?"

"I don't know, Frank."

"And you keep firing after he's down. But from a distance, like you're squeamish. You don't lean over and finish the job. Why? It's almost the way a woman would do it."

"I suppose you shoot a guy six times, you figure he's finished no matter how close you are."

"Maybe. Let's look at the bedroom."

We padded up those carpeted stairs.

"Her description of the suspect is just right," Frank said. "Not too detailed, not too vague. It rings true, not like something she made up. Maybe she's a good liar. She seem like a liar to you?"

"I guess if she was any good you wouldn't notice."

"Very true. I can usually tell, though. I've had so much practice. The truth is almost impossible to make up, I've found. What's phony has a certain ring to it, like a cracked bell. But there are born liars, no doubt about that."

We walked into her room, still maneuvering through the dark house. He switched on the bedside lamp. He sat on the edge of her bed beside the flagrant stain.

"Stay there, just inside the door. Now hold your arm out. No, wait . . . you carrying? Hold it out."

I reached down and unclipped the pistol from my ankle holster. I held it out, pointed it above his head. He stared at me. I wasn't sure if he could detect the tremor in my hand from that distance. For a long silent moment he just looked.

"Boy, I love a puzzle," he said finally. "There are so many pieces here. The victim—he's an asshole. He's the type of guy who makes enemies. He's into drugs—that may or may not mean anything. He's pretty well fixed, look at this place, so maybe it was a robbery gone bad. Maybe it was extortion."

"I thought you had a suspect," I said, putting my gun away. "I thought it was just a matter of finding him."

"Layers, Ray. Every crime has layers, like an onion. The trouble is, if you keep peeling away layer after layer, eventually you come to nothing. The question is, Where do you stop? Where does that truth lie? At the surface? Maybe, but that can be set up. At the deepest part, the core? Not usually. Most people aren't deep. They're greedy or horny or angry or crazy or just mistaken. The truth is in one of those layers. To solve your crime, you need to go just deep enough, no farther."

He moved over to Sheila's dresser. I stood in the doorway. My eyes kept straying to the bed, to her blood.

"I'm getting used to having her gone," Frank said. I stared at him. "Elaine. I always put her on a pedestal more than she deserved. I'm glad she's gone. I'm a new man. A new man."

"And you're on the track of a bad guy."

"Exactly." He sniffed the air. "I can smell him. I'm taking this case down, one way or another. This is going to be my masterpiece."

He started looking through the dresser drawers.

"She says they'd always had separate bedrooms—they both liked it that way. I asked her, Was the marriage on the rocks? They had their problems, she said. I said, Problems? I understand problems. Oh, yeah."

"It was pretty obvious they weren't hitting it off."

"Either of them step out?"

"I wouldn't know. I didn't see that much of them."

"No. Hey, look at this." He held up a pair of panties, so white they seemed to glow. He stretched the fabric with his fingers. "Would you have separate bedrooms, married to a broad like that?"

I had always liked Frank, loved him in an odd way. That night, though, I hated him. Hated him and feared him.

"Who knows what goes on in a marriage."

"You said a mouthful there, boy. Look." Now it was a silk camisole. He held it against his chest. "Yeah, everybody has their problems. And what do you think I found out? She didn't tell me, forgot to tell me, so I had to find it out. Insurance. Nice fat term life policy."

Anything I said would ring false. I had a right to remain silent.

Kaiser said, "Guess who's the sole beneficiary?"

I shrugged.

"The wife. A million dollars." He studied my face.

It's amazing how cool you can stay. A thousand emotions flashed through my mind, but none surfaced. Was I too cool? Was I overdoing it?

"Yeah, one million dollars," he said. "You take any case, a million insurance, how far do you have to look? That's where I think I'm missing something."

"He was in the insurance business." I immediately wished I hadn't said it.

"I know. The policy was a fringe benefit. I know why he had it, but when was the last time an elephant walked into your living room, pure coincidence? A million dollars is never a coincidence."

"I guess anybody is capable of anything, when it comes down to it."

"Ray, that's why I keep telling you to go for the gold shield. You think like a detective."

He crossed to the window and looked out. I was clenching my teeth. Insurance.

"Hey," he said, "isn't that your house right there? I didn't realize you were so close."

"That's me."

"Christ, they built these places practically in your backyard."

"I don't mind, except for the lights. I like it dark for the telescope."

"Of course, your stargazing. You have a clear view from over there. She ever forget to pull her shade?"

He turned to me, smiling broadly.

I BEGAN SEEING LIGHTS in her house again, the hard kitchen light, the creamy wash from the family room, the amber glow of her bedroom. I couldn't help noticing.

I stayed away. I was working overtime almost every day. The chief wanted the maximum number of bodies on the street. Lance's shooting was one of those cases that had to be solved, no excuses. The press was grandstanding it.

A couple of days after she returned, one of those gray, dank afternoons that fill up Manchester Januarys, I was getting ready to head down to the station for a four o'clock tour. I had been up most of the night—I had made a DWI arrest at eleven-thirty and it had taken me three hours to process the drunk.

I was shaving when the phone rang. I let the machine answer. I heard Sheila's voice, but the message was over before I could pick up.

I pressed the button. "Ray, it's me. Please, call as soon as you can. It's important. I have to talk to you."

She shouldn't have been leaving messages on my machine. She

shouldn't have been calling me at all. The sound of her voice was flagrant. I punched her number.

"I need you, Ray. Come over."

"I don't think that's a good idea."

"Come. Please. I'm losing it."

"Okay," I said. "Keep calm. Take a deep breath. Everything's cool."

"No, it's not. It's not cool. Hurry."

This was all wrong. We shouldn't be communicating. I wanted to keep as much distance between us as possible. You can always be overheard. Nosy neighbors are always watching, always noting how often you visit, what time. I knew from my police training that everything a person does leaves traces. Those traces could hang us.

If I was going to go over, I was going to do it in the open. I would drive around the corner, a neighbor visiting a neighbor. I would park in her driveway and walk into the house in plain view.

Sheila answered the chimes and stepped toward me and wrapped her arms around my neck. I pushed her back and closed the door. We clung to each other for a long moment. The taste of her mouth lit me up.

I was intoxicated. I began to work on her delicious throat. She slid her bare foot up my calf. I started to pick her up, but she gave a little gasp. I'd nearly forgotten about her injury.

I held her away from me, gripping her shoulders between my hands.

"What is it? Why did you call? Don't you know—"

"He woke up," she said.

"What?"

"Lance."

I searched her face.

She said, "I hate seeing him. I go in every day and play the wife, but it kills me, Ray. This morning—Brie went with me—no change. We sat there staring at him, talking to him once in a while as if he could hear us. Then we went to the hospital cafeteria for lunch."

"What the hell happened?"

She pressed her finger to my lips. "Brie's taking a nap," she whispered, and pointed upstairs. Grasping my hand, she led me toward the family room.

"Hello?" Brie's voice said. We could hear her coming downstairs.

"It's Ray, honey," Sheila called. "He just dropped by. I was telling him the good news."

"Hi," Brie said to me. "Isn't it great? Isn't it fantastic?"

"It's a good sign, that's for sure."

"He has a long way to go, of course. I was reading up on it. The rehabilitation process can be very slow."

"We have to be thankful for every little improvement," Sheila said.

"He looked at me," Brie said. "I know he recognized me. I'm going to help him get better. I've been, like, a jerk. I see that now. But I can be there for him, now that he needs me."

"You're so sweet," Sheila told her, stroking her cheek.

"You don't think," Brie told me. "Until something like this happens, you just don't think."

"We learn from everything," I said.

"When he opened his eyes I realized that I really care about him. I wanted to—"

We heard the low rumble of a car exhaust from outside. Brie skipped to the front window.

"It's Justin. I'm just going to talk to him. I'll be right back."

"Put on a jacket!" Sheila called, but her daughter was already out the door.

Sheila and I stood in the living room where we could see Brie talking to a boy in a Camaro.

"She used to stay out till all hours, always breaking curfew. Now I can't get rid of her."

"Tell me what happened."

"He knows, Ray. We're coming back from the cafeteria, a page comes over the loudspeakers, Mrs. Travis report to room three-eighteen—his room, right? I figure, this is it, he's gone. I'm getting ready to go into my grieving widow act, tears and all."

Brie leaned on the car door. The driver was the one who had let her off the morning of the shooting, not one of the punks she had been joy riding with. She trotted around to climb in the passenger side. I didn't think they could see much through the window, but I nudged Sheila and took a couple of steps away from the dull light.

"We get to the room, my heart is beating. I'm actually telling Brie to prepare for the worst. The doctor meets us outside, says Lance has been stirring, they think he might be coming out of the coma. A good sign, he says."

"He was awake?"

"We go in, no change. Beep beep, flash flash, the ventilator going. He's lapsed back. Brie goes over very close to him and talks to him. Nothing. She keeps it up. After a few minutes of this, he actually opens his eyes. I thought I was going to faint. I couldn't stand it."

"But you were happy, you acted happy."

"Sort of. I knew I should join Brie, or say Lance, Lance, or cry, or something. I was too scared, Ray. He was a heartbeat away from saying I did it."

We were talking in low voices, but I didn't like to hear her say that. Maybe Kaiser suspected her enough to plant a bug in her house. It was far-fetched, but we had to consider every possible angle.

"He's not going to remember what happened," I whispered.

"He does remember. I know it. He looked at Brie, just moving his eyes. Brie started crying, clutched at his hand. I forced myself to come up beside him. Lance, I'm going. Lance, baby. Then his eyes are on me. He's looking at me, I'm looking at him. There's nobody else in the room, that's the way I felt. It was like being haunted, only worse. He knows who I am and what I did, and I know he knows. Ray, it was more horrible than you can imagine. I wanted to take my fingers and jab them into those eyes and rip them out, so help me."

"Keep it low," I said. "What happened then?"

"He stared. He didn't say anything, of course—he's still on the ventilator. Then he slowly closed his eyes. I called him again, he didn't respond. Let him rest, the doctor said. We stayed awhile longer, but I had to get out of there. The strain. Good idea, the doctor said. Tomorrow we can hope for more progress."

"He doesn't know."

"He does! I saw it in his eyes, the look he gave me. I saw the frustration—not being able to speak. But it's just a matter of time, the doctor said. Just a matter of time before he accuses me. He's going to point the finger, Ray. I know he is."

I shook my head. "Aphasia—where you can't think of words, can't speak properly—it's the most common symptom of brain damage. And recent memories are almost always wiped out. You can remember summer vacation in fourth grade but you can't remember what you do for a living. Good chance he didn't even see you clearly."

"First, he was a goner," she snapped. "Then they said he might never come out of the coma. But miracles happen. That's what I'm worried about, a damn miracle."

"What you have to worry about is yourself. You're the one who's going to give up this case. You can't think wrong. You can't talk wrong. And you can't play games. I told you—"

"You told me he was dead."

"Listen to you."

"I depended on you."

"I'm telling you, gunshot wound to the head, I know the prognosis. You're worrying about the wrong thing."

"What's the right thing?"

"A million dollars."

"You know? I was going to surprise you. That was a secret I was going to spring on you."

"But you forgot?"

"Ray, we could be rich. If only he would—"

"Here she comes." Brie was out of the car and waving as the Camaro backed into the street. I said, "We have to stay away from each other. Every time we're together it's a risk."

"I know that."

"You should have told me about the insurance."

"You're right, I'm sorry. But the money just sweetens it, don't you see? And we'll get through this if we're together. Just don't leave me. Don't stop loving me. I need that." Her eyes flashed.

I wanted to kiss her and hug her, and I wanted to strangle her.

I wanted to put all the perfume back in the bottle. I wanted not to have ever seen her.

I stepped back from her as I heard the front door open. I said some exit words and got out of there. The gray twilight looked like the end of the world.

THE JANUARY THAW that year was three days of cloudy skies, the temperature creeping up to fifty. A cold rain began to fall, the storm sewers backed up with runoff, the snow turned to dirty slush.

The last brightness had leaked out of the sky by four o'clock, reflections of streetlights were smeared across the pavement. I was climbing into my patrol car to start my tour when I saw a figure approaching, gripping an umbrella against the gusts of wind. I unlocked the passenger door and Leanne Corvino slipped inside.

"You don't owe me anything," she said. "I'm not saying you do. The fling, whatever, means nothing now, zero. But I thought we were friends."

"We're friends, why not." I turned on the engine to warm up.

"I leave messages, I don't hear from you."

"I'm not good at returning messages. I meant to."

"Did you? I don't think so."

"You need help?"

"I need to know. Who shot Lance Travis? It's the question every reporter in the city is asking."

"You've seen the sketch of the perpetrator. It's all we have to go on."

"Yesterday's news: unknown black shoots homeowner for unknown reason with unknown gun, goes upstairs, shows his face, plugs wife, same reason, same gun. Home invasion, suburban nightmare, fearful gentry. Been there, done that."

"What are you looking for?"

"I met Lance Travis. You knew them, you live practically next door. He dabbled in cocaine—he offered me some the night we were over there. We both know he liked to rub up against the hard boys. Why are you guys making out that this is some random shootout, robbery attempt, or whatever it's supposed to be?"

"I don't think the police are saying it's one thing or another. We have a situation, we have a description of a suspect."

"Was this a drug thing? They must have found some evidence in the house."

"The department's not going to point the finger at drugs for two reasons. First, they're protecting the privacy of the victim."

"Come on."

The rain drummed against the roof, washed down the windshield in sheets. I turned the heat up.

"Let me finish," I said. "He was shot, he doesn't deserve to have his vices sprayed all over the papers, the television, if the dope isn't connected to the crime. If it is, they still want to keep it out as long as they're looking to close a big case."

"And this one is big."

"Maybe drugs will factor in later, but for now they want Lance Travis simon-pure. If the case turns difficult, looks like they won't crack it, then they can drag out the dope angle and use it to dampen public outrage. People hear the victim took drugs, dealt drugs, they tune out. He tangled with the devil and got burned, so what? Don't quote me on any of this."

She said, "Ray, I've got some hot stuff on this story and I need confirmation. Frank Kaiser's a friend of yours, right? Is he keeping you up to date on the investigation?"

"He doesn't talk to me about it, why would he?"

"But you can talk to him. Just confirm a rumor. I want to go with it on tonight's news. I want to have something fresh."

"What's the rumor?"

"She had an insurance policy on the husband. One million dollars and she's the sole beneficiary."

A gust of wind tore big drops of cold water from the tree branches and pelted the car with lead bullets. I stared across the seat. She had very eager eyes.

"Go with it," I said.

"It's true?"

I nodded.

"A million?" She whistled a falling tone.

Don't argue, I said to myself. Don't act as if it means something or nothing. It's information that's bound to come out. Better now while the chase is on for the killer. Better from me. My giving it to her would put me in solid with Leanne. If she was going to be poking around in this case, it would be smart to be her pal. If I was helping her, she'd be less likely to imagine I was a piece of the puzzle. I was thinking like that now, always thinking.

Insurance doesn't mean anything. Everybody has insurance. He was in the insurance business. She had nothing to do with him taking out the policy. They had plenty of money already, she didn't need insurance. But don't explain. Don't try to justify.

She said, "You know how much is riding on this case, don't you?"

"Two people have been seriously injured in their home."

"That, too. But there's a bigger story. Mayor Catlett wants to be Senator Catlett. He has momentum, everybody agrees about that. If he doesn't shine in the election this year, it stops him in his tracks. The Keshawn Pitts incident hurt him. If his police force can break the Travis shooting, which has the suburbanites' underwear in knots, Catlett looks good again."

"The pressure's on from the top—that's no secret."

"You guys get it wrapped up quick and neat, Catlett's a can-do mayor. A few African-American citizens might scream about their toes getting stepped on, but everybody can feel safe, and that's what counts. Catlett has pushed a whole stack of chips onto the crime issue, and now here's crime in technicolor."

"I'm just down here in the trenches doing my job."

"You and me both. This insurance thing is an interesting little angle, though, isn't it?"

"Is it?"

"Would you kill for a million dollars?"

"No."

She smiled broadly. "That's why I like you, Ray. You're a decent human being. And a cop. What a combo. I have another favor to ask."

"What's that?"

"I plan to keep on this—I've already started digging. What you can do is put me in touch with Kaiser, give me an inside track on what's happening in the department."

"Always working the connections."

"That's my job."

"Any reason I should help you stay ahead of the pack?"

"Because you're my friend. Because we're both interested in truth. Because there are angles to this that need looking into."

"I'll do what I can. I'll talk to him."

"You're a real doll, you know that?"

She opened the door and climbed out. I turned on the wipers, watched as she crossed in front of me and hurried down the street toward her own car.

Once, I had thought of her as my salvation. I imagined she could head off my fate. That notion seemed absurd now.

"ELAINE CALLED—THE DIVORCE, filing the papers, whatever. I said, fuck it, file your damn papers. Do I care? I've got a case, baby. I've got a life here."

We were headed across town in Frank's car. It was the second time he had picked me up at the station after my tour.

"I want to show you detectives can have fun, too. I want you to get a taste of it."

"A taste of what?"

"Everybody's looking for some meaning in life," he said. "I've found it. I put people away. Forget cheating wives, screwed-up marriages, all that. I am doing good work. I take nothing—a description that could be anybody—I take that and turn it into a case. That's what I'm on earth for. That's what I live for."

"You're the master, Frank."

It was just after six. The streets were clogged with traffic. Frank checked his watch a couple of times as we worked our way through downtown and onto the jammed expressway.

"I'm going to make this one pay," he said. "I've even started thinking, chief of detectives. I never would have dreamed about it before. But you get your name in the paper, your picture on television, they have to sit up and pay attention. Suddenly, you're a valuable commodity. Frank Kaiser, they start saying. Yeah, get Frank Kaiser."

"Nobody in the department deserves it more than you do."

"I'm beginning to taste it. You know I've never been a pusher. I've done my job, put one foot in front of the other. But now, why not? Why the hell shouldn't I be on top? And when the opportunity comes along, you grab. You don't catch many cases like this one. Everybody's eyes are on you."

"I guess it makes sense if you get a conviction. What happens if you come up empty?"

"Then it backfires and I'm the goat. But I'm not letting this one get away. And I'm going to play the game. That broad you introduced me to, the one from Channel Ten? She's very cooperative. I figured, she made you a hero, why not me? I give her an inside edge on a story, she makes me look good."

"She's a hustler, all right."

"I don't like newspeople, but you have to play the game."

Frank leaned on his horn, pulled around a tangle of cars to get down the ramp at the Oak Hill exit.

"The suspense is killing me here, Frank," I said. "What's coming down this evening?"

"I've got the guy who did it."

"The Travis case?"

"That's right. I have him. I'm bringing him down and I'm going to make a circus of it. I'm going to get noticed."

"You have a lead?"

"Anonymous tip. This is going to be rich, Ray. Catlett's going to love this. Talk about hero. He'll be giving me two medals. Hell, he'll probably want to take me to bed. Snuggle in there between him and Mrs. Mayor."

"This guy looks good for it?"

"Tailor-made. We had him in for questioning earlier, routine. No alibi. Drug connection. Dead ringer for the composite. Tattinger and Powell are exercising a warrant on his residence as we speak. He's got a room in a slum on Empire Street, common-law wife. We're headed for the main event, close the trap. In fact, here we are."

"Our Lady of Sorrows?"

"He eats here every day, the soup kitchen. The padre is one of these holy Joes with the save-the-poor, gay-is-okay, fight-city-hall bullshit. The bishop doesn't like him any better than we do."

I worked this sector regularly and was familiar with the neighborhood. Frank had ordered up a tactical force, Special Services, close to a dozen officers in helmets and face shields, with the type of oversized batons they use in riot control. Another smaller group was armed with shotguns, battering rams, even a few automatic weapons.

"This is for show," Frank said. "Plus, I want the bust to go down smooth. Nobody tries anything. We're going in, nice and clean, bag ourselves a murderer."

"You're getting a little ahead of the game, aren't you, Frank? The victim isn't dead yet."

"Travis? Didn't I tell you? He cashed in at three thirty-seven this afternoon. This is homicide all the way now. It's better that way, cleaner. Guy would have been a vegetable anyway. Let's go."

LEANNE CORVINO LOOKED COLD. Her dark gray skirt stopped a few inches above her knees, showing off her prizewinning legs. Her camel-hair coat hung open. Her creamy blouse exposed her throat. She held a microphone in one black-gloved hand while she thrust the other into her pocket. She threw me a quick wink and turned her smile on Frank Kaiser, who was crossing the street to meet her.

I wandered over and talked to some patrolmen I knew. They were glad for the overtime. They knew the show of force was an act—a church, for Christ's sake. They were looking forward to going home that night and watching themselves on television.

"It'll be the number-one story, I know that," Terry Lofton said. "That's why they're doing it now, get it on the eleven o'clock news."

"Here comes some more television," somebody said, pointing out the two remote vans that were pulling up the side street where we were congregated.

This wasn't a typical Frank Kaiser play. He never wanted to talk about a case, even when it was over. He rarely gave interviews.

Now he was having a cozy little chat with Leanne, gesturing, pointing toward the palm of his other hand as if tracing a map.

Three other detectives had shown up to take part in the arrest. I was told that Monica Hargrove, the DA, was waiting at Central, ready to grab her share of credit and join in the news conference. But it was clear Frank had set himself up to be the star of the show. He had broken the case of the decade. His face would be on every front page, lead off every report.

Neighborhood people were watching as we made our way around the corner to Our Lady of Sorrows. Few stared openly. They had spent too many years not looking at cops. In poor neighborhoods, black neighborhoods, nobody looked right at you. They watched but never met your gaze. They knew it meant trouble. Look at a cop—Hey, buddy, come here—you're hooked.

So people let their eyes slide past us.

Our Lady of Sorrows spoke of a day when Oak Hill had money and more Catholics. The facade of carved limestone boasted elegant gothic arches and a big rose window of stained glass. Lit from within, it poured rich hues onto a street of ashes. A well-used stairwell at the side of the church led to a door on the lower level.

What attracted the crowd were the television cameras, the lights that were now scalding the scene, turning us all into actors, technicolor robots.

Frank called my name and gave me the high sign. We were going in. Three uniformed officers, two of them managing the battering ram, led the way. We got to the bottom of the iron stairs, where a smell of stale piss hung in the air. The detectives gathered on both sides of the door. As they prepared to heft the ram, one of them reached over and turned the knob. The door swung open as easy as milk.

In an instant we were all inside. I saw drawn pistols. Shouts of "Don't move!" and "Stay where you are!"

No one was moving. No one screamed. Exposed pipes ran along the ceiling. Radiators hissed. Long tables were filled with folks eating, old men, not-so-old men, young mothers with their kids, people on the edge. The room smelled of fried meat and cabbage.

A priest—he wore a flannel shirt but had the Roman collar under it—was hurrying toward us.

"Hello, Father," Frank Kaiser said. "How can you help us out here? you want to know. Jerome Johnson? Name ring a bell? We need to talk to him."

"I'm afraid you can't come in here without permission. This is a church. A church is a sanctuary."

"We have permission. In writing. We also have a warrant. We want to get this done quickly, smoothly, without any aggravation."

"I have to object. No one contacted me about this. This is my parish."

"The diocese holds the deed."

"You cannot come onto this property to arrest someone without—"

"We can, we are."

The name Jerome Johnson hissed along the tables until it reached a black man near the end.

Kaiser gave a signal and three of the uniformed officers started forward.

The man was young and used up at the same time. He had the wary, three A.M. look of a junkie. He spoke quickly to the woman beside him. She whispered to him. He looked everywhere but at us.

The people around him spoke rapidly. He shook his head. He said something else to the woman. Then he stood and started moving along the wall opposite where the officers were approaching. Kaiser pointed. Two more cops moved to block his exit.

"Jerome!" someone shouted.

Jerome shouted back something I couldn't understand. The whole basement suddenly filled with shouting. Everyone began to move at once.

Just before the officers reached Jerome, he jumped onto one of the rickety tables and down into the next aisle. A mad scramble broke out. Chairs toppled.

The priest tried to get between the police and the man they were after. In the rush, a cop pushed him and he tripped. That made a lot of people angry. They surged toward the police. The tactical boys formed a phalanx against them.

Jerome dodged a cop's grasp and made it to the end of the room. He was through a door that led to a staircase. The cops, the priest, and a few of the soup kitchen patrons all tore through the door after him.

I followed them. Upstairs the church was dark. The air rattled with echoes of shouting. Jerome was pinned to the floor of the altar by two big patrolmen. He continued to struggle as they handcuffed him.

I had been a Catholic myself before I asked questions the priests didn't want to answer, before I substituted my own rules. It still seemed a kind of violation to me, that kind of commotion going on in God's house.

Frank Kaiser leaned against the front pew until they brought Jerome to him. He read the prisoner his rights.

"What is this about, man?" Jerome kept asking. He was thick-tongued and inarticulate. "What the hell's this about?"

"What you're doing is not right!" the priest insisted.

"It's right as rain, Reverend," Kaiser said. "We have a warrant for his arrest."

"What the hell's the charge?" Jerome screamed.

"Murder."

The young man actually grinned. "Murder? You're crazy!"

"I'm crazy? You're crazy if you think you can walk into a man's house and shoot him in the head, shoot his wife, leave them both for dead, and get away with it. Not in this city, brother. You're going down for this one."

"It's the police department of this city that should be put on trial," the priest insisted. His face was flushed purple. "Do you think we've forgotten Keshawn Pitts?"

Frank Kaiser shrugged.

The woman pushed her way through the crowd and tried to grab onto Jerome's arm.

"What are you doing to my husband? He has not done anything wrong!" Several other women gripped Johnson's wife and consoled her.

"Let's go," Kaiser said.

They marched the prisoner down the main aisle and out.

In the few minutes we had been inside, maybe two hundred people had congregated in front of the church, had materialized out of nowhere.

Presumed innocent—the words had never meant much to me before. Everybody I had ever arrested had been guilty. He might plea bargain, he might get off on a technicality, or on a lack of evidence, or with the help of a connected lawyer. But you always figured he was guilty—and you were always right.

Jerome Johnson was not guilty.

The television lights blazed. The cameramen scurried to get the best shot. Johnson dropped his chin to his chest. The two detectives who gripped his arms hoisted them a little so his shoulders hunched. He sure looked guilty.

The reporters yelled questions, jabbed their microphones at the prisoner. "Why did you do it?" "How do you feel?" "Did you know Lance Travis?" "Did you kill?" "Did you kill him?" "Did you do it?" "Did you?" "What do you have to say?"

He turned his head from one side to the other as if the lights were slapping him in the face.

After Jerome had endured the gauntlet of cameras, Kaiser eased him into the back of a squad car. Another detective pushed in beside the stunned prisoner.

An ugly mood permeated the street. I wanted to get away, but I had to wait for Frank. He was on the corner, giving Leanne an exclusive interview. The arrest, on top of Lance dying, would make for a juicy story.

From a distance I watched her putting on her look of grave concern, nodding in response to Kaiser's words. Frank kept turning away from her to speak directly to the camera. Five cops held spectators well back from the circle of clean light.

I wandered over to see what I could pick up.

". . . trying to make this a black-white thing," Frank was saying. "This is not about race. This is about being safe in our homes. Citizens of this city, no matter what their race, will be glad to know that we've made an arrest."

"Lieutenant Kaiser, how confident are you of your case against Jerome Johnson? Can you assure the citizens of Mansfield that they can rest easily in their beds tonight?"

"Definitely. I think this case is solved. Period."

"Thank you."

"My pleasure, Leanne."

She turned to the camera, which moved in close on her. "This has been an exclusive Channel Ten interview with . . ."

THE WAY THE LIGHTS were arranged, it was impossible to see any-thing from up on the platform, no matter how you shaded your eyes. The witness sat in the dark and made the identification. The tech boys had video cameras trained on the platform, microphones to pick up the sound.

"A defense lawyer questions the lineup," Frank Kaiser was telling me, "you have to be ready. Every step of the way you're trying to outthink these guys."

"The wife's coming down here?" I asked.

"Right now. She gives us a positive ID, this case is grease."

"What if she doesn't?"

He looked at me. "You trying to jinx it?"

"I'm just saying. How good a look did she have?"

"She saw the guy, all right."

The room was crowded with half a dozen detectives, some tech-nicians, a couple of guys I knew who worked in the forensic lab. Everybody was interested in this one.

"We're going to do a dry run before she gets here. Bring them out," Kaiser said.

The room went dark, high-wattage lights illuminated the platform. A minute later, the door opened. A bailiff from the jail directed six men onto the little stage.

They all had the deliberately funky aura of plainclothes cops— the sneakers, army jackets, shaggy hair. As they paraded across the platform and took their places under the numbers, a rustling of laughter snaked through the room. Everyone had been tense, now they let out a roar.

I laughed myself. It's hard to avoid the infection. Or maybe it really was funny: five of the men were white, one was black, a narcotics cop I knew pretty well. He gave a couple of shuck-and-jive moves to show he was into the spirit of the joke.

"Now, Mrs. Travis, look closely at these men," Kaiser said. His words set off another spasm of merriment. "Do you see him? Take your time. Number four, is it? Thank you."

The black cop, who stood under that number, put on a show of outrage. He pointed at himself, waved his arms, made faces. His act went over well. Detectives were actually stomping their feet on the floor, wiping away tears.

They messed around awhile longer before the lights went off and the men left. The rest of us waited uneasily for the main event. Detectives filtered in and out, conferred briefly with Kaiser, brought him reports, a fresh cup of coffee.

He had surprised me by inviting me in for the lineup. He kept saying he was trying to get me hooked on the idea of going for my gold shield. But I had to wonder if there was something more to it, some suspicion whispering in the back of his mind.

I didn't want to be in Sheila's presence with Frank Kaiser in the room. If she looked at me and put anything into it, I knew he would spot it.

Still, I was glad it was happening. This would be Sheila's chance to back away from her description of her assailant. She could say she didn't really get a close enough look. Then the whole thing would start to cool down.

After about twenty minutes Kaiser indicated to most of the spectators that they would have to leave.

"This isn't a show," he said.

I got up to go with the others. Frank grabbed my arm.

"You want to see this through, don't you, Ray? You were the first on the scene. Play detective awhile longer."

It would seem odd for me to refuse. I sat back down. A minute later the door opened.

Louise Newman, a black woman two years younger than me, who had recently made detective, led Sheila into the room. The idle chatter died immediately. Three men moved to open seats in front.

Sheila nodded a vague greeting to everyone. Dressed in somber colors, she crossed toward Kaiser, her limp more noticeable than usual. Her face suggested tears lurking behind her controlled features. She was playing the perfect widow, solemn and courageous.

She looked right at me. Jesus. Without wanting to, I glanced at Frank Kaiser. He was watching her, but in that instant his eyes jumped toward mine. I looked away and crossed my arms.

Frank placed her in the seat beside his. He asked her if she wanted coffee. She declined. He arranged the microphone. He had her speak a few sentences in a low voice to test the recording level. He asked her if she was ready.

"Okay, let's hit those lights."

Again the room went dark and a wall of light sealed off the platform in front. Kaiser ordered them to bring in the lineup.

This time all the men were black. They were all roughly similar in height, weight, age, and complexion to Jerome Johnson, who stood in the number four position. Whether Frank had planned this arrangement as a sort of tag to his earlier joke, I didn't know.

Each of the men squinted slightly against the glare. Each wore the hard expression of a potential murderer. Two of them I recognized as off-duty patrolmen.

Kaiser spoke into a microphone connected to a loudspeaker on the platform.

"Number one, take a step forward," he said. The volume was too high. For a second, the whine of feedback filled the room. A technician adjusted it.

"Turn to the right," Kaiser's voice continued. "Now to the left. Point your right arm straight in front of you. That's it. Thank you. Step back. Number two."

He went through the routine with each of them, slowly and methodically, his voice absolutely even. After the second one, Sheila turned her head briefly and looked at me. Her eyes widened, as if she expected me to give her a cue, to indicate which man was the suspect. I averted my gaze and swallowed hard.

I had no idea what she was going to do. I wanted her to say she couldn't identify any of the men and leave it at that.

"Number four, step forward."

Jerome Johnson went through his paces like all the others. Deadpan. Bored. Nonchalant. No more guilty or innocent than anybody in that room.

"Number five."

I didn't dare look at Sheila again. I yawned. Or did I pretend to yawn? A wave of sleepiness can come over you in a crisis.

I heard her ask Frank if she could get closer. Of course, he said. They can't see you as long as you stay out of the light.

She left her seat and moved toward the narrow platform. She walked along, peering at each man carefully. She stood in front of Jerome Johnson, almost seemed to be sniffing him. She moved on. Turning back toward Frank, she was frowning. She sat.

"Are any of these the man you saw in your home that night?"

She looked them over again, left to right, right to left. The room fell absolutely silent.

"That one," she said. She slowly pointed her finger.

"Number . . . ?" Frank asked.

"Four."

"You're positive?"

"That's the man."

"Is there any doubt in your mind?"

"No. That's him. That's the man who shot me. I'm sure of it. I can see him doing it. That's him."

Over the loudspeaker, Kaiser said, "Okay, that's fine."

The bailiffs opened the door and the six men left the room.

Frank and another detective escorted Sheila out of the room, which immediately filled with an eager buzz. We waited for Kaiser to return. The chatter died down.

Frank came back and looked gravely around the room. Breaking into a grin, he made a fist and took a wild swing at the air.

"Yes!"

The rest of the detectives erupted into cheers. I went along with them. What else could I do?

WE DRESS OUR BRIDES and our widows in veils. Under the veils they are beautiful. Under the veils they are radiant and joyous and stunning, or they are sad and mournful and lovely.

Sheila's face, behind the dark gauze, was delicate and strong and sorrowful and robust. Her grief, her pretended grief, enveloped her in an aura of mystery, of sanctity even. She followed the casket down the aisle. She glanced at me before slipping into the front pew.

I was in the sixth row next to Frank Kaiser. We stood behind the family and close friends, behind the gaggle of city officials who had shown up. Mayor Catlett was now gripping Sheila's hand in both of his, whispering to her, nodding. Chief Preston's lips were moving as well. Some Democrats, contenders for next year's election, had also come to bask in the glow of the event. Sandy LoPresti was murmuring to his wife in the pew just ahead of us. She wore her flagrant mink.

Sheila appeared to me as a picture of dignity. Her eyes brimmed. Her lips managed a pained smile. Each movement, each gesture was solemn and deliberate. I would never have imagined it was all an act.

I remembered other funerals. My father's. Cops had liked him. Officers came from all over our end of the state to say good-bye, a sea of uniforms. Comforting, I suppose, to have all those men, those replicas of him, gathered to do him honor. Yet for years, my nightmares were filled with rows and rows of white gloves.

Now winter light barely illuminated the stained-glass windows.

Does anybody believe anymore? I had not thought about God for a long time. I couldn't remember exactly when I had stopped believing. I just knew I was a long way from salvation. It's funny to think that a change like that, the loss of faith, comes over you so casually.

Sheila now knelt in a fervent semblance of prayer. She and Lance had joined this Episcopal congregation because Lance felt a salesman needed a church. I had never thought to ask her if she believed in any of it.

The priest came down and blessed the casket. He led the congregation in a prayer. He mounted the pulpit to deliver the eulogy.

You would have thought he and Lance had been best friends. He mentioned Lance's sense of humor, his generosity, his hearty laugh, his caring and compassionate soul. He praised him as a father, a husband, a brother, a businessman, a devoted member of his community, a Christian. He talked about how each of us was a child in Christ. He cautioned us not to try to fathom God's will, not to let out understandable anger over Lance's murder turn to bitterness.

A professional spiel. A few more hymns, some prayers, and it was over. They rolled the casket down the aisle.

Outside, the television technicians fiddled with the clear plastic covers that kept a cold rain off their camera lenses. They were waiting along with about fifty intrepid gawkers drawn by the news accounts. Always the gawkers.

Sheila had already gone when I emerged. City dignitaries were climbing into half a dozen limousines. The long line of cars, all with their lights on, wound toward the cemetery. More curiosity seekers had stationed themselves there, in spite of the rain.

The canopy near the grave sheltered only a handful of the mourners. Sheila and Brie sat on folding metal chairs. Brie's boyfriend, the kid with the Camaro, looked stiff in a new suit. Lance's brother had shown up from Elgin, Illinois. I had met him at the funeral home. He had brought his two sons, who both played on the offensive line at Northwestern. A sister, a mousy woman from Ohio, was red-eyed and sniffling from a bad cold.

The rest of us had to let the rain drip down our necks. As the coffin was being carried across the slick snow, one of the pallbearers slipped. He went down on the seat of his pants. The casket wavered, tilted, but they steadied it in time.

An emerald all-weather carpet covered the mound of dirt from the grave. It showed up neon against the snow. Rain pattered onto the mahogany lid of the box while the priest recited more prayers. Surely goodness and mercy shall follow me.

We filed under the canopy to offer our final condolence. Frank was right behind me in line.

I came to Brie first. Her puffy face made my chest tighten. She wrapped her arms around me. I patted her back.

"Why?" she said. "Why did he have to die?"

"You're doing great," I said. "There are no easy answers. You're doing everything right. Be strong for your mom, okay?"

I grasped Sheila's hand. She gave mine a little squeeze. I had prepared some things to say, but I couldn't bring any of them into my mouth. We just looked at each other.

Finally she said, "Lieutenant Kaiser," and turned. "I wanted to thank you. It's such a relief to know that you've . . . that we don't have to worry. I can't tell you. It's a relief for my daughter."

"You made it possible, Mrs. Travis," he said. "You were very brave."

"I just wish they would respect our privacy. These television people just won't leave us alone."

"One of them said he would pay me for an interview," Brie put in. "Can you believe that?"

We nodded in sympathy.

"I can't bear the idea of facing them for one more second," Sheila continued. "Not today. I was wondering, Ray, if you're going home, maybe you could drop me. Brie can go with Justin."

"If you want a police escort, Mrs. Travis," Frank said, "I can easily—"

"I think this will work out better, just to slip away. That is, if you're willing, Ray?"

"Sure," I said, shrugging. "Anything."

"I'd just like to go home and be alone for a while. You don't mind, do you, honey?" She stroked Brie's face.

Ten minutes later Sheila and I were in my car, the wipers slapping back and forth in front of us. Except for fleeting moments, it was the first time we'd been alone together since the night of the killing. I was nervous about it. I was nervous about everything.

Neither of us said a word until we had driven a couple of miles away from the cemetery. When she moved, her clothes rustled.

"Was that smart?" I said at last.

"Yes."

"Kaiser standing right there?"

"It's natural, Ray. It's the way innocent people act. Plus I couldn't wait to see you. Jesus, I've missed you."

"I've been thinking and thinking about you."

She twisted and wrapped her arms around my neck to kiss me. The car lurched. I had to pull away to focus on driving.

"You were very convincing back there," I said.

"Wasn't I? Academy Award performance, I think. I told you I always wanted to be an actress."

"Real tears."

"Which is not easy when you're exploding with happiness. God, I hated him. Love, that's a tragedy waiting to happen. With love, you're always going to lose in the end, one way or the other. Hate, you can hold on to right to the end and past the end, past the grave. I thought about that when I was pulling the trigger. It was satisfying, Ray. Horrible, but satisfying, too."

I didn't want to go any further down that road. I didn't want to know what she was thinking or feeling while she was killing him.

"We have to talk about the lineup. You were taking a hell of a chance."

"I knew it was him. He looked like the picture."

"A picture out of your imagination."

"I took a guess, I guessed right."

"Don't you realize that some of the guys they put up there are cops? What if you had picked one of them? How would that have looked?"

"There's no way we're going to make it through this without taking chances. You know that."

"Exactly!" I said, pounding on the steering wheel. "That's why you keep it simple. Now there'll be a trial, you'll have to take the stand. Keep it simple, a man in a ski mask, didn't I say that? Don't play games."

"It's all right to play games if you win."

"What have we won? We're just in deeper."

"If they didn't have a perpetrator, they would still be looking. That goddamn Kaiser would still be grilling me about it. I know he's your bosom buddy, but he's a monster, Ray. He was the one who made me do this. He was so damn suspicious, I had to come up with a suspect."

Part of me saw she was right. She had taken a chance and it had paid off. But the whole thing left me with a bad feeling.

"Later you can tell them you were on medication for the pain and it threw you off," I said vaguely. "Tell them you're not sure anymore."

We rode along in silence. A glaze of ice was forming on the small branches of the trees. When we reached her house, we sat outside for a few minutes just listening to the hum of the heater. Then I looked at her and she gave me a nod that meant everything. We entered the front door and she led me upstairs.

"What about Brie?" I asked her. "You don't know when she'll come back."

"So? I'm a free woman now. Can't I entertain a gentleman if I want to?"

"We have to be careful, Sheila."

"You'll be careful, I know you will. You always are."

I was careful. She said my name in a voice that was pure want. She kept saying it, whispering it into my ear, until it became a prayer.

"I'll always have this scar," she said afterward, pointing to her belly. "Your mark on me."

I kissed it.

"We did it, Ray."

"It's not over."

"Don't say that. Say 'We did it.' "

"We did it."

"Look." Sheila pulled open the drawer of a night table and took out a stainless-steel revolver. "Look what I got."

"Why? What's the point of that?"

"The point is"—she aimed the gun at my chest—"the point is, I feel vulnerable. This is my security. Now if anybody tries to shoot me . . ."

She mimed firing at me. Her cheeks ballooned in little puffs, her hand jerked with the recoil. She laughed and slipped the gun back into the drawer.

She said, "You're the one who taught me how."

"What about the insurance?" I said. "The million dollars? Why did I have to find out about that from someone else?"

"Ray, every cake has to have a little icing. Doesn't it?"

I climbed out of bed and stepped to the window. I said, "It points right at you. Don't you see? You don't know what Frank Kaiser is thinking. This whole thing with Johnson may be a ruse to throw you off your guard. You have to stop toying with the police."

She pulled the sheet over her head for a second. "Why do you keep going on about that? I did good, Ray. I steered them away from us. They don't suspect a thing."

"A cop suspects everybody."

The rain began to mix with sleet. It clicked against the windows.

"It's not just the danger to us," I said. "You've accused this guy. They've charged him with murder. There won't be any bail. He sits in the can until the trial."

"So?"

"It's not right."

"Why?"

"Why? He's innocent. Didn't that occur to you? The man is totally innocent."

"Innocent?" She said it in a loud whisper. "Are you kidding? Nobody's innocent. We don't know what crimes this guy's committed. He's probably been getting away with murder all his life. Now he gets caught. Innocent? Ray."

Laughing, she pulled me to her again.

I've had dreams where I'm falling. I feel frightened, but also exhilarated—out of control but past caring. Right then, I had a taste of that terrifying bliss and wondered if it was something I would ever wake up from, or ever wanted to.

THE NIGHT AFTER the funeral, Frank Kaiser came up to me in the station house and touched me. That didn't usually happen. Frank Kaiser was not a guy who touched you. I was not a guy who encouraged it.

Maybe it meant nothing. Maybe it was my own state of mind that made me wary.

I was living in a world where the light had a permanent glare, where every object had moved a fraction of an inch from its true place. Nothing was right. It was a world that was accusing me. I walked down the street through a gauntlet of eyes. When people laughed, they were laughing at my absurdity. When they looked, they were looking at my transparent guilt.

I had worked my tour as usual. Afterward, I carefully typed two reports into the computer, one about an attempted suicide who had been transported by ambulance to the county hospital, another describing a car that had had the rear window broken. They had taken a radio, a pair of ski boots, and a clarinet.

I changed my clothes and was heading out the door when I ran into Frank. That touch bothered me, that heavy arm.

"I want to talk to you. Come in here."

He guided me into the interrogation room. He closed the door. He steered me toward the straight-backed chair. The tiny room held no desk. Only the two chairs, fluorescent light in the ceiling, mirror that was one-way glass, on a shelf along the opposite wall a tape recorder. He sat opposite me.

"When was the last time you went to confession?" he started.

"Been awhile."

"You're Catholic, right?"

"You know I am, Frank. Raised, anyway."

"Sure, altar boy. I always thought you Catholics were lucky, confession. Protestants, we're kind of stuck with our sins. A Catholic can run down to church, tell the priest. You can get the blessing and walk out feeling holy. I always thought that must be wonderful. Isn't it?"

"I guess it is. People pay shrinks a lot of dough for the same thing."

"Must make you think God's a good guy, let you off so easy. You ever want to be a priest?"

"I thought about it. My mother wanted me to."

"I would have made a good priest," Kaiser said. "I could have listened to all the world's sins. I'm not even so bad at the celibacy part, I'm finding out. Since Elaine, I've realized I can get along without it. Never thought I would reach that point. It used to drive me crazy. Now I don't seem to miss it. Isn't that funny?"

The room was warm. The noise of the station house seeped in as a distant hum. It was easy to see how you could lose your bearings in here.

"How's that going?"

"Elaine?" He shrugged and changed the subject. "We all have sins. We all need to go to confession. Who hasn't got a few sins on his conscience?"

"Like I said, for me it's been awhile."

He looked at me, stroked his chin, leaned a bit closer. "But you don't want a lawyer, do you?"

"What?"

"You didn't do it, right? So whaddaya want a lawyer for? Just tell the truth."

"What are you talking about?"

"Stay with me, Ray. You didn't do it—you say. Man, every perp I've ever talked to, they didn't do it. But if none of them did it, who did? See my logic? Because *somebody* did it. So don't waste my time with you didn't do it. Don't waste your own time. Life's too short."

I could smell his breath, stale coffee and pizza with garlic. His knee jutted between my legs.

"Sure, somebody did it."

" 'At's the spirit. We agree. We agree about that part of it. Now, you say you didn't do it, but if you had done it, just if, how might it have gone down? How could it have gone down?"

"I don't know." You think you'll be able to control yourself, stay cool. But you start sweating, your mouth goes dry, little quavers creep into your voice, you can't help it.

"Just speaking hypothetical now. The big if. What do you think?"

"Look, if you're trying to get me to say something here . . ." I stopped myself. He was joking, wasn't he? I knew he was jerking my chain. Or was he testing me? If he really suspected, he wouldn't let on, wouldn't tip his hand.

I made a series of quick calculations. If he was joking and I took it seriously, I might plant suspicion where there was none. If he was serious and I joked around about it, then what?

"You didn't mean to kill him. You didn't want to kill him. Is that what you're trying to tell me?"

"Frank, for Christ's sake."

"Maybe you went over there, you argued with the guy. He was a real prick—I know that, you know that. He tried to fuck with you. He's the kind, give you a hard time for the hell of it. Pissed you off. And you lost it. You lost it, right? Say it. Say it for me."

What the hell was he getting at? I felt that Frank and I were both swaying on a high wire.

"I lost it."

"That's right, you lost it and you pulled out your piece. Not to kill him. Not to kill him. You just wanted to show him this was serious business. You just wanted to wipe that shit-eating grin off his face. And the gun went off. All by itself. And something snapped. And *Bam! Bam! Bam! Bam!* Is that what happened?"

I shook my head. Was I smiling? I could feel my face wrinkle. Where was the joke? Where was he taking this?

"But it could have, right? Remember, we're just talking about what could have happened. It could have happened all by itself. Like you were watching it, right? Slow motion, right? You shot him."

"You're saying that."

"You know the wife is upstairs. Maybe she's seen you. You have to take care of her. But when you look at her, you can't bring yourself to finish her. You fire a shot, you know you've hit her, you run."

"Is that what happened?" I said.

He grinned. "What happened was, I spent twenty-one hours in

here. We're just like this. No distractions. Nothing to hang on to. No judgment, no blame. Hour after hour."

"You mean . . . ?"

"Johnson gave it up. He went to confession with Father Frank. He gave it up, Ray." A laugh burst from his mouth.

"He told you he shot Travis?" I was thrown off balance again.

"And the wife. Drug deal gone sour, just like we thought. All the details. A neat package. Threw the gun in the river. Divers are going down as we speak."

Was it a trick? Was he saying this to see how I would react?

"What about his lawyer?" I asked.

"I laid it on the line. Jerome, you refuse to talk to me, it's your right. Just, you're going to be spending a long time inside. You work with me, you could walk. Pretty much all we got is the word of the wife. That's what I told him. And the wife, shit, that insurance money, maybe she set you up. Maybe she was behind it herself. Who knows? So if you trust me, I might be able to get you off. You tell the truth, you could breathe fresh air."

"The cop who's trying to put you away is your only friend."

"That's the way they see it. I spotted him as somebody who's weak, jail weak. He can't take the confinement. I see it in his face, whenever the cuffs go on. All I had to do, talk about six months inside, he was ready to try anything."

"You brought him in here?"

"Right to this room. I didn't want to question him uptown. Here it's nice and cozy. I just said, tell me your story. I want to hear it."

"What did he say?"

"He never met Travis. That night, he says, he was over at his pal's house helping him fix his furnace. After they get it going, they have a couple of beers, shoot the breeze awhile."

"That's his alibi?"

"Not exactly. Jerome goes home. He watches television with his wife. She goes to sleep. He can't sleep. He goes out to get some smokes. The store's closed. He hits a bar, but only to use the cigarette machine. He comes home. Watches some more tube. Finally falls out. That's it. It's morning."

Frank leaned back and stretched his arms.

"So he denied it."

"At first. I said, 'You have to help me understand. We've got two people shot. You have to help me understand how it went down. You say you're not into dope, you have to help me understand these convictions you have, peddling rock. You never met Travis? Help me understand why the wife described you to a tee, picked you out of a lineup.' "

"He wants to help you."

"Like you say, I'm his only friend. I go over his story again and again. Pick up on every little discrepancy. Anytime I feel the line go slack, I reel in. He tries to explain a slip, he makes another slip. I break down his version, build up my version, until he has no choice but to accept it the way I lay it out, to accept the truth."

"And he gives it up." I leaned back and folded my arms. I had been wanting to ever since we sat down, but I knew how Frank could read body language.

"Not right away. It took time. Ever see a spider capture a grasshopper? The grasshopper gets a leg caught in the web and he tries to kick it off, no big deal. The silk wraps tighter. Pretty soon he has another leg tied up, another. The grasshopper starts to get frantic. With every movement he's more and more wrapped up. All the spider has to do is wait."

"Then suck his juices."

"Exactly. It's over, I tell him finally. Admit it. Don't keep holding out. We've got you. It's late, Jerome. It's getting late for you. I'm your friend. Trust me. Sign the statement, the way I've laid it out for you, the way we laid it out together."

I could see it. Frank wouldn't force anything. He would let you writhe for hours. He would sympathize with you all you wanted. Except, his eyes would be on you like two weights. Watching. Pressing. The eyes and the voice. That monotonous, hypnotic, coaxing voice.

"He bought it. He signed. We shared a smoke. We laughed about it. It was a damn relief for both of us. I'll tell you, this case was thin ice, before. Eyewitness is nice, but an eyewitness can break down. You gotta have a confession or he's always got a chance to beat it."

"Congratulations." I was relieved. I knew I shouldn't be—this was one more complication. But I was beginning to swing toward Sheila's point of view. Innocent? Who's innocent? Johnson had not killed Lance Travis, but maybe he had a good reason to confess. That was the kind of seductive thinking that was flooding my head.

"Ray, as I was walking out of this room, I was thinking, if I had to choose, Elaine or this, I'd choose the job every time. You know what I'm talking about? You puzzle over a case. You wake up at three in the morning sweating it. You try to ease the pieces together. If they won't ease, you pound them into place. Gradually, gradually, the picture comes into focus. There's no satisfaction like it."

"I'm glad for you, Frank."

We walked out of the interrogation room. I took a few deep breaths, felt the muscles in my thighs, my belly, begin to relax.

"You know what gets them in the end?" Frank said. "Loneliness. They're used to a gang, a family, a crowd. Get them alone, they need somebody, and you're the only one there. Want me on your side? You have to tell the truth. Go to confession. They'd rather put their head in a noose than be lonely."

He laughed at that idea. I joined him. My face was stiff. I knew there was more to it than that. Cops learn to manipulate people. They're good at it and they have authority on their side. Jerome Johnson wasn't the first suspect to walk into an interrogation room an innocent man and walk out a confessed killer.

WINTER WENT ON and on. In the two months that followed Johnson's confession, the Travis case faded from the headlines. The wheels of justice ground slowly forward as Johnson's public defender tried a series of unsuccessful legal maneuvers.

I let things ride. In the back of my mind, I allowed myself to imagine that somehow Johnson really was guilty. I dreamed that Sheila would get away with her crime, that a time would come when we could be together openly, that all this darkness would lift.

I had not even spoken with her since the day of the funeral. I had long since stopped looking toward her window. Those glimpses did nothing but frustrate me now. I dreamed of her, I talked to her in my head, but I never tried to contact her. It was too risky.

People were hanging plastic Easter eggs on their shrubs and still the snow lingered. The tired earth was reappearing, but in the shadows the sooty artifacts of drifts remained.

I lay in bed one Saturday morning listening to a relentless rain and then to another sound. It seemed to start in my unconscious and slip bit by bit into my front brain—a pounding, someone hammering insistently on my door. It made me tense all over.

I knew in a flash that it was Frank Kaiser. I knew he had come to make the arrest. I knew he had brought a tactical team. Flak jackets. Face shields. Riot guns. Gas. They wouldn't be taking any chances. They were here to confront an armed man, a desperate man. Their cars were stacked in the street in front of my house, a nervous row of flashing lights.

The whole thing—Jerome Johnson, the confession—it had all been a ruse. Kaiser had set it up to lure us into complacency.

Nothing had worked. We had been careful, we had been discreet. We had stayed away from each other. We had kept our appetites under control. Nothing had worked. Nothing ever does, against fate.

Moving at dream speed, I opened the drawer of the night table by my bed and took hold of the .38 revolver I kept there. It had been my father's gun. The checked wooden butt was nicked and worn. It reminded me, every time I touched it, of the way his palm used to feel.

I knew it couldn't be a dream because I wasn't asleep. I couldn't sleep anymore, my mind wouldn't let go. I had been lying there making an effort not to think. I had been trying to fill my head with bright thoughts. I had been clinging to images of backyards in summer, of the sparkling spray of a lawn sprinkler, of the wet print of a bathing suit on the seat of a chair.

Kaiser had seen through the bullshit. He had calculated the winning move, arranged the checkmate. Now it was my turn to go under the grill, my turn to tell my story and tell it again. Tell it until it became his story, until it became the truth.

I climbed out from between the sheets. I was wearing only a

pair of briefs. I felt the cold floor against my feet, the chill air pricked my skin. The gun, though, had a comfortable heft. It reassured me.

The pounding had stopped. Now it started again, stubborn and angry.

Nude descending a staircase. I gripped the revolver and held it in front of me. What was I planning to do?

Go out in a flame. It was in my genes. Why fight it? Now was the time. It will be clean, I thought. This way, it will be clean.

I eased the hammer back, watched the cylinder slide over to bring a cartridge under the pin.

I would fire a shot to alert them. Not aiming. Then I would run out, run and fire, go for them. They would open up.

When I reached the kitchen, I saw that it wasn't Kaiser, it wasn't the Mansfield Police coming to arrest me. It was Sheila.

She was still pounding on the door. She had run through the wet spring grass in bare feet. Bare legs. Only a green cardigan sweater. She was hugging herself, hopping on one foot, puffing her cheeks.

I opened the door. She threw herself against me. I breathed her smell, the cold damp of the rainwater. She gripped my neck and twined both her legs around my waist. Her mouth tasted like fire. We couldn't get close enough.

I was still holding the cocked pistol.

She dropped her head back. Her eyes looked at me, vulnerable and penetrating. What wouldn't I do to attract the gaze of those eyes?

"We're rich!" she said.

She stared at me and nodded. A wild grin spread across her features.

"It came," she said. "It just arrived. I had to tell you. One million dollars and no cents exactly."

My reaction to this news astounded me. I don't express emotions—a lot of cops don't, a lot of men don't. Overwhelming joy or abject sadness are not in my repertoire. I have a keel. I keep my balance.

Yet in that moment, in that cold kitchen, an almost unbearable sense of jubilation flooded my chest. I was holding in my arms a woman for whom I felt a desire I had not thought possible. And all that money.

I never thought money could matter to me that much. You don't become a cop in order to get rich. I always thought I could take it or leave it. But money is seductive in ways you don't suspect until it comes within your reach. The voice of shame may have been whispering somewhere inside me, but the much louder roar of pure want was drowning it out.

"Hey," Sheila said. I put her down. She undid two big buttons on her sweater and pulled it open. She wore nothing underneath.

I heard myself laugh like a hyena. We ran upstairs to my room. All those weeks apart, all that dreaming and doubting and wondering and fearing, it broke wide open into a flood of grasping and clinging and pushing and kissing. The bed giggled and laughed and finally guffawed wildly as we let loose.

Money is a great healer of guilt. It's a great lifter of mood. It's a great easer of burdens. And I swear to God, money makes you horny as hell.

"We're rich," she said. She pulled the sweater back on and danced around the bedroom. "We have to celebrate."

"We just did."

"I mean really. Go out. Blow some cash. Tonight."

"No, no celebration. Don't you see? This means we have to be more careful than ever."

"It's the natural thing to do."

"No, it's not," I insisted. "What's a million dollars compared to a woman losing her husband? We have to stay in our roles. How would it look? That's the question to ask yourself. Do widows celebrate insurance settlements?"

Her mouth turned down. "I just wanted to be happy with you, Ray."

"It's blood money." I knew right away they were the wrong words. "No, I don't mean that. I just mean we have to be extra careful."

"Blood money?" The look on her face scared me. "This is our future. Yours and mine. Where do you get off saying that?"

"The money won't mean anything if we don't get away with it," I said.

"They've got the killer. The case is closed."

"No, it's not. They aren't going to convict Jerome Johnson. We both know that. If you hadn't picked him out of that lineup, the case would be cold by now. Instead, it goes on and on."

"He confessed, Ray. I can't change that."

"It's no good."

"It's going to work," she said. "With this we can go anywhere. We can get lost in the world. We have to celebrate. Don't we? Let's celebrate."

I thought about it. Maybe she was right. Maybe you could be too careful in this game. You could play it straight so long that you fell on your face. Planning was essential. But playing fast and loose was essential, too. You had to let off steam. Anyway, I needed to see her, needed to spend time with her. The craving for her had been tearing me apart. I was only beginning to see how deeply it went.

THAT SAME NIGHT Sheila and I were driving in my car out to Tre Scalini, a top-shelf Italian joint on Lake Erie. She rolled her window down in spite of the chill.

"I feel good, Ray," she said. "You don't know how hard this has been for me, the nightmares I've had."

"I can imagine."

"What got me through it was you, knowing you were there, knowing you would support me. I don't have anybody else. I feel as if, in this world, there's only you and me."

I swung into the parking lot and climbed out. The restaurant overlooked the lake. The sun had left an orange smear above the water. Higher up, the sky was already fading past indigo. She grabbed me. "Look," she said, "first star. Right there. I wish I may, first star I see tonight."

"That's Venus."

"I made a wish. For us. I know it'll come true. It already has." Her smile warmed me.

The maître d' called me sir and led us across a spacious dining room with glass walls. He placed us at a table with a view of the water. Shore lights were sending out their reflections to dance on the waves. Far out, a few boats showed red and green beacons.

"It's magical," Sheila said.

Her girlish excitement charmed me. At the same time, I couldn't help looking around for a familiar face, for some anonymous diner regarding us with curiosity.

A pianist in the opposite corner was shaping abstractions that were as clean as the double strand of pearls that hugged Sheila's throat.

She prompted me to order a bottle of Dom Perignon. She said we deserved the best. We chatted about champagne. She knew a lot, how they have to turn the bottles to settle the yeast, how they freeze the wad of sediment in the neck and ease it out.

The bubbly spoke for itself. It tasted like golden air and instantly brightened the inside of my skull. The waiter brought various delicate and colorful hors d'oeuvres, small jewels of food on sparkling china plates. We killed the first bottle and were starting on another.

"I want to offer a toast," Sheila said. I lifted my glass. "To Ray Dolan. I love you, baby. Really and truly, I do."

She lifted her glass and drank. Yes, she was a little sloshed. But the sentiment made a knot form in my throat. My mind went back to that first time, when we had made urgent love on her bed, and how I had discovered love that night, and how I had never told her in so many words. I couldn't say it now, even, except with my eyes. She hooked her arm around my neck and pressed her forehead to mine.

But again, I couldn't help thinking that somebody was watching. What kind of a scene were we making? Were we advertising our guilt?

Our dinners came. Sheila's dish of scallops was a work of art. I sliced into a beautifully charred T-bone and watched the blood run out.

"Six more months," she said. "I figure six months and we can be out of this town. Put Brie in a boarding school and go."

"What do you mean?"

"Say good-bye to Mansfield, New York. What did you think? Were you planning to go on being a cop? A millionaire cop? You won't need to work, lover. Never again."

I really had never thought about that part of it. I had imagined lying low for years, I guess, seeing each other on the sly indefinitely. Part of it was caution, and I suppose part of it was my ingrained reluctance to commit myself.

She read my hesitation. "Nobody can prove anything. Nobody will ever be able to prove anything. We're free. We have to enjoy life. I've been waiting for it for a long, long time."

The thought of a change like that made me nervous. I liked the idea of being her secret lover. I guess I liked being a cop, too.

"When I was a little girl," she was saying, "I used to lie in the grass and watch the clouds and imagine I was up there floating and looking down on everything. I hated my family. They were trash. They never drank champagne. My mother used to go around cleaning office buildings nights. They wanted me to be trash, too. I ran away over and over. Always running away."

I was feeling pretty sentimental, thinking about her as a girl. Seeing her again after being apart lightened my head more than the champagne did.

"Lance was supposed to be my knight in shining armor," she went on. "Take me away from all the shit I had grown up with. But I found out he had this snarl inside him."

She looked down at the table and her face turned sad. I reached over and took her hand. The piano player swung into an easy rhythm and I pulled her up and we danced right there beside our table.

It didn't matter who was watching. The light was gold and the music was as sweet as maple syrup. Her eyes were naked and intimate when they looked at me, a smiling invitation.

I wanted to know everything about her, yet at the same time I didn't want to know anything more than just that lovely shining surface.

Soon the piano player was saying, "Thanks, that's all for tonight." Then we were outside. The brisk air didn't touch us. Before we unlocked the car, she turned and kissed me.

I felt something click open inside me. I found myself saying, "I love you, Sheila." I could barely control my smile. Yeah, I was flying.

We climbed into the car and headed back along the mostly deserted highway. The moon was shining so brightly I could have driven without my headlights.

When you're drinking, you always imagine you can drive just as well, maybe even a little better, than when you're sober. I had soaked up quite a bit of booze that night and I thought nothing of going heavy on the gas. Weeds and fence posts and patches of leftover snow rocketed past in a long blur.

"We're lucky, Ray. We're lucky we found each other. I can't imagine my life without you."

"I know" was all I could say. "I know." What I wanted to say was something I had thought about a long time ago, one night when I had caught one of those pristine, virgin glimpses of her through her window. That she was the one who had wiped away the rules for me. That I loved her for setting me free.

I don't know what happened. Maybe I looked at her, glanced over at her lovely, excited face. All I remember is catching the gravel on the side of the road and feeling my insides go hot as the car fishtailed. I wrestled with the wheel. We went sideways and I knew we were about to roll and there was nothing I could do about it. But we didn't go over. We skidded onto the far side of the road and I was able to get some purchase and swing it around and feed it some gas and finally straighten it out. An instant later we were flying down the road as if nothing had happened.

Sheila was laughing. The exhilaration of it, the relief of it, got me to laughing, too. We continued on for a long time that way, laughing and laughing, speeding through the darkness.

THE ATMOSPHERIC PRESSURE on the surface of Venus is ninety times what it is on earth. The temperature reaches six hundred degrees Fahrenheit. A choking dust storm rages without end. Thunderstorms pour down a rain of concentrated sulfuric acid. Yet this planet of love appears to us as the mild evening star, a tiny seed pearl in the twilight.

I could already make out its placid glow as the sun slid below the horizon. I was preparing my telescope. I hadn't had it out all winter. I was anxious to bring the celestial images to my eye.

It was summer now, end of June and already hot. Sheila and I had been seeing each other secretly since that day she received the insurance settlement. We came together as often as we could. Sometimes I had dinner at her house. Or she snuck over to my place when Brie was away and we enjoyed a brief bout of ecstacy. But we agreed it wouldn't do to be seen in public again, at least not until the Jerome Johnson trial was over.

Most of the legal wrangling had been completed, and the trial was set to start in a few days. Johnson had hired a hotshot lawyer by the name of Ephraim Carr. The case was becoming a cause.

It was making me nervous. I didn't want to see Johnson convicted for something he didn't do, and the trial could easily cause the whole thing to blow up in our faces.

I was just aligning my scope when I heard a voice say, "Aren't you going to watch her?"

I looked up to find Brie standing quite close. Her hair was growing in now, dark like Sheila's.

"Watch who?"

"Didn't she tell you? She's going on television. You know that talk show—Donna Jordan? She's going to talk about the murder."

Sheila had told me nothing about it. She knew I would have objected. All my warnings about not playing games and now this—to go on television and be cross-examined, to put the whole thing at risk for no reason. It was crazy.

"Let's have a look," I said, as casually as I could manage. "I can do this later."

We walked across the patio together.

"She said she was going to reveal something, a surprise," Brie told me.

Surprise? A hot flash passed over me as I imagined her confessing on television. Would she point a finger at me? Would she leave me to take the blame? No, that was just paranoia, just nerves.

Brie stopped before we reached the door.

"This whole thing has been so odd. I mean, it's so bizarre that he would be killed and all. But it's affected my mother, too. She's so strange at times. I don't mean strange, but, like a stranger. She's a person I don't know."

"Everybody has to adjust to trauma in their own way. I think she's still trying to come to grips with it. You have to give her time."

"I know that." She paced up and down the patio. "I can't explain it, but I have a sense of something dark. Like in a dream, where you feel this presence but you can't see it, you can't turn your head fast enough. I feel that with her, with this whole thing. You know how I said I was psychic? I'm beginning to wonder if I really am. It scares me."

"You've been through a lot yourself." I said no more. I wanted to offer her comfort, but her intuition was coming too close to the truth.

We went inside. She had already ordered a pizza and a delivery boy soon pulled up in an old VW Rabbit with a lighted sign on the roof. I could hear her joking with him at the door.

"Do you like pepperoni? I should have asked."

"Love it."

We ate at the living room coffee table. She sat on the floor. I settled on the couch and leaned my elbows on my knees. The program had not started yet.

"Sometimes I get so confused," she said. "I can't sort out my feelings about anything, especially the murder."

"It's natural you would have mixed emotions about it."

"Mixed emotions . . . what do you mean?"

"Nothing." I said it too fast and too casually and I wished I'd kept my mouth shut.

She squinted at me. "Why did you say that? You meant something."

"I just meant that this has been a difficult thing for you to cope with."

"No, you didn't. You were referring to something."

I could have simply denied it and held my ground. But maybe suspicions were lurking in my mind that I needed to have clarified. Maybe I wondered why Brie *didn't* seem to have mixed emotions. Maybe I thought that it would do her good to talk about her feelings.

Whatever it was, I found myself saying, "She told me a little about your problems with your father."

"What problems?"

Our eyes locked. I couldn't back away from it now.

"The abuse."

"Abuse?"

"You don't have to say anything. I know it's hard."

"Like, sex, you mean? That's absurd. She said that?"

"She mentioned it. She's concerned about you."

"But it's not true. It didn't happen."

"I might have misunderstood."

"How could you misunderstand something like that?"

"Maybe she meant—"

"Meant what? He never abused me. Never. Nothing remotely like that ever happened. That's so weird, that she would say that."

I vaguely remembered something Sheila had said about hate, how satisfying it was, how you could depend on it. I had hated Lance for what he had done to his wife, for how he had abused this innocent kid. Hate had been my touchstone. I had hated him so much that it had made me happy to see him dead.

Now one reason for my hate was being thrown into question. I had the sense of ice cracking underneath me. I knew I had to step very carefully.

"Anyway," she said, "Lance wasn't my father."

"What do you mean?"

"Didn't she tell you? My real father was killed in a car crash."

Doubts were flying all through my head again, more than
doubts. Sheila and I had joined together to lie to the world. Was
she lying to me? The idea scared the hell out of me.

Why? Because we had bet it all on one roll of the dice. If the
flame went out between us, whether in a sputter or an explosion,
we would both be plunged into darkness.

Brie pointed the remote control. The sound came up on the
television. Donna Jordan and Sheila were seated in cushioned chairs
facing each other.

Jordan used to be a gossip columnist for the *Mansfield Chronicle*.
I had seen her show a few times. Sometimes it was Junior League
do-gooders and school board members, other times local nobodies
who had overcome a prescription pill jones or lost a hundred and
fifty pounds after praying to St. Jude. Getting Sheila must have been
something of a coup for her, especially with the Jerome Johnson trial
looming.

Sheila had chosen her clothes with care, a simple dark dress,
subdued but not somber. The skirt was not short, but when she
crossed her knees, her legs looked good. Her features came across
more vividly than in real life. Seeing her image, I realized what a
beautiful woman she was—her dark eyes and the strands of hair
curling around her forehead gave her just a hint of wildness.

Her personality turned out to be perfect for television. She seemed
more natural, smoother somehow, than Donna Jordan herself.

"I think the unreality of it has been one of the hardest parts to
deal with, Donna," she was saying. "It's something so far out of my
experience, my everyday experience, that at times I just can't believe
that it happened. I can't shake off the feeling that I'm walking around
in a dream."

She had all the gestures down. She paused at the right times.

She spoke with something of that measured cadence that news announcers use. She was having fun. The light of publicity made her glow. It was a hell of an act.

"What about the media attention?" Donna asked. "What's it been like dealing with reporters and TV people through all this?"

"I wish they were all as sympathetic as you are, Donna. Yes, it's been hard at times. But I've told myself: They have a job to do. The only thing that peeves me, really, is the speculation about Lance's being involved with drugs. That's really putting the victim on trial. I don't think it's fair. People spread rumors, but they didn't know Lance. Lance was a decent, decent man. Doesn't he deserve some privacy, even in death—especially in death?"

"Who said he used drugs?" Brie commented. "That wasn't in the papers."

She was right. It was exactly the kind of loose talk that could hang us. Was Frank Kaiser watching all this? Of course he was.

". . . what this says about violence in our society?" Donna Jordan had a knack for asking empty questions in a tone of voice that made people take her seriously.

Sheila paused thoughtfully. "Until something like this happens, you always think that violence is limited to people who aren't like you. One thing I've taken away from this is a better understanding of the victims of crime, a deeper compassion, I think, for those who have to deal with violence every day."

I could sense that she was getting tremendous satisfaction from putting something over on the world. That was why she had gone on the show, to flaunt the lie. She said she had always wanted to be an actress. This was her chance.

"One of the issues raised by this case," the hostess said, "is the question of race. The police have been criticized for insensitivity to minorities. The arrest of your husband's killer—alleged killer—has generated a great deal of controversy. What's your take on the whole race thing?"

"Donna, race has nothing whatever to do with what happened. Violence can happen to anyone, at any time."

She was talking to the television audience, but she was speaking to me as well. There was a private irony in her words. I was the only one in the world who understood her, who got the joke.

Donna asked her about the grieving process. Sheila talked about the stages—denial, guilt, how loss was something you carry for the rest of your life.

"But I feel that Lance is still with me, in some strange way. Looking down on me. We never really lose those who are gone. I know that in my heart."

"You told me, when we talked earlier, that there was something you wanted to announce on the show."

"Yes, Donna." Sheila turned directly toward the camera. "My husband was a generous, caring man, and I want to share with others in his name. So I'm taking this opportunity to announce that I'm establishing the Lance Travis Foundation for the Victims of Violent Crime. We plan to be working with crime victims from all across the country, to help them get their lives back together."

"That's a wonderful gesture."

"It's part of the healing process for me. I think it's a fitting tribute to the memory of my husband. And I have here a check, in the amount of ten thousand dollars, which will be the first grant from the foundation and will go to the Citizens Alliance right here in Mansfield. I think we all know the great work those folks have been doing."

"And to accept the contribution, we have in our studio today Hazel Turner, executive director of the Citizens Alliance. Hazel?"

Hazel was a slender, energetic black woman. A lot of handshaking and hugging went on. They talked up the Citizens Alliance for a few minutes. Then Donna Jordan thanked her guests and it was over.

A commercial for microwave popcorn filled the screen.

"Sometimes I think she's glad he's dead," Brie said, something of the old bitterness in her voice.

"Don't say that. People make the best of a situation, that's all."

"She encouraged him to drink. It didn't take much encouragement, but when he would try to stop, she would laugh at him. She was always egging him on. Now he's dead and she's so sorry." She clicked off the set.

I said, "People's relationships are always complicated. Death doesn't end that. Issues still need to be worked out. Feelings still conflict. You have to understand that." I felt I was saying too much.

"You like her, don't you?"

Her question caught me by surprise. I took a swallow of iced tea.

"As a friend, yes. A neighbor."

"That's all?"

"What do you mean?"

"I'm not blind."

She didn't say anything more and I wasn't in any mood to continue the conversation. I made an innocuous remark and headed back to my telescope.

I wanted to see Sheila and I didn't want to see her. I was on the last-out tour that night, so I wouldn't be around when she got home. It was just as well. This was no time to stir things up, even though my head was buzzing with doubts—about her, about everything.

I looked into the eyepiece and scanned the sky. Venus had already set that night.

EPHRAIM WALSTON CARR. Stonewall Carr? Everybody said he could have played in the NFL. They even speculated about which teams might have drafted him, the kind of player he might have been, the records he might have broken as a middle linebacker. Around here they dreamed of him bringing to the Bills the same lethal brilliance that he'd shown at Mansfield South High the year of their iron defense. His freshman year at Michigan State, he terrorized the Big Ten.

But a terrible thing happened. Drunk driver. Head on. The collision snapped both femurs and shattered his pelvis.

Swinging on crutches and against his doctor's orders, Stonewall entered the courtroom to witness justice dispensed to the well-connected Ann Arbor building contractor who had robbed him of his dream. The defendant cried on the stand. A single moment of carelessness. Now in treatment. Never drink again. Sorry. So sorry. Even the judge wiped away a tear. The performance won the defendant a fine and five years' probation.

Carr never said a word to the press, but the incident made him change his career plans. He switched his major from accounting to prelaw. He graduated third in his class. Columbia Law School. Job with Buffalo's top white-shoe law firm. After five years studying the mechanisms of power, he went out on his own.

The lawsuit that made him famous was the Rin Tin Tin case. A Niagara County landlord wanted to convert a big single-room-occupancy hotel into upscale condos. Impatient, he brought in hired muscle and a couple of German shepherds. Carr took up the case of the former tenants.

The defendant pleaded that German shepherds were not necessarily intimidating dogs. He cited Rin Tin Tin to prove his point. The jury wasn't buying. The homeless plaintiffs collected a cool two hundred grand each. The press went wild. Carr's name was all over the papers. His ego swelled up like a Macy's parade balloon.

Carr traveled all over now, jumping into any case that promised a good mix of civil rights and headlines. Always on the side of the little guy. You could say that for him. Always ready to stand up for some dirtbag who hadn't been treated like the king of Siam. Or for some poor schmuck who really had gotten ground up in the wheels of justice, somebody like Jerome Johnson.

Carr also made a healthy six-figure income defending some of Sammy Corvino's cronies on labor racketeering and other charges, but he didn't publicize that facet of his career. We all have to eat and Stonewall was a big eater.

I had been sitting in court all morning waiting to testify about an assault case. As it turned out, the victim failed to show and wasted everybody's time. The judge had no choice but to put the perp back on the street. Out in the courthouse hallway I came face to face with the famous Mr. Carr.

You couldn't miss him. Six-seven. Two seventy-five. Black.

Shaved head. A physique that bulged every seam of his very expensive suit. A face that could flash from granite frown to butter-melting grin in an instant.

This was it: The case of the *People v. Jerome Johnson* had begun that morning. Carr was just emerging from State Supreme Court. The lackeys in his entourage waved off the questions of the reporters who were waiting. Mr. Carr would be giving a press conference outside, they said.

Back in the seventies, the urban renewers had carved a big gash out of the center of Mansfield. They had demolished grimy apartment buildings and dingy storefronts to make way for a paved square surrounded by glass towers. They called it Municipal Plaza. The new city hall was the focus, along with the courts, police headquarters, the motor vehicle department, some county offices. The various buildings were connected by underground passages. The plaza itself was without shade or shelter, decorated with big bronze sculptures nobody could quite figure out.

For the press conference, they had set up ranks of microphones. I was surprised to see that, in addition to the reporters, a couple of hundred people were waiting, obviously supporters of Jerome Johnson. The trial was hot news to begin with, and Carr's involvement stamped it as a bone fide Big Story.

The crowd greeted him with cheers. Many were teenagers. They began to chant: "Free Jerome! *Free Jerome!*"

"Today, in this building," Carr boomed, "we have taken the first step toward justice."

Cheers.

"Judge Pennwalt has ruled that my client's statement to the police, the coerced statement that supposedly implicated him in the killing of Lance Travis, is *not* admissible as evidence."

Wild cheers.

"Furthermore! Furthermore, the judge has admonished the police department of the city of Mansfield, and most especially the detective in charge of this case, for savage and unjust tactics in forcing my client to sign a bogus confession. We now call on the police chief to take immediate action to punish these thugs with badges."

The crowd ate it up.

"I say 'First step toward justice' because the trial that is beginning today will prove that my client is innocent, that he is the victim of a conspiracy by a racist police department desperate to solve a crime."

"What prompted you to get involved in this case?" a reporter asked him.

"I received a phone call from Mrs. Olivia Johnson." Carr gestured toward the small woman I remembered from the church the night of the arrest. " 'My husband,' she told me, 'is being crucified.' The chief priests are yelling 'Crucify him,' just the way they did when our Lord was on trial. I came back here, to this city where I grew up, and I saw bigotry and injustice, and I could not turn her down."

"Are you saying Johnson was framed by the police?"

"Look." He was suddenly the voice of reason. "A man gets shot. He lives in a big house. He has money in the bank. The cops are going to get somebody for it. They make an arrest, you people take the heat off of them. It doesn't matter who they get. It doesn't matter who the actual killer is. It doesn't matter that an innocent man's life is destroyed, or that his wife and children suffer. Of course he was framed."

"What about Mrs. Travis's eyewitness identification?"

"A hysterical woman, a fleeting glimpse—it adds up to zero. Everybody knows that. My client will be exonerated. That is a fact."

"... about rumors of a plea bargain arrangement?"

"False! Absurd! We will win this case. We have scored already. We have scored very big here today. We will not give up until we have achieved the final victory."

"Are you actually going to sue the police officers who investigated this case?"

"We are going to bring to his knees any cop who thinks he stands above the law and above the people. Once our client is cleared, yes, we plan to file a multimillion-dollar suit against the city of Mansfield and numerous of its henchmen."

I didn't want to hear any more. I walked across the plaza toward my car. On some level, I was relieved about the confession, but I was scared, too. I didn't want them to convict Jerome Johnson, but I didn't want them to turn their attention to Sheila. Maybe, just maybe, we could slip through the narrow gap between those two calamities.

As I reached my car, Frank Kaiser called my name. He was cutting across from the courthouse.

"You heard?"

"You lost the confession."

He nodded. "I put this investigation together piece by piece. It was not an easy case. Then this media hotshot walks in, kicks it all apart in twenty minutes. The judge was completely taken in by him."

"It's a hard one."

"You win some, you lose some. I think they still might hang the son of a bitch, confession or no confession. But it's a crapshoot now. And I don't like to gamble."

"You did your job, Frank. That's all you can do."

"You're right. You do your job, you get your reward. So what's my reward? A fucking lawsuit."

Behind us the "Free Jerome!" chant was building. A band of maybe fifty teenagers broke away from the crowd and went running across the plaza, shouting and whooping.

"So much for my dream of making chief of detectives," Frank went on. "I'll be lucky to get out of this with my pension intact."

"It's not your fault. Everybody knows that. The system stinks."

"Yeah." He smiled a sad, ironic smile. "I guess I had better see about getting a lawyer myself. If Johnson gets off, I'll be in court for years."

"The city will stand behind you."

He shook his head. "Catlett? He'll jump on whatever horse has its neck out front. We both know that."

We turned to watch the Johnson supporters stream across the sidewalk and into Main Street. They jumped over cars and pounded on hoods, formed little bands that brought traffic to a honking standstill. As three police cars swooped in, the kids cheered and ran, disappearing down alleys and side streets.

"Too bad the suspect wasn't a white man," Kaiser said, "somebody like you. I could have made the case easily then, none of this racial bullshit. Yeah, I think I could have convicted you in a snap, Ray."

He forced a laugh, but I saw something in his eyes that I couldn't interpret. Was it discouragement? Frustration? Or something else?

"Frank, let me buy you a drink," I said. "We'll get together later and drown our sorrows, whaddaya say?"

"Sure, that sounds good. I've got a reason to celebrate in spite of this shit. I'll tell you about it tonight."

As he headed off toward his car, he had the look of a beaten man.

32

As THE FIRST OFFICER on the scene, I was scheduled to testify at Johnson's trial the next day. Monica Hargrove, the district attorney, was a Republican with a toothy smile and a lot of ambition. She was glad for her time in the limelight.

The judge was Milton Pennwalt. I remembered him from high school, a skinny kid who had won the Section Four golf championship his junior year. He was the type of guy you imagined would still have his trophies on display.

I was supposed to take the stand early, but the lawyers argued procedural issues all morning. Then they started with the dispatcher who had taken Sheila's 911 call. I came next. Sheila, who would testify later as a witness, was not in the courtroom. Neither was Frank Kaiser.

I glanced briefly at Jerome Johnson, who sat at the defense table with an expression of quiet outrage etched into his features. He glared back at me.

As Hargrove walked toward me, I could hear her stockings scrape and smell her perfume. I was used to being in the witness box. I let her lead me through what happened. I had already gone over the story with one of her assistants.

She asked me about the murder scene, what I had observed when I entered the house that morning. She asked about Sheila. She wanted me to emphasize that Sheila had walked out on her own and had spoken coherently to me.

"Officer Dolan, how you doing today?" Carr said at the beginning of his cross-examination.

I told him I was doing fine. He had a genuine warmth, a real charm.

"You say you didn't check to see whether Lance Travis was dead or alive when you first went into the house. Why was that? I'm just curious."

"The policy of our department is you make sure the house is clear—that the perpetrators are not still inside—before anything else."

"But you testified that Mrs. Travis had already told you that the assailant was gone."

"I needed to check that for myself. It's one of the rules."

"I see. Did you walk around the outside of the house that morning? See if there was anybody hiding out there?"

"No, I didn't." I thought about the hole I had left in the snow. No one had ever mentioned it.

"Was Mrs. Travis upset when you encountered her?"

"Yes, I think you could say that."

"Very upset?"

"She was shaky, a little short of breath, pale."

"On the point of collapsing?"

"Probably."

"She had lost a lot of blood?"

Hargrove's objection rang out before I could answer. Sustained.

"What did she say to you after you carried her behind your patrol car?"

"I didn't carry her, I helped her."

"What did she say?"

"She said a noise had awakened her. She had heard a gunshot. A man appeared, fired at her several times. She had come downstairs and found her husband shot."

"That's all?"

"That's all she said."

"No description of the man?"

"No."

"Did you ask her for a description?"

"No, I didn't."

"Why not?"

"I wanted to get into the house, make sure it was clear, see about her husband."

"Didn't you think it was important to get a description?"

"Very important. But I felt that the things I mentioned should come first."

"You knew the Travises, didn't you?"

"Yes."

"Had you ever been inside the Travis home before that night?"

"Yes, I had."

"Could you tell us about the other times you went there?"

"Irrelevant," Hargrove called out.

Again, Pennwalt sustained the objection.

"Would you say they were happily married?"

Hargrove was on her feet before the question was out. Carr couldn't cross-examine me about a matter that hadn't been touched on in direct. The judge agreed.

"Did you see any sign of forced entry at the Travis residence that morning?" Carr asked.

"No."

"Did you see any signs of a struggle within the house?"

"If you mean overturned furniture, things like that, no."

"When you were arriving on the scene, as you were approaching, did you see anyone leaving?"

"No, I didn't."

"I have no further questions."

That was it. I stepped down and walked out of the courtroom.

I suddenly felt the full weight of responsibility for Johnson's fate. The twelve dough-faced jurors weren't the ones who would decide. The thing rested with me. I had devoted my life to justice, I really believed that. Now I was perpetrating a terrible injustice.

But without the confession there was a good chance the prosecution wouldn't be able to win the case. Maybe Sheila would waver on the witness stand, express some doubts about her identification. Maybe she would take my advice and say "I thought it was him, but now I'm not sure." I was hoping for some miracle that would take the responsibility off my shoulders. Isn't that what we're all hoping for?

In the hallway outside the courtroom I ran into Frank Kaiser, who was waiting to testify himself. We nodded at each other but didn't exchange a word. Frank looked old. I was cruising and he was taking it in the neck.

The night before, he and I had shared some drinks at Mullin's. Frank had dropped a double scotch back in two swallows and ordered another. I had asked him what he thought about prospects of a conviction.

"It's touch and go," he said. "What kind of show can the wife put on? That's what's going to decide it. If she can convince the jury, we have a chance. The rest of the case is toilet paper. But I'm still hoping. I'm still looking to nail this one down."

He had been eating and sleeping and breathing the Travis case for months. That wasn't what he wanted to talk about. When we reached the third round of drinks, he raised his glass and clicked it against mine.

"I'm a free man," he said. "The divorce is final as of today. She's a free woman and I'm a free man."

"It's going to be good to get it behind you."

"Sure, real good. I like living alone. I tell you that? I love it. Love it so much it scares me. Every night, me and the four walls. Silence. Nobody to think about except myself. The single life, it's terrific."

"It's going to take some adjustment."

"Did I tell you, she didn't even end up with the Paki? She dumped him, too. It wasn't that she fell for another guy, somebody who paid more attention to her, or who wined and dined her more than I did. That wasn't it. It was me. She couldn't stand living with me. She hated my guts."

"Elaine isn't a hater."

"That's what I thought. She hired a lawyer, he was a fucking chain saw. She got everything—the house, the car, the furniture. I got in the habit of counting my balls every morning, make sure I still had two. The marriage didn't work, okay, fuck it. But why would Elaine turn on me like that, after she was the one? Why would she do that?"

I didn't have any answer except to buy him another drink.

"And this bullshit on top of it. Carr, the lawsuit. I've had it. This Travis thing is my last case, Ray. I'm done."

"What do you mean?"

"I'm retiring, hanging it up."

"Get out, Frank, you'll always be a cop. You'll end up a dino-saur."

He looked at me with antique eyes. "I'm done. It's over. I already put in my notice. I'm gonna sit back and collect my pension and fish."

"You hate to fish."

"Time comes for you to move on. If you're doing your job the best you can and they tell you you're out of line, it's time. I'm going away—California, Hawaii, I don't know."

We talked about a lot of things that night. We went back over his early days on the force, my early days. We talked about the hairy situations we had been in, the perpetrators we had arrested, the stories, all those stories.

At one point, I was on the verge of spilling the whole thing—one of those spasms of honesty that come over you during a night of drinking. I was going to tell him about Sheila. I could feel the words in my throat. An almost uncontrollable urge to admit what I'd done boiled up in me, an urge to come clean, to go to confession. I even had a sneaking suspicion that Frank wouldn't be surprised, that somewhere in the back of his mind he suspected the truth.

But everyone has a survival instinct.

Frank was drinking doubles of Johnnie Black, I was just having beer. When they started putting the chairs on the tables, he was definitely too far gone to drive. I took him home in my car.

He was living out in a little A-frame he had rented in the country. I had to help him out of the car. A chorus of frogs jeered at us as I walked him to the front door.

He slept on a convertible couch. I opened the sliding glass door in back to let the night air in. I helped Frank get some of his clothes off and put him to bed.

Driving home, I started thinking about friendship. I had had plenty of friends when I was younger. Now I knew a lot of people, but I wasn't close to any of them. Only Frank.

They say the universe is expanding. Every galaxy is moving away from every other galaxy at a tremendous speed. Every one of them is becoming more and more alone.

THE DAY AFTER I testified, Sheila was scheduled to take the stand. I hadn't spoken to her in a couple of weeks—it was just too danger-ous for us to be together.

I had already told her over and over not to point the finger at Johnson in open court. Sometimes, I thought she would take my advice. Other times, I felt she had actually convinced herself Johnson was guilty. I had no idea what she would do.

I was glad I was scheduled to work the day tour. It would give me something to do.

The trial was being televised. Everybody in town was glued to a set. It was a pleasant amusement for a hot summer day, watch a man being tried for murder.

I told myself I didn't want to see her. I knew that wasn't true. There were holes in my eyes, in my soul, that could only be filled by her image. I lived on memories of her, on glimpses, gestures, scraps of images.

Maybe it was no accident that I happened to be cruising Clinton Avenue in my patrol car about the time she took the stand. About ten blocks from downtown was a place called Mad Manny's Television City. Manny was the biggest electronics retailer in Mansfield.

Three full-size plate-glass windows stretched along the front of the store. Behind each, stacked from floor to ceiling, television sets formed a wall of picture tubes. Manny claimed it was the largest display of its kind in the state. The effect was hypnotic. Any image that appeared on the screen took on a strange significance by being multiplied so many times. That day, Manny had every set tuned to the trial, half a block of lurid color.

The place had always attracted a lot of loiterers. If one TV catches the eye, a hundred of them really make people stare.

Everybody in Mansfield knew Mad Manny Goldberg. He starred in his own commercials, sprinting breathlessly through his store to point out the specials, and always ending the spot by snatching off his toupee to expose his shiny bald scalp. "It's the bare truth!" he'd yell. "We will not be undersold!"

Manny had gone bankrupt twice, but he always seemed to rise from the ashes with a bigger store and steeper discounts. His place was open every day of the year, including Christmas.

Today a small crowd had gathered out front to watch the trial. I double-parked and sat staring at the show. Hargrove's face was on each of the screens. She was supporting her elbow with one hand and holding a pair of reading glasses in the other. When she finished speaking, she bit on the bow of the glasses.

All the pictures switched at once to Sheila. I stopped breathing for a second. She seemed confident, nervous, sympathetic, courageous, sincere.

For a second the idea gripped me that everything that had happened was just a television show. It wasn't real. Nobody was dead. It was a soap opera. It was only actors and a staged murder and fake blood. And now the phony trial. I found myself smiling, first out of relief, then smiling at the way my mind was working.

I climbed out of the car. Quite a few of the gawkers were senior citizens with time on their hands. Also young mothers, their strollers parked in ranks.

No sound came from the bank of sets, but a few people held plastic radios. Now and then the words would drift through the air, competing with the noise of talk and traffic and a salsa boom box playing farther up the street.

"I was afraid," Sheila was saying. The movement of her lips, her hundred pairs of lips, was not perfectly synchronized with the sound. "I felt paralyzed, I couldn't make myself move."

The spectators were watching the screens intently.

". . . took me a second to realize I'd been shot." The words materialized and were gone.

Yes, Sheila was saying on all the screens. She was answering some question from Monica Hargrove, but she was saying yes to me. Yes, we're going to pull this off. Yes, we're going to get away with murder. Yes, we're going to be rich. Yes, we're going to have it all.

She was nodding. This was the moment. Everybody along the sidewalk began to focus now. They stopped chatting. They turned up their radios, stared at the barrage of images.

". . . any doubt in your mind about the identity of the man who entered your home that night and shot you?"

"No, I remember it vividly. Vividly."

"And is that man in this courtroom today?"

"Yes, he is."

"Could you point him out?"

"Right over there. The defendant, Jerome Johnson." A hundred fingers pointed. The camera panned to Johnson, who stared back at Sheila. He frowned and leaned over to say something to Carr.

The judge's face flashed onto the screen, looking grave as he spoke to the jury. Then the scene changed—a man in a button-down shirt and wire-rimmed glasses was giving an earnest analysis of what we had just seen.

An old guy, with a big belly but practically no torso above his belt, came back from a deli up the street with sodas and sandwiches for his friends, three women and another man. They started to fill him in on what had happened. Sandwiches and little plastic containers of cole slaw.

Life was going on. I climbed into my patrol car and started the engine. Life was going on. You can't look back or mourn the way you thought it should be.

The trial was over as far as I was concerned. Fate, not salvation, was the hidden clockwork that made the universe tick.

THE SAME DAY that Sheila testified I was scheduled for a marksmanship test. It was a piece of cake for me. I almost always held top ranking in the department.

The city had built a shooting range in an abandoned gravel pit on the north side. They had erected a little cinder-block building where you could change your ammunition and clean your piece. You had to qualify every three months.

You fired one clip on the regular range, at ten, twenty, and thirty yards. The combat range had a series of facades and barricades stretching away from your location. Targets popped out or jumped up from these. You blew away the evil-looking men pointing guns at you. The schoolgirls and businessmen you let live. It happened fast—hesitation was not rewarded.

Some cops see the gun as the basis of their authority. Do what I say or I'll shoot you. I didn't look at it that way. To me, the gun is only a tool. As a cop, your authority comes from who you are, from your guts. I believed in being prepared to use my weapon and

I liked to shoot, but I never thought about the gun when I was working. I relied on me.

I was waiting to take my turn on the combat course. The heat had been mounting all day and the air was getting sticky. It was the first time that year I had heard cicadas buzzing their fanfare to summer.

"Ray?"

I knew the voice before I turned. The sound of it gave me an icy feeling. I twisted to see Leanne Corvino smiling at me.

"I told you I'd keep on it," she said.

"Keep on what?"

"The Travis thing. I needed to talk to you about it, but I didn't want to leave you a message. It's kind of urgent."

"I'm always glad to see you. Sit down." She took one of the plastic lawn chairs.

"I've been piecing things together for months. Now I feel as if I'm getting somewhere, as if I'm on the edge of breaking it open."

"I thought it was over, as good as over."

"It stinks, Ray. They're railroading Johnson." She clutched my arm as she said it. Her eyes glittered with intensity.

"I don't know what you mean." I pointed and slipped on my ear protectors. She put her fingers in both of her ears. A deputy from the sheriff's department fired off his clip on the combat range, fifteen heavy claps of sound.

"Yes, you do," she said when he was done. "They're playing a deep game, somebody is. They're trying to convict the wrong person. It never made sense. I talked to people who knew Johnson. He just didn't fit."

"Things happen. People who don't fit kill people." Don't argue it, I told myself. Let her talk.

"Except I know who did it."

The world stopped and took a breath. Her eyes blinked at me a couple of times, playing coy. The cicadas began again, a yearning drone.

"You're next, Ray." Vinnie Otto, the weapons instructor, was calling me.

You can't think. Thinking always gets in the way of shooting. It's all in the body. That's why you need to practice. You need to make it automatic, pure reflex.

But my mind was being pulled in another direction. I was thinking as I walked to the line and drew my pistol. I was thinking as I looked over at Vinnie and gave him the nod. I was thinking as the first target popped out and I shot at it. A bad guy, a hit. Another bad guy, another hit.

The third target lurched from behind a brick barricade. A woman. She was holding a purse. Dark haired. Slender. A secretary, maybe. My bullet caught her in the throat. I missed the next one, a biker with a sawed-off shotgun. The rest of them went down in order—I fired or held my fire for each.

Vinnie was smiling. How long had it been since I had failed to qualify? It meant a mandatory two-hour pistol class and an hour of target practice.

"The broad threw you," he said. I thought for a second he was talking about the target, but his eyes flicked over toward Leanne.

I took my sheet and went in to clean my pistol. Leanne joined me heading for the parking lot.

"So give it to me. Who did it?" My voice was supposed to sound casually curious. I hoped it did.

"The wife."

I kept walking. One step, two steps, three steps. I kept putting my feet in front of each other as we crossed the blacktop.

I said, "Because of the insurance?"

"That started me thinking, sure. That started me looking into their background, her and Travis—this happy couple, right? They lived in Arizona, before they moved up here, a town called El Mirage, just outside of Phoenix. The police there have a laundry list of domestic disputes, some of them violent. They were not happy campers."

"Which makes them pretty much like every other married couple walking the streets."

"Maybe. Except there are other angles. She killed her first husband, too."

Now I stopped and looked at her. She threw me a little pixie smile. Cute. This was a dangerous woman.

"You've been busy." I kept a straight face. "Why don't we get a cup of coffee and you can tell me about it."

She followed me in her car to a hot dog stand down the road. I bought two coffees at the window and we sat on a picnic table in the thin shade of a locust tree.

We smiled at each other. I was waiting for her.

"She married young, a glamour-puss named Carl Lewin who had served time for grand theft auto, drugs."

"Where did you dig this up?"

"Marriage records in Ohio. It's not hard. That's part of what bothers me. Why didn't the cops look at this themselves?"

"How do you know they didn't?"

"Just a feeling. This Lewin was a womanizer. Maybe Sheila couldn't take that. At least this is the way I put it together. Jealousy. Police in Cleveland knew them, had been to their apartment. She threatened to kill him, Ray."

"I've seen domestic disputes. People say things. Threats. They kiss and make up, it's forgotten. What does it mean?"

"Except, one night, with her help, he drank himself over the edge. They were partying at a roadhouse. He was way too plastered to drive. She got behind the wheel, put the car into a tree. She was wearing a seat belt, he wasn't. He went through the windshield. She fractured her hip."

"Sounds like an accident," I said.

"That was the idea."

"So why do you think—"

"She collected a hundred thousand dollars insurance."

I let my eyebrows rise and gave a silent whistle. Was that how I should react? I felt as if I were pulling the strings on a marionette, trying to get my body to mimic the gestures of an innocent man.

"Why tell me about it?" I said.

"You know her, you've met her. Does what I'm saying make sense?"

I thought about it for a minute. "It's true she and Lance weren't happy. They had a blow-up in December—"

"I know about that from the court papers."

"But some kind of murder plot? That's soap opera stuff."

"Somebody's dead. Somebody's been accused of it. Is that a soap opera?"

"It just seems a stretch to me." No, don't argue, I told myself. Don't take a position.

"Strange things happen, Ray. When there's big money involved, they happen pretty often. And I found out something else interesting. Lance Travis was way over his head in debt."

"They seemed pretty comfortable to me."

"That was a facade. In realty, they were practically bankrupt. They were living on the edge and they were this close to losing the comfortable life. That insurance money came in handy. All in all, you'd have to say it was pretty lucky for her he got shot. And sometimes people create their own luck."

"You're missing one little fact. She was a victim. She was shot, too. That's the catch."

"That's what I'm coming to. It's why I need your help. Somebody else was in on it. I know who he is."

The day was hot. Why did I suddenly feel cold? I just stared at her.

"He admits he was her lover," she went on. "He admits she talked about getting rid of her husband. He admits they discussed the insurance. He swears he didn't have a hand in the killing, but I'm not sure. He's a slippery character."

"Who are you talking about?"

"He's a mob wannabe named Dante Lucas. I hope I can get you to meet him."

"What about Johnson? First he confesses, then they find blood evidence in his car."

"Possible blood evidence. The DNA didn't prove anything. Maybe the wife and Lucas set him up, I don't know."

"Why bring it to me?"

"I need more. I need somebody who can meet the man, give me a sense of his credibility, somebody who can back me up. If I take it to Carr's people, I'm sure the guy will spook. Same thing with the cops. Anyway, I don't trust the cops. They've got Johnson and they're not looking beyond him. I need you, Ray. And I'll tell you the truth, this Lucas scares me. I'd feel a lot more comfortable if you went with me to see him."

I rubbed my mouth and tried to bring into focus this new version of the picture. It was one thing that Sheila had lied to me about her first husband. That was history now. This was something recent.

This was a man she had seduced and recruited to help kill her husband. The thought opened the door to a cave somewhere inside me, and a dank, dark wind was blowing down all my fragile ideas of who she was and what I felt about her.

"A man is on trial for murder," she said. "We have to follow this up for the sake of justice."

"Justice?" I laughed a little too loudly. "That's what you're after?"

"Well, it's a great story, too. I don't deny that."

"When do you want to do it?" I knew I had to see the man, had to meet him and size him up. I had to find out the truth about Sheila.

"I'll start working on it right away. I won't tell him you're a cop. Like I said, he's very cautious."

"You'd better be a little cautious yourself." I gave her what I hoped was a smile.

"I will. I'm glad to have you on my side." She reached out and gave my hand a quick squeeze. "I'll call you when it's set. Soon."

I watched her stride back to her car in the sunlight. Sure, I'd go along with her. I had to meet Dante Lucas. I had to stay close to Leanne Corvino, too.

I don't know how long I sat there listening to traffic on the highway and sipping the dregs of my coffee. When I next looked up at the sky, I imagined I caught sight of some of that blackness you're supposed to see from the bottom of a well.

Q: (Mr. Carr): You must have been afraid. Anybody would have been afraid.
A: (Mrs. Travis): Yes.

Q: Of course you were. Paralyzed, you said. Didn't you say that? Paralyzed?
A: I was scared.

Q: You were scared to death. This is a terrible thing, a man comes right into your house, into your bedroom, it's the middle of the night. I'd be afraid. Who wouldn't be afraid? You were defenseless, weren't you?
A: What do you mean?

Q: You didn't have a gun, did you?
A: No.

Q: So you felt vulnerable?
A: Yes, of course.

Q: You weren't wearing any clothes, is that correct?
A: I don't see . . .

Q: You were naked, you testified to that.
A: I didn't have anything on. I always sleep that way.

Q: That made you feel even more exposed, didn't it? More
   helpless?
A: I suppose, yes.

I was reading the transcript of her testimony in the paper while
I ate breakfast. I didn't envy Carr. He had to make the jury question
her credibility without seeming to attack a widow, a victim. He had
to raise doubts while appearing sympathetic. It was a narrow line.

Q: It was dark.
A: I had turned on the lamp beside my bed. I said that.

Q: But it was night, wasn't it? That was the only source of
   light, correct? That one lamp.
A: Yes.

Q: You were upset. You were confused. You were afraid.
A: I wasn't exactly . . .

Q: You didn't know what was happening, did you?
A: No, how could I?

Q: You knew nothing about what was going on?
A: No.

Q: You heard a gunshot in the middle of the night inside
   your house?
A: Yes. I didn't know what it was, whether it was a gunshot
   or what.

Q: So the situation was confusing.
A: I guess you could say that.

I cooked three strips of bacon until just before they turned crisp.
Some people like their bacon crisp, but I don't. I poured the grease
into an empty orange juice can. I fried two eggs slowly, leaving the
yolks liquid. I toasted an English muffin. I poured a glass of juice.
Salt, pepper, and Tabasco on the eggs. Half of the muffin plain to
soak up the egg, half buttered and spread with orange marmalade.
I ground three scoops of Colombian beans and made a pot of coffee.
The first cup with the meal, the next two while I finished the paper.
The old familiar ways.

Q: You looked up and you saw a man silhouetted against
   the doorway, isn't that right?
A: Yes.

Q: Just his shape.
A: No, not silhouetted.

Q: You said silhouetted.
A: No, you said. There was no light behind him. Only the
   lamp by my bed. I saw his face.

Q: He was twenty feet away from you, correct?
A: About.

Q: What was the first thing you noticed about him?
A: I don't know.

Q: Was it the color of his skin?
A: No.

Q: What was it? His height? The shape of his ears? What?
A: I don't know. I just saw him.

Q: You saw what he looked like, didn't you?
A: Yes, I saw him very clearly. I didn't notice just one thing.
   I got an impression of him.

Q: A general impression?
A: That's right.

Q: So you saw what he looked like, but you didn't notice if
   he was black or white? Is that what you're telling this
   court?
A: I saw he was black.

Q: That was the main thing, wasn't it? Yes or no?
A: Yes, I mean no.

Q: Of course it was. You saw a black man. That was all you
   saw, isn't that right?
A: No, it's not.

Q: You saw a black man for a bare instant when you were
   in a state of tremendous fear and tremendous confusion.
A: I saw that man sitting over there. I saw him.

Yes, Carr did a good job, I thought, given the circumstances. Some of the newspaper columnists in town were already saying the district attorney was putting up a weak case. Even the state's own experts couldn't prove that the blood found in Johnson's car was Lance Travis's.

But you couldn't underestimate Monica Hargrove. She pulled out the heavy guns and ended her case with a bang. First Sheila, then the shocker that made everybody sit up and reconsider.

The final prosecution witness was a crack dealer named Abdul Hakeem. He testified that Johnson had talked to him while they were in adjoining cells in the county jail.

"He said he had gone out to this house in the 'burbs, this Travis place," he explained. "The next thing, Jerome just flipped. Guy tried to burn him, Jerome pulled his piece. First, it went off by itself, but then he just kept shooting. He couldn't stop himself, he said."

Court had to be recessed for twenty minutes because of an outburst by Johnson's supporters in the spectators' area. When the trial resumed, Hakeem continued to lay it on. "It happened like in slow motion, he told me. He said he knew the man's wife was upstairs. Had to take care of her, too."

Carr moved in on cross and established that, of course, Hakeem believed his cooperation with the DA might help his own case, which involved wounding three people with a TEC-11, a dope deal gone sour. But the witness stood his ground, insisted that he had been promised nothing, that he just wanted to tell the truth.

Carr's own case proved to be short.

He brought in half a dozen blood experts to make it clear that, given the sketchy DNA results, the blood found in Johnson's car was more likely from the nosebleed he said he had had two months before the crime. They couldn't absolutely rule out a match with Travis's blood, but it was a long shot.

He brought in other experts to prove that the money clip found on Johnson, which Sheila had identified as having belonged to Lance, could easily have been purchased, as Johnson said it had.

Carr put up Donnie Stapleton, the guy whose furnace Johnson had helped fix that night. But Stapleton couldn't testify to anything after ten o'clock. Hargrove got him to admit to smoking a spliff that night, which made him even less believable.

Next, three experts witnesses cited a slew of studies showing that eyewitness testimony often proves unreliable, particularly when race comes into it. In fact, they said, seeing the crime with your own eyes, which is usually considered the strongest evidence, is often the weakest.

Finally, Carr paraded half a dozen character witnesses into court, including the priest we had run into the night of the arrest. They all claimed Johnson had broken free from drugs, that he was turning his life around, that he was now devoted to his wife and his two kids, that he went to church, worked a job, washed his car, trimmed his toenails, and did all the things a civilized person does.

Carr gave a masterful summation. He attacked the police for their incompetence and the prosecutors for mounting a case against his client that was little more than a house of cards. He assured the jury that Mrs. Travis was simply mistaken.

Hargrove's case rested squarely on Sheila's ID and everyone knew it. The only question that remained was whether the jury would believe her.

Some of this I got from Leanne, who had been at the courthouse for the finale. She called me at around seven-thirty in the evening to arrange for our meeting with Dante Lucas later that night.

Ever since I had talked to Brie about Lance, since Leanne had wised me up at the shooting range, I had wanted to rush over to Sheila's and force her to explain. I wanted answers about her first husband and how he died. I wanted answers about Lucas. I wanted to know how I fit into the picture, how she really felt about me. I wanted very badly for her to be able to explain it all away.

Of course, I did nothing. The situation was too delicate. Or maybe I knew she would have no answers, only more lies.

I told myself I needed to talk to this Lucas. I needed to hear it from the source, to be absolutely sure.

After dark, while I was getting ready to go, I looked out my upstairs back window. As she often did on warm nights, Sheila had turned on just the pool lights and was swimming. I could look down into the glowing blue water. She swam mostly underwater, pushing off from the shallow end and slithering along as far as her breath would hold. She would stream bubbles, surface to take in air, and go back down.

I watched her for a long time, as she glided through the water alone, content in herself, oblivious to the world. She was beautiful. Beautiful, wicked, alluring, reckless, without remorse. She was, to me, a creature as remote and lovely and untouchable as some distant star.

"He runs a skin club on the far west side," Leanne was saying. "He's skittish. I can see him bolting, denying the whole thing."

"What does he say happened?"

We were driving west in my car, out along Culver Avenue, the truck route. Ten-thirty at night, but it was still hot enough to keep the air conditioner on.

"She talked murder to him. He went along, he says, not really thinking she was serious. When he realized she meant it, he cut bait."

"You met him how?"

"Friends of my uncle.

"Sammy Two-Fish heard of this guy, even down in Atlanta?"

"No, but I asked around, guys who know that world. They trust me. Not just because of my uncle—I've made a point of developing contacts. You're a reporter, you want to have friends in low places."

"What did you find out?"

"He'd been talking, bragging to his pals how he knows this Travis woman who's in the news. I went to him and said I'm doing a story. He's dying to get on television. I'm trying to play on that."

"Why is he talking?"

"He's stupid and arrogant and he trusts me. He wanted to tell me things off the record. When I started to explain how I would put him on the tube, put him in the public eye, he got interested. I suppose he imagines it'll be publicity for his place."

"He wants the light to shine on him."

"You're not real these days until you've been on television. When we get there, you'll make out you're a producer at Channel Ten. I told Lucas I couldn't move ahead on the project without approval from upstairs. He's going to be nervous about it, but I insisted that you had to check out his story."

I kept pace with the traffic. We talked about the closing arguments in the Johnson trial.

"Carr's a master," she said. "I think he played his hand perfectly. Whether he'll succeed in getting Johnson off, I don't know. If we get the right breaks, it won't matter."

I pulled into the parking lot of a long stucco building. A sign shouted "Starlight Club" in hot neon. The barred windows in front made it look a little like a wild-west jail. A man with tattooed twenty-inch biceps greeted us just inside the door.

"How you doin' tonight?" he barked.

Leanne explained that we were there to see Lucas. The muscle man pointed toward a table in the front corner.

A bar stretched across the back wall, or you could sit at a counter that wrapped around the stage on the far side. Two girls were working the snort poles. Occasionally they squatted to give a customer a closer look and pick up a tip. Two others, wearing oversized boxing gloves and nothing else, were dancing and mock-fighting. When they went into the clinches, a couple of guys in the audience started to howl.

Dante Lucas was in his early thirties. Height, my height. Weight, about the same as me. Health club physique under some expensive threads. Good-looking guy with a couple of pounds of Rolex on his wrist, a monogram on his shirt. A beauty mark just above the corner of his mouth gave his face an insinuating, slightly feminine cast.

He pointed to the seat opposite him in the booth. We sat and Leanne introduced me.

"My theory," Lucas said, "this guy Johnson was in on it. In fact, he might have been plowing her, I wouldn't be surprised. I'm sure he was in on it."

"Maybe," Leanne said. "In order to assemble the picture, we need all the details. You hold the key links."

"I'm the man," Lucas said, cracking a big smile. "I figure . . ."

A sudden uproar obliterated his words. Chairs scraped. One of the girls on the stage had clipped the other too hard. Now they were going at it in earnest, pummeling each other wildly, spitting insults. Finally one of them fell on her bare rear end and the other clasped her hands over her head in victory. The crowd hooted.

"Part of the show," Lucas said. "All part of the show. Let's go into my office, be quieter."

We slipped behind the bar, past a storage room, and entered a small office. On the left, fish swam around a big aquarium under black light.

"She gravitated to me, I gravitated to her," he said as he settled into the high-backed leather chair behind the desk. The wall behind him was covered with ego shots, posed photos of Lucas with Wayne Newton, Lucas surrounded by half a dozen young ladies with pillow-sized breasts, Lucas shaking the hand of Mayor Catlett.

"Where did you meet her?" Leanne said. "I know we talked, but Ray needs to hear the whole thing."

"Oh, it was at a party. It must have been a party, I'm a party animal." He smiled to himself. "I remember them being there, her and Lance, both crocked, but he was more crocked. She knew me right away. Understand? She knew me before she met me. She knew things about me. I don't know how. I never knew how."

"You met at a party," Leanne prompted.

"So we get to talking, we hit it off. I see her around afterward. I call her—want to go for a drink? She says, 'I'm married.' I say, 'So?' We meet, we drink. Friendly, that's what it was. She was a friendly broad. What did I care if she was married?"

I sat there examining my fingernails, as if my first priority was deciding whether to go for a manicure or not. The best way to get information out of somebody is not to show any interest in what they're saying. If you're bored, distracted, or seem like you just don't give a damn, they'll talk themselves silly. As soon as you start paying attention, they wonder if they're saying too much.

"This is when?" Leanne asked.

"Year and a half ago. They were renting a house on Patowa Drive, looking to buy. I told her some of the shit I'd been into. Told her I knew guys, which I do, who are connected up to their eyeballs. She was interested in that. She was cool, nothing shocked her. A real pleasure to talk to that broad. Real pleasure."

He liked to play with his cuffs. French cuffs, big gold links with his initials in diamond chips.

"She wanted me to tell her about the life. I hinted around. She liked it, so I made up some shit—things I heard other guys did, only I said I did 'em. She wanted to see this."

My tongue pressed against the roof of my mouth as he pulled out a stainless-steel automatic from under his coat. It looked like a

9 mm. He held it out in his palm. A lazy smirk spread across his mouth; he liked to put on a show.

"What was he like?" Leanne asked, ignoring the gesture. "The husband?"

"Lance?" He slipped the gun back into its holster. "Nice guy. An asshole, but a nice guy. She said he beat her up. I never saw it happen, but I believed it. I've got a temper myself. But the things he did to that broad, it wasn't right."

He patted his hair, which looked like he had it trimmed every afternoon. He waited, enjoying the attention. I rubbed my mouth, pretending to stifle a yawn.

"When she brought up the idea of offing him," he said, "it was the most casual, everyday thing in the world."

"The two of you were intimate at this point?" Leanne said.

"Intimate?" He laughed. "Oh, we were intimate, all right."

My hand was clutching the arm of the chair. I had a strong urge to pull my own gun and shoot him in the face.

Lucas went on, "One day, she says, out of left field, 'Wouldn't it be nice if Lance was dead?' 'Why's that?' I say. I mean, Lance ain't causing me any problems I can see. She says, 'Get him out of the way, I'm free.' 'Just leave him,' I tell her. 'You've got feet at the ends of your legs. Walk.' That's when she brought up the million. See, Lance had this insurance policy. If anything—"

"We know about that," Leanne said.

"That changed the picture. A broad, no matter what you say, is a broad. But a broad plus a million, that is one attractive package. I mean, wouldn't you?" He looked straight at me.

"What was the split?" Leanne asked.

"Depended on her mood. I would get a hundred thousand. That

was minimum. Sometimes she'd say a quarter million. Sometimes she talked as if we would live together and share it all. Travel the world. We had lots of plans."

He smiled, remembering. I glanced at Leanne, who was looking over at me. I realized I was grinding my back teeth and I forced myself to relax.

"We talked about how to set him up," he continued. "How we would lure him out by the dump, or to a road I know that goes around the airport. Different ways we could play it. Ways to kill him. She liked talking about it. It gave her a thrill."

"Did you think she was serious?" Leanne asked.

"Hell, yes. She was serious. No question. She always knew exactly what she wanted. I'll say that for her, no bullshit."

"Why not do it?" I said. The words felt rusty in my throat. "Why walk away?"

"Why?" He pondered the question as if it had never occurred to him. "Broad was in the ozone, man. I didn't trust her. There were times I thought maybe she was running a sting of some kind. But she didn't have on no wire. I checked." He forced another laugh.

"So you never intended to kill him?" Leanne asked.

"A million bucks, you think about it. But she turns, I burn. I didn't like that angle. The people I know, people who are in the life, you can trust them. This broad, maybe she's solid, maybe she goes screaming to the cops as soon as they say boo to her. Plus, to kill a guy, that's a heavy load. To kill a guy who's never done nothing to you? Heavy."

He made a show of looking for a cigarette. He searched his pockets, opened a couple of drawers.

"Hey, babe," he said to Leanne. "Mind going out to the machine and picking me up a pack of Newports?"

He held a frozen smile on her. She looked at me, finally nodded. When she was out the door, he said, "I want to tell you something, not in front of her. I want to give you the real story."

"Oh, yeah?"

"Listen, I'm up for any woman on God's earth. Any. Believe me. But this Sheila was too much. She was a truly dangerous broad."

He was grinning and at the same time moving his mouth as if chewing gum.

"She scared you?" I said.

The smile went away. "That's it." He was suddenly earnest. "You're a man, maybe you get what I'm talking about. The broad was a phenomenal piece of ass. But she was taking me right over the edge. First time she mentioned capping the husband, I'm going, 'Sure I'll kill your fucking husband. I'll kill every male on this planet, baby, you say the word.' Yeah, she scared me. She scared me plenty."

I stared at him. A cold rage was gripping my mind, part contempt for this animal, part amazement that she had had anything to do with him, part fury that she had lied to me from beginning to end.

Leanne returned. Lucas lit a cigarette and dropped the match into a clean glass ashtray.

"We have to talk about the affidavit," Leanne said.

"No," he said, "first we gotta talk about the money."

"So you're going on about truth, justice, and the American way," I said to Leanne as we drove back to pick up her car, "and at the same time, you're paying this guy for his information?"

"That's the way the news business works these days, Ray."

"But what's it do to his credibility in court?"

"That's not my worry. Each of us plays his own game. I'm a reporter, I put the facts out there. If the cops or the DA want to prosecute her, fine. I think he's believable, don't you?"

"I think he's a professional bullshitter."

"Sure he is. But I've already followed up a couple of leads he gave me, people who knew the Travises. They confirmed that Lucas was around them, went to their parties. What he says may be smoke, but it's not *just* smoke."

"Anybody can manufacture a story."

"Look at the pattern, though. If you isolate on one thing, you miss it. If you look at the whole, a picture emerges—money, jealousy, murder."

At a stoplight I watched a teenaged couple ambling along the sidewalk holding hands. She leaned way back and slapped him playfully on the arm, then grabbed him and kissed him.

"I need an interview with her," Leanne said. "I have to have a go-between. You know her. Convince her to give me a chance. She talked to Donna Jordan, she can talk to me. I want to get her on camera and put this stuff in her face. Tomorrow we'll have the affidavit. I think she'll crack. If she does, I've got what everybody in television is after, maybe save an innocent man on top of it. If she doesn't talk, I still have her reaction. I'll hand what I've got over to the police. I just don't know whether they'll do anything with it."

"Why is that?"

"Cops don't always play straight. You know that better than I do. They want a conviction, period. Johnson is a good bet to get one. They have a vested interest in nailing him. I mean, I did some running around, but it didn't take a Sherlock Holmes to dig up this stuff. How come the police couldn't?"

"They had an eyewitness, a suspect, a confession."

"They never considered any other possibility, even with the insurance angle. That seems odd to me. It seems as if she took them in a little too easily. Anyway, I want to do this my way. I want to make an impact."

I pulled into my driveway and left room for her to back her car out. It was one of those summer nights when the air never cools down. The moon lolled in the west, a soft slice of orange.

She came in to use my phone—her cell phone was broken. She punched the number of the television station and talked in the clipped code used by people who work together.

"Could I offer you a drink?" I said when she'd finished.

She looked at me. Her mouth tried on a couple different flavors of smile before folding into one that was friendly and a little ironic.

"I didn't mean anything more than a cold one on a hot night,"
I said.

"I know you didn't. I think I'll pass. I'm doing the Miss Mansfield thing at the mall tomorrow morning. Plus, everybody's going
to be on edge waiting for the Johnson jury."

"I have to work myself."

"What's your answer? Are you going to help me get to the wife
or not?"

"I need to think it over."

"And I need to know. Things go stale in the news business damn
quick."

"Let me sleep on it."

"Tomorrow. But I have to have a definite yes-no."

"You will."

I walked her out to her car. The air was skin temperature.

"Thanks, sweetheart," she said. "We'll talk tomorrow."

"I'll be in touch."

Her headlights dazzled me as she backed out. I heard a sound
behind me; someone was lurking there. I moved cautiously around
the corner. Stepping into the shadow behind the house, I caught
sight of Sheila. She must have been swimming and spotted us from
her yard. She was wearing a suit like the one she'd worn the day I
first met her. Her bare arms and legs practically glowed in the dark.

"What is that bitch doing here?" she hissed.

"Come inside," I said. I led her up the back porch. Her hair was
wet. I could see the glow of their pool.

"I warned you about her, Ray," she said.

We stepped into the kitchen. "She's on to you."

"You're crazy. You're planning something with her."

"She's building a case against you."

"What are you talking about?"

"You weren't married before?" my voice boomed. I was breathing hard.

"Married?"

"Lance wasn't your first husband, was he? You killed your first. Killed him and collected the goddamn insurance. You did that. You did it!"

Her eyes looked me up and down coldly, as if I were a stranger. Then she casually shifted gears and said, "How about a drink? We could both use one."

I took the tequila from the freezer, poured a couple of fingers of it into two tumblers, and handed her one.

She said, "I didn't want to talk about Carl. You're right, he was my first husband, my first love. His death was a tragic, tragic—"

"Get off it! Tragic? You were driving the car."

"I was hurt, too. I could have been killed myself. You think I crashed it on purpose?"

"Of course you did. To collect a hundred thousand dollars."

The words gave her pause. She crossed her arms and stared at me.

"She knows you were broke," I said. "You and Lance."

"Broke? Are you kidding?"

"Lance was drowning in debt and you were afraid of losing the good life. You had to do something."

"Did I?" She toasted me, sipped her drink.

"The insurance money wasn't icing," I said. "It was all you were ever interested in. You killed a man to get it and you used me to pull it off. End of story."

"That's not true, Ray. I wanted to be with you. That's why I killed him. I did what I had to do. You think I enjoyed it? My God.

It was necessary. For our sake. Now you go around listening to stupid gossip and pointing your finger at me. How do you think that makes me feel?"

My blood was racing. I looked at her and said, "She just took me to see Dante Lucas."

She tried not to react, but her eyes betrayed her.

"No need to pretend you don't know who he is," I said. "He's already agreed to sign an affidavit. He'll tell how you recruited him to kill Lance. How you used your lovely body to twist his head around. And when he backed out, you had to find somebody else to be your dupe."

She shook her head and said, "Damn you."

"You don't know Lucas?" I said.

"Sure, okay. So what? I knew him. He was a lowlife creep."

"You talked to him about Lance having an accident."

"Maybe I did. You know the way Lance treated me. He cheated on me, Ray. He beat me up. You saw. He molested his own daughter. He didn't deserve to live."

"You're a liar. He didn't abuse her and she wasn't his daughter. He never touched her."

"What do you know about it?" She drained her glass.

"She told me." I felt suddenly drunk myself.

"Haven't you ever heard of denial? Denial is very common. Anyway, I told you in confidence. I trusted you."

"Stop it. It never happened."

"I saw them at it. I caught them. She's trying to defend his reputation now that he's dead."

"You're a liar!"

"Don't call me that," she said in a low voice.

"You recruited Lucas and you offered to split the insurance with him."

"Why not? Why shouldn't I free myself of that bastard? Lucas didn't mean anything to me. He was a tool."

"He was a tool and I was a tool. You used me." I wanted her to deny it. I wanted her to convince me it wasn't true.

Instead, she said, "You're feeling the fear. That's what it is. You're getting cold feet and you're blaming it on me. This thing is going down perfectly. Perfectly! But you haven't got the guts to see it through."

I shook my head. I could feel my fists opening and closing.

She was almost screaming. "You're terrified. I was willing to put a bullet in a man's brain. Do you know what that's like? I thought you were strong. But you're weak. Weak! You goddamn fucking cop!"

Her glass floated through the air, tumbling over and over. It sparkled, catching the light and fracturing it. It grazed my temple and continued on. I heard it crash against the wall behind me.

Her face, aged with anger, was mouthing words at me. I was surprised to see my hand snake out and sting her face. I heard the smack, felt the heat on my palm.

My ears were filled with a rushing sound. When I went to hit her again, she grabbed hold of my wrist. My hand lit up with pain.

I jerked back from her. I looked at the gash her teeth had made in my palm. Blood was dripping.

She came at me now, beating with her fists, kicking my numb shins. I held my hands up against the flurry of blows. I pushed her. She stumbled back against the counter, slipped, and fell awkwardly.

She threw an animal glare at me from the floor. Blood smeared the corner of her mouth. I grabbed her by her arm and yanked her to her feet. She weighed nothing.

I didn't know what I was doing. She twisted, tried to squirm away from me. I yanked her to me, kissed her throat, kissed her reddening cheek, her mouth. Her arms came around my neck.

It was all happening in a rush. We stumbled, locked together, into the living room. In our urgency we knocked a piece of my mother's cut glass to the floor. It shattered. We fell onto the couch.

I won't say it wasn't good. But even as we tore at each other, even as we mounted the summit of pleasure, I knew it wasn't love I felt for her. Not anymore. No, it was nothing like love.

THE BEAUTY CONTESTANTS were sweating. I don't know if the air-conditioning was broken or if it just couldn't keep up with the roaring sun outside, but the food court of the mall was a sauna that morning. As the pageant went on, you could see the damp darkness spreading down the satin under the girls' arms.

It broke my heart to watch them. They weren't used to walking in high heels. This was Mansfield, not New York City. They weren't used to being looked at, to being judged. And each wanted so badly to win, wanted so badly to be told she was beautiful. A girl with pumpkin-colored hair stepped carefully, unsteadily up the steps to the plywood stage they had set up. She flashed a metallic smile at the audience, walked in front of the judges, a tiny tremor in her step.

It wasn't just the sad spectacle that broke my heart. The night before, after Sheila had gone, I had cracked open a beer and had sat on my back porch until dawn. I had sat there sweating and trying to bring it all down to a single idea that would guide me or at least explain what had happened. Appetite? Lust? Cowardice? Desire? Disaster? What was the one idea that would let me say, Oh, yeah,

that's what this was about? What was it, when you stripped it to
the bone? Could you call it love? Or had I only been played for a
fool?

I had decided there was no single explanation. The path had
been laid out for me and I had never had a choice but to travel it.
It had just happened. And now I had come to one of those crossroads where you have to choose, where it doesn't just happen.

On stage, a black teenager was singing "Over the Rainbow." Her
thin soprano was as fragile as glass. Some. Where.

The equations I had had to solve that night were complicated.
Dante Lucas. Lance Travis. Her first husband. A million dollars.
Whispered words. Stolen glimpses. Moments of breathtaking love.
Promises. Lies. Betrayal. Hatred.

The calculations had been too much for me. Finally, I had to
turn to practicalities. Leanne Corvino knew too much. Whether they
convicted Jerome Johnson or not didn't matter now. Leanne
wouldn't let it rest and in the end I wasn't going to let somebody
else take the blame. It was going to come undone no matter what I
did. I decided it was time to tell my story.

If love blurs our vision, fear clarifies it. Sitting in the dark staring
at her dark windows, I knew, suddenly and certainly, that if Sheila
were cornered she would turn on me. She would not hesitate.

Yes, I needed to tell my story first. I needed to tell the truth.

After months of pretending, months of lying, months of worrying about being found out, it seemed odd now to imagine telling the
truth. But it was the only strategy that made sense. Survival. When
everything else goes to pieces, you have to let survival be your guide.
A new rule.

I had never liked being lied to.

Watching the sun come up the way it does at the beginning of a really hot day, I had felt as if I had just returned to myself after a long journey. It felt good. I took a shower and put on my uniform and went to work.

I knew I had to talk to Leanne. Not to tell her the story. It would be Frank Kaiser I would tell that to. I just needed to be honest with her, to give her an answer, as I had promised I would.

"And here to announce the winner of this year's Miss Mansfield contest and place the crown on her head is Channel Ten's own Leanne Corvino. Let's give her a big hand."

She looked absolutely fresh in a cream-colored suit with blue trim. She hit the MC, each of the finalists, and then the audience with a smile so convincing and radiant that it seemed to take on a life of its own. Her eyes continued to blaze with gladness as she spoke about what an honor it was.

After a few minutes of drama and the announcement of the runners-up, Leanne proclaimed that the new Miss Mansfield was the wobbly redhead. Tears streaming, the girl let Leanne pin the awkward tiara to her head.

The show finished up quickly then. I had a chance to catch Leanne's attention. I indicated a nearby exit. She nodded.

We walked through the shimmering air in the parking lot, which was fast filling with cars. We walked a long way. I knew what I wanted to say, but the words didn't come easily. We were almost out to the weedy fringe where grasshoppers swarmed.

"I think you're on to something," I said at last.

"I'm so glad to hear you say that, Ray. I was beginning to wonder if I was reading all this stuff right or not. You don't know how I've agonized. My God, if I got it wrong."

"No, I feel very strongly that you're right about her being involved."

"Will you talk to her?"

I shook my head. "I'm going to have to work it out my own way. You can't turn this into a spectacle for the gawkers."

"Now, wait a minute."

"Whatever happened, it was a tragedy."

"Listen, I developed this. I did the legwork. You're not going to take it away from me."

"I understand that."

"Do you?"

"You'll get a story, I guarantee it."

"An exclusive."

"Exclusive, inside, just for you. I promise. But not to make a show of it. Not to play it for sensation. It's not a circus."

"Ray, it's going to be a circus no matter which way you cut it. A husband murdered, a big insurance settlement, an innocent man accused—it's a dream story. The public is going to eat it up. If we can prove she did it, it will be a circus—networks, tabloids, the whole nine yards. Nothing I can do or you can do is going to prevent that."

"I'm not going to help you ambush her. I'm going to do it my way."

"But when? The Johnson jury could come back any minute. There's no more time."

"Today. By this afternoon. Trust me."

She stared at me through narrowed eyes. I could see doubts flickering across her face. Maybe she was suddenly making connections that she should have made a long time ago, suddenly wondering where I fit into this picture. But then her features cleared and she smiled.

"Okay, I trust you," she said. "You'll do the right thing, won't you?"

I nodded. I could see the Channel Ten van angling across the parking lot at a pretty good clip. The driver pulled to a halt just behind Leanne. He was a young guy with a ponytail.

"We gotta go, babe," he said. "We have a breaker on the west side."

"Okay, Teddy." She turned to me. "Ray, call me, okay? Don't let me down. I want that exclusive."

"Don't worry."

She climbed inside and the van took off.

BEING A COP is more than a job. It's a role, a mission you might call it. You feel it from the first day you graduate the academy. It's a feeling of power, of purpose. You're a somebody, a person citizens respect. You can take off the uniform, but you're always a cop.

I was going to miss that. This hot July day would be my last on the job. My career was over. What lay ahead I didn't know, but I was sure it wouldn't involve driving a patrol car around the streets of Mansfield.

From the mall parking lot I used my car phone to call the station. Sergeant Phelps, who was on desk duty that day, told me he didn't think Frank Kaiser was there. He checked. No, Kaiser was working a crime out on Culver Avenue, he said. He gave me the address.

I don't know why it didn't register. I wasn't thinking as I drove over there. I was imagining what Frank would say, what he would think, what he would not say.

I was thinking about Sheila, too. I was imagining how it would actually happen, the knock on her door, the detectives, the warrant, the interrogation. She would know I had betrayed her.

Sure, I had qualms, plenty of qualms. But I hated her lies and I was afraid of her. One of us was going down for this, I knew that now.

I was driving out Culver, as I had driven out Culver the night before. Then the car dealerships had been closed. Now the ranks of shiny Chevys and shiny Buicks and shiny Volvos glistened in the sun. Now the strings of red and yellow and blue triangles flapped excitedly. Now customers were prowling the showrooms of furniture stores or hunting for bargains in wedding dresses and aboveground pools. Now the bars and clubs sank into the background, their raucous neon diluted.

It still didn't register with me. It was just a funny coincidence, just the same neighborhood, pure chance.

Driving out there, I had other things on my mind. What kind of a deal could I cut? That was police thinking—justice means plea bargaining. I was going to sell her out, betray her, and my mind had already started calculating the deal I would be able to arrange.

Exotic. It was the only light flashing at the Starlight Club. It hung from the bottom of the sign out front, the one word lit from within. *Exotic.* It flashed and flashed in the fierce sun.

I saw the patrol cars. I saw the detectives' cars. I took it all in, the handful of gawkers, the crime-scene tape, the television crews. I parked my cruiser and asked one of the patrolmen on duty where Kaiser was. Inside.

I saw Leanne motioning to me, wide-eyed and eager. She tried to reach me. One of the officers held her back. She called my name. I waved a meaningless gesture and entered the club.

Inside, the air conditioner chilled the darkness but took away none of the stale beer and cigarette smell. Empty, the place looked small and squalid. The forensic crew, dressed in their white suits and latex gloves, were collecting trace evidence. My sweat turned icy.

I waited while Frank Kaiser finished interviewing a woman who, judging from her makeup and physique, was one of the dancers. She kept crossing and recrossing her legs, which were encased in knee-high fringed boots. She kept glancing at the bar. From behind it, a pair of feet protruded, one wearing a tasseled Italian loafer, the other just a gray sock.

I could see she was scared, but the set of her mouth was defiant. She had come in that blistering Saturday morning to do her job and make some money and instead she had found a dead man.

Kaiser thanked her, then watched the bounce of her hips as she left. He rubbed a hand down his face and moved his jaw back and forth.

"I have to talk to you," I said.

"Medical examiner here yet?" he asked one of the other detectives.

"Just arrived."

"Let's get moving. Look at this, Ray."

We stepped to the end of the bar.

Kaiser said, "White male, mid-thirties. That girl claims he runs the place."

We stared at the body. Dante Lucas was lying with his lips pressed to the floor, as if he were trying to sip his own blood. One side of the head was blown away. He wasn't handsome anymore, though the beauty mark on his cheek stood out more than ever. Blood matted what was left of his neatly trimmed hair.

"She came in to open up," Frank said. "He usually doesn't show till later. I said, 'Why do you want to work in a joint like this, show your titties to every perverted fuck who has the price of a beer?'

She laughed in my face. What am I, a missionary? Hell, I can't wait to retire."

The medical examiner had the face of someone laughing at a private joke. He pulled on gloves and knelt by the body. He picked up Lucas's hand and looked at the fingers, waved the wrist around. He slowly rolled the torso halfway over. As the head twisted, the dead man seemed to glance at us over his shoulder through dull, wide-open eyes.

"Preliminary is multiple gunshot wounds to the cranium. Body's cold but not stiff. I would say six hours, maybe eight."

"We have a Ruger P89, three gone from the clip," Kaiser said. "Possible?"

"Very."

"Young lady found the body claims he packed, so it could be he got done with his own iron."

"Robbery?"

"Maybe. Maybe sex, maybe drugs, maybe who knows? Maybe he argued with some guy, what's the capital of South Dakota."

"Well, it wasn't suicide, that angle. Is it Bismark?"

"That's North. I've seen too many of these."

The medical examiner let the body roll back. You can't imagine how loose a lifeless body is. It can sicken you, if you're not used to it, to see gravity take over so completely.

I was used to it. The sight did not bother me. Lucas being dead did not bother me. He had known Sheila. I was glad she had killed him.

Frank's men went through Lucas's clothes while the medical examiner and his assistant prepared the big plastic body bag.

"I have to talk to you, Frank," I said again.

"What about?"

"This. And the Travis case. It's important."

He spoke to the other detectives. "Carson, you and Manning do some preliminary canvassing. Gunshots, cars, strange people, anything. And get a list of the employees."

Frank motioned me toward the door.

"Travis is history, boy," he said. "Got that? Travis is history. This guy, he's history, too. A dead man is history. Forget about it."

"I have new information."

He stared again, a man trying to solve a complex math equation in his head. Finally he said, "I've been up all night on a boon shooting in the third ward. I'm going to get the guys started on this, turn it over to Davy Makowski. How about we meet over at my place later? It's quiet, we can talk. We can talk about everything."

"I think we should talk now."

"Later."

His hand gently but firmly turned me toward the door.

The heat slammed into me as I walked outside. I squinted against the glare.

I quickly climbed into my patrol car and started the engine. In my mirror I saw Leanne Corvino hurrying toward me, waving.

I put the car in gear and drove off.

A BALCONY JUTTED off the back of Frank Kaiser's A-frame house. Below that was a patio that extended from the walk-in basement. We sat on the balcony at six that evening drinking Johnnie Walker, the ice clinking in our glasses. I was telling Frank the story, telling it from the beginning, from when I first saw Sheila's shape in the window one hot summer night.

I was telling him about our doomed romance and about her lies, about her shooting Lance and me shooting her to cover up. I tried to give him a little of the why of it all, but I couldn't seem to find the words to capture that angle. Frank took it in. He seemed bored by it all.

Frank's house was in the middle of nowhere—Mansfield's suburbs hadn't reached out that far yet. The backyard needed a haircut. It sloped down from the patio and ended in woods. Somebody had landscaped it once, turned it into a charming glade, but it had been let go. A couple of forlorn weeping cherry trees jutted out of the tangle of brambles, goldenrod, and sumac. Above them, clouds of insects caught the last glow of the sun. You could feel their drone resonate with the hum of the heat.

As I sipped the icy, smoky taste of the scotch, I imagined it might be my last drink for a long time. I didn't know what lay ahead. I had never had a knack for charting the future.

Both of us glanced from time to time at the little black-and-white television that Frank had propped in the corner. The rumor was that the Johnson jury was on the verge of a verdict, that they could be coming back any minute. We were waiting for the bulletin.

"She was counting on me," I said. "That's the way she played it. She made me believe I couldn't let her down."

"They have their tricks, all right."

"I was literally mad about her. The craving went right through me. I committed myself. Me, Ray Dolan. Can you believe that? I told her she could depend on me. I've never told any woman that. I felt responsible. I loved her. I really and truly loved her, Frank."

He shook his head slightly, maybe in sympathy.

I said, "You tell somebody they can count on you, what the hell do you do?"

"You come through. If it's in you, you come through for them."

"I'm not making excuses. I guess I'm trying to explain it to myself. She was counting on me. As you say, I came through. I didn't think about the fact that I was doing something wrong. Not really. I was doing what a man does."

"Of course. And you weren't doing anything wrong. The husband was dead already, you thought. You were just cleaning up. You were using your judgment. We all do it every day. For a cop, a crime is what we say it is. Was she guilty, or innocent? You judged her. You had every right to. I don't blame you."

He meant it. Frank took in what I said without ever judging, without ever registering shock or surprise. He asked just the right questions and then sat there silently while I struggled to answer, to put it into words. No blame.

The story wasn't like in a movie where everything makes sense. Even I could see that it was a crazy mix of love and hate and greed and blindness and betrayal. I brought Frank right up to my meeting with Lucas the night before, to my final encounter with Sheila.

"I thought about killing Lucas myself," I said. "Not because I imagined it would get me off, or get her off. I hated him for knowing her, for looking at her, touching her. I hated him for being just like me."

"Who do you think clipped him?"

"I can only guess."

"The wife? The Travis woman?"

I nodded. "She's capable of it. I knew that all along. I knew she didn't kill her husband in a rage. She executed him. She broke the rules. I guess that was one thing that fascinated me. Last night, knowing she had been lying to me, using me, I was still fascinated by her, still caught. Hell, I am even now."

He nodded.

"There are all these rules, Frank, but not for her. She was beyond rules. Does that make sense?"

"Sure. That's why you're a cop. Cops are beyond rules, too."

I didn't know what he meant by that. We stared at each other.

He lifted the bottle and splashed generous slugs into each of our glasses. We were drinking hard, burning it up.

He said, "I know all about what a woman can do. I was the one who always let them twist my head around. You, I thought you had it under control."

"I never chose any of it. Or I guess I did choose it, but it didn't seem as if I were choosing. It just seemed to happen."

He nodded. "I admired you, do you know that? I admired your cool. Old married man like me. Messy divorce. You kept women in their place. That was quite a knack, I thought. Yeah, I admired you."

"You've seen her."

"I've seen her. I don't blame you, boy. What did you think would happen? How did you think it would play out?"

"I didn't think, period."

"That million bucks, you must have thought about that."

"I didn't even know about the insurance until you told me. Is that crazy? I didn't do it for money. I don't know if that makes a difference, but I definitely didn't do it for money."

"You're telling me you did it for her. Of course. You're a god-damn romantic, you know that?" His laugh went floating off into the warm air. I even chuckled myself. The scotch was loosening me. Between the scotch and lack of sleep, reality was losing its edge.

Leanne Corvino's image appeared on the small screen.

"This looks like it," Frank said. "Damn funny they should be coming back now. Let's see if the jury believed her." He leaned over to turn up the sound.

". . . that the jury in the murder trial of Jerome Johnson has indeed reached a verdict in a case that has had the city of Mansfield on edge for so long. We are about to take you live inside the courtroom at the Mansfield Municipal Building to hear that judgment."

"Leanne," a voice said, "what's the mood outside there? We can see people gathered around."

"In a word, Chuck, the atmosphere is tense. Feelings about this case have run very high, especially in the minority communities, and everyone is waiting to see just what this jury will decide. Now I understand the jurors are filing back in. Let's go live inside the courtroom."

The picture switched to the idle activity in the court as the jurors took their seats off camera.

"Madam Foreperson," Judge Pennwalt said after an endless pause, "would you please open the envelope and check the condition of the verdict forms?"

The camera focused now on the defendant.

We could hear a woman say, "Yes, Your Honor."

"Are they the same forms you signed, and are they in order?"

"Yes, they are."

"Before we have the reading of the verdict, I would ask that everyone in this room refrain from any kind of demonstration or display. If there is a disruption, I will instruct the bailiffs to remove any and all persons involved."

He stared sternly around the courtroom and continued, "Mr. Johnson, would you rise and face the jury."

Johnson, wearing a neat dark suit, stood, along with Stonewall Carr and his other attorneys.

"Mr. Warner, please read the verdict."

The clerk stood in front of the bench, glanced quickly at Johnson, and read, "In the case of the *People v. Jerome M. Johnson,* we the jury find the defendant guilty of the crime of murder in the second degree in violation of the Penal Code of the State of New York, in that he did willfully take the life of one Lance Travis, a human being, as charged in count one of the indictment."

Johnson kept staring as if he didn't quite understand what the words meant.

The clerk continued reading. The jury also found the defendant guilty of attempted murder for shooting Sheila. They found him guilty of robbery for taking money from the Travis home.

Johnson's head swiveled toward Carr, who had his hand on

Johnson's shoulder. Johnson's mouth opened and the word *No!* rang out. Carr said something to him. Johnson just repeated the word, screamed it, "*No! No!*"

Three bailiffs moved toward him. He bolted. Carr tried to grab him, but he was already over the railing and into the spectator area. There he scuffled with several more bailiffs, big men in uniforms. His supporters yelled and moved to his aid and were pushed back. A fist was thrown. More security officers crowded around. Johnson was handcuffed and led away. The bailiffs quickly cleared the spectators.

The judge thanked the jury. He casually announced that the court would stand in recess.

The television picture switched back to Leanne.

"And so, as you heard, a guilty verdict in a murder case that has riveted the attention of this community. The defendant, Jerome Johnson, obviously, understandably, very upset by the jury's decision."

"Leanne," the anchorman said, "how has the news been received there?"

"As soon as word reached here, Chuck, I heard a lot of shouting, a lot of anger."

While she was speaking some of those waiting started to crowd around her. Most of them were black teenagers, a few older people. They were mugging for the camera, grinning, but also making angry, closed-fist gestures. Some hooted.

"Right now, perhaps you can pick it up in the background, I'm hearing glass breaking down the street. I'm not sure if that's a direct consequence of what we've just heard, but clearly the atmosphere here is becoming very uneasy."

The kids behind her were shouting now, practically drowning

her out. She glanced over her shoulder but maintained her on-air demeanor.

"Thank you, Leanne Corvino, reporting live from the Mansfield Municipal Plaza. This case began many months ago when . . ."

Kaiser turned down the sound. The picture showed a montage of familiar scenes: the Travises' snowy house, Johnson's arrest, shots of Carr's harangues, footage of Sheila.

"The jury fell for her just like you did," Frank said. "There's going to be hell to pay in this town tonight."

I nodded.

"You know I have to do my duty here," he went on. "After what you told me, I have to do my duty. I hate to say this, Ray, but I'm going to relieve you of your weapon."

"I understand." I unsnapped my service pistol and handed it to him. I pulled up my pant leg and extracted the Walther auto from the ankle holster. I felt funny handing them over.

"Cuffs, keys, everything."

I removed my equipment belt and emptied my pockets onto the rust-pitted surface of an old patio table. Frank slipped my handcuffs out of their leather case.

"This stinks," he said. "This wasn't the way it was supposed to work out. I didn't want it this way, I really didn't." As he stepped behind me, he made a gesture to indicate I should stand.

"Cuffs?" I said. "Is that necessary?"

"Procedures. You know about that, about by-the-book."

"I know. I guess it has to start sometime."

The feeling of handcuffs, their hardness, goes all through you. It's not just in your wrists, you feel it in your teeth, your ankle bones, your skull.

"Don't worry too much," he said. "The first one to talk is always in the best position to bargain, you know that. You're only an accessory. You turn state's, she's the one who'll go down."

He picked up my service pistol, ejected the clip. He checked the ammunition, slipped the packet of bullets back into the butt.

"It's a shame, really," he said. Taking me lightly by the elbow, he opened the sliding screen door and led me inside. "Here you have a man already convicted of the murder. All you had to do was keep your mouth shut. You're the only one who can burn her, she's the only one who can burn you. A million bucks. I don't get it. I really don't get it, Ray. Let's go downstairs."

The stairs led to a damp-smelling rec room. The old pool table and bar must have come with the place. Frank had added a television, his rack of rifles and shotguns.

"You go into something, you go in all the way," he said. "That's where you made your mistake. You got sucked in, you found yourself in over your head. I understand how that can happen. But then you panicked. Instead of riding it to the end of the line, you decide to bail out. Have a seat." He indicated a torn leather couch. I eased myself awkwardly onto it.

I said, "Part of it, I guess, was Johnson. I knew, ultimately, I couldn't sit by and see him pay for a crime he didn't commit."

"Why not?"

"Because he's innocent. Look, I'm no hero, I know that. I know it wasn't just him. I did it to save myself, too."

Frank said, "Sure, I understand. You're afraid of her."

I nodded. "It wouldn't have worked anyway. The whole thing was coming apart."

"So you whack the dink at the strip joint. The girl reporter, too.

Do what needs doing, Ray. If you have to kill, you kill. Don't you
get it?"

You have an idea of a person, an image in your mind. An image
has momentum. Mass times velocity. My idea of Frank Kaiser had
kept me from seeing what was happening. Now I began to wake up.

I said, "You knew about this before I told you."

"It doesn't matter what you intended. You start it, you take it
to the end. That's the way you do it."

"Oh, Jesus, Frank."

"Whether you like it or not."

He stood across the room by the bar, holding my gun casually
in one hand as he pulled a latex glove onto the other. Then he
switched, gloving his right hand.

He said, "Did you really think I wouldn't see through that broad
in two seconds and have her admitting it in two more? I walked
into that hospital room the morning of the murder and I knew. I
smelled it. As soon as she opened her mouth, I knew. I laid into
her, she broke down."

"So the two of you were working together from then on."

"You and I were working together, too, only you didn't know
it. You were damn lucky it was me, because she sold you over, first
chance she got. Tried to convince me that it was you who whacked
the husband. You planned it, you were the shooter. All your idea.
Forced her to go along. Shot her to make it look good. That was
her fallback, lay the whole thing on you. I saw through it. I said, I
know Dolan. He's no actor. I saw through everything. So we talked.
We made a deal."

He laid the gun down and poured himself another big slug of
scotch. He swirled it in the glass and took a swallow.

I said, "You fell for her."

He laughed. "No, no. I saw the temptation. But I wasn't bitten like you were. Tempted, sure, I was tempted. But I didn't fall."

"So what was it? What made you?"

"The money for starters—she brought that up right away. I wanted the money bad, not like you. And, you know, maybe it *was* her. Maybe she had me by the balls and I didn't even know it. Maybe I just thought, 'Fuck it.' "

He snorted through his nose, looked down at the gun. "Maybe I wanted to save your ass. I did, you know. She was ready to ice you. You didn't make it easy, all that shit you told her about not playing games. I steered the whole thing away from you, Ray. Saved your fucking ass."

"You set Johnson up."

"Sure I did. I picked him out. He was a nobody. He was expendable. It turned out the poor sap fit. Just luck. If he'd had an alibi, I would have picked up somebody else. The confession, years of being a detective, that's easy. That's just knowing how to get people to give you what you want. Anybody can arrange a jailhouse stoolie. That blood turning up in his car was pure luck. I created a story and it became the truth. Jury said it was the truth. What the hell more do you want?"

"You killed Lucas?"

"Rich, isn't it? Pop him and five hours later I'm investigating it? Always wondered what it was like, kill a man. All the murders I saw, I wondered what it felt like. There's a satisfaction, Ray. Great satisfaction. Great pleasure in erasing a man. Found out I liked it. Turns you into God fucking Almighty. Now it's only that reporter."

He tossed back the rest of the scotch, wiped his mouth with his wrist.

I said, "Not her. She's got nothing, really. She's just guessing. Without Lucas, she comes up empty. Don't."

"Guessing? Her guesses are too good. The Travis woman wanted to handle that end. Got a green eye for her, I think. I'll take care of that bitch, she tells me. I'll take care of her."

Instead of pouring himself another, Frank drank from the bottle. A trickle of scotch dribbled down his chin.

I said, "And what's my story going to be?"

"Whaddaya think? Cops are under a lot of stress. We've both known guys, couldn't hack it. Bullet in the brain can seem like the sweetest thing in the world. I guess you know that better than any-body—your dad. You came over here. We did some drinking. I knew you'd been under some stress. Suddenly, *bam*. The good part is, you die a hero. I'm doing you a favor. The tragic case of the hero cop. I'm letting you off the train at the right station."

I think he kept talking to put off what he planned to do. My brain was galloping ahead.

Under pressure, I knew, you fall back on your training. You don't think. You act on what's hard-wired into you. Before you fire the gun, you cock it.

"Frank, for God's sake."

When you cock the gun, you point it down and pull on the slide. It brings a shell into the chamber, under the pin. It sets the hammer back against the spring. You point it down, you cock it, you let off the safety. You do it all without thinking.

"You thought you were betraying her. Fact was, she'd been tak-ing you for a fool the whole goddamn time."

He would have to get close. He took a step.

"A blind fool."

I braced my feet on the floor.

"I guess you're right, Frank."

"And you . . ."

It came right then. He lowered the gun to cock it. The metallic click.

Not thinking, pure reflex, I left the couch. I threw myself at him. The gun exploded, shook the room.

Frank fell, I went down on top of him.

I pounded my head furiously into his face. I kneed him. I scrambled to my feet and stomped at his gut. Stomped him in a frenzy.

When it had gone off, the gun had wrenched itself out of his hand. He rolled, reached for it.

I stumbled across the room. I twisted and tried to open the sliding door. Locked. I heaved against it with my shoulder. The glass held. I stumbled backward.

I drew my foot back and slammed it into the glass. The force of the kick knocked me down.

From the floor, Frank fired off three rounds. The hard roar of the pistol numbed my ears. Two spiderwebs etched the glass.

I was not breathing. The ringing inside my head gave the scene a slow-motion, underwater feel.

Frank was climbing awkwardly to his feet. He must have remembered now that the shot had to be from close enough to look like suicide.

The booze he'd soaked up had fogged his head. He staggered a little as he came toward me.

I heaved myself at the door one more time. I aimed my forehead for the center of one of the radiating cracks. The pane shattered.

I tumbled onto the stones of the patio outside, stunned.

The gun boomed once more.

I rolled. I managed to get to my knees.

The stone was slippery with shards of broken glass. But I was an acrobat, my feet came under me like magic. I ran, bent at the waist, across the lawn.

The weeds clung to me, grabbed my legs. I lifted my knees. I kept my head bobbing. At every moment I expected a slug to break open my skull and blast my life into the sky.

I zigzagged, sprinting toward the highest bushes. A bullet whispered through the weeds beside me just as another pistol crack reached my ears. I sank to a squat. The air throbbed.

I hesitated for only a second. I was up and running again.

Handcuffed, I couldn't push the brambles out of the way. They tore at my face.

The sky still held some brightness but the light wasn't filtering down to earth. Darkness was seeping rapidly from the ground, gathering in the branches of bushes and under trees.

Darkness. I could lose myself in darkness. I stopped zigzagging and ran flat out. I was jacked up on the pure rush of it all.

I tripped and went down hard.

I jerked my legs, crablike, trying to stand. I glanced toward the house. Now the beam of a flashlight was bouncing toward me.

I got up and ran again. I reached the undergrowth and pushed on into the woods. I came to an outcropping of rock. It formed a ridge that dropped fifteen, maybe twenty feet into the trees. It was the type of landscape where you imagined Civil War battles being fought.

I hesitated. Jumping off that cliff into the gloom, when I couldn't see the ground below, would be suicidal. Thick brambles on both sides kept me from moving down the ridge.

I started back. But the beam of the flashlight was coming right toward me through the brush. It winked at me.

I had no choice but to conceal myself. I looked around frantically. I spotted where the roots of a maple downed in a storm had pulled up in a disk of soil. I tucked myself into the loamy cavity at its base and waited. The odor of clay and fungus filled my head.

All I could hear was the seesaw of my own breathing. I struggled to quiet it. My lungs were throbbing. Muscles twitched up and down my legs. My shoulders ached. My forehead burned.

I waited.

I heard uncertain, staggering steps. Frank was passing about ten yards beyond me. He stopped to listen, swung the light and probed the bushes with the beam. Then he went on. He scouted the edge of the rocks.

He stopped again. He was listening for me. He must have sensed I was near. I could hear him breathing.

The light swung toward me. I burrowed my head into the clay. The lethal beam caught my shoulder but moved on.

There was no way I could outrun him wearing handcuffs. If I waited, he would find me.

I groped in the dirt. I had no time to plan. My hand touched a stone the size of a cigarette lighter. My fingers closed around it.

I rose slowly. I twisted. I flung the rock with my wrist as far as I could.

It went over the ridge just to Frank's right. He spun. He fired three times at the sound. The muzzle blasts flashed in the gloom.

While the explosions were still compressing the air, I moved. I slipped getting out of the pit. I sprinted, knees high, right at him.

He realized his mistake. He spun back toward me. He lifted the gun and fired. The shot blew by my head. The sound of it lacerated my eardrum.

I ran right through him. He was two steps from the edge of the rock. We both went over.

For an instant that felt like an hour, I was soaring. The air pillowed me, lofted me to the tops of the trees. Up and up, along a wild, giddy arc. I stared at Frank's house from far above. I watched it fade to a dot of light in the dark. I spiraled above Mansfield. I saw downtown glowing like a furnace. I saw the city itself shrink, become a fuzzy speck of light. I saw Lake Erie, Lake Ontario, Canada. I was being drawn up and up and up. Toward Venus. Orion.

Maybe I dreamed all of it after I landed. I don't remember being unconscious. I remember the crash of leaves, but I don't remember the blow of the ground. I remember sliding, knocking into a tree, sliding some more.

Then I was lying against another tree in the middle of a deep silence. I could not take a breath. I opened my mouth and tried to bite the air. My teeth clacked stupidly.

I lay there, I don't know for how long. Maybe I lost consciousness. Finally, I opened my eyes. The faint summer glow of the sky still reached me through the trees.

I listened. I waited. I held my breath. Nothing.

Something urged me to try to get up. An epic struggle, a fierce grappling, brought me to my feet. I fell immediately.

I stood again. Fifteen feet away the beam of a flashlight shone steadily. I stumbled toward it.

Frank was wedged upside down between two rocks, his head twisted and laid onto his right shoulder. His eyes caught the diluted light, two dull pools of darkness. He wasn't moving. He wasn't breathing. Blood had seeped from both corners of his mouth and left him with a clown's grin.

Then the sky exhaled the last of its light and the silence expanded to fill the darkness.

HE WAS DEAD. Frank. After everything, to have it come to this.

I made my way along the bottom of the ridge to a low section where I could scramble up. I trudged back to the house. Glass crunched under my feet on the patio stones. Inside, I found my keys and opened the cuffs.

My wrists were bleeding. My scalp and neck were bleeding, my shirt was drenched with blood and sweat. Glass was embedded in my forehead. My scratched face was beginning to swell.

I buckled on my equipment belt. I found a pistol—Frank had plenty of guns. I checked it for ammunition, slid it into my holster. I retrieved my backup gun. I went to Frank's kitchen sink and washed the dried blood from my hands. I cupped cold water to my stinging face. I eased a sopping dish towel around my neck.

There was no time to think. I had to stop this thing, had to stop Sheila. I had to make sure it didn't reach Leanne.

Then I was driving. Him or me. He was dead, I was alive.

The radio crackled with activity. Something was happening downtown. I switched it off.

It seemed foolish to think. I was beyond thought. At a certain point, you switch over to reflex.

I was heading for Sheila's house. I had to reach her. I had to see her. To talk to her. To stop her. But mainly to see her. Once more.

Night had descended completely by the time I pulled into her driveway. In the dark, the heat seemed all the more oppressive.

I climbed out of the car. It had not occurred to me that Sheila's betrayal, my own betrayal of her, made us enemies. It had not passed my mind that she might want to finish the job Frank Kaiser had started. What was between us went beyond that. So I thought.

But reflex, training, something made me hesitate. I found my hand unclipping my holster and easing the pistol out. I held it by the side of my leg.

In the heat I could smell the cedar bark mulch, the asphalt, somebody's backyard citronella.

I tried the door. Locked. I rang the bell. Waiting, I almost collapsed.

Brie's face appeared in the narrow window along the frame. She swung the door open. Her features recoiled. One hand went to protect her throat while the other hovered, fingers trembling, at her lips.

"Is your mother home?" That was what I meant to say. It came out a garbled groan.

"What? My God, what's going on? What happened to you?"

"Your mother!"

"She's not here. Were you in an accident? Come in and lie down."

"No, no time. Where did she go? When?"

Her hand floated toward me. "You're bleeding."

"Have to see her."

"Has something happened to her?"

"When did she go out?"

"I don't know. I got back and she was gone."

I tried to map the thing in my mind. Sheila gone. Leanne. Frank dead. Him or me.

"I have to go upstairs." The words trailed behind me.

"Wait, Ray. Jesus, what— Where are you going?"

I walked mechanically through the house, remembering. I remembered a party one summer night long ago.

Glancing into the dark kitchen, I saw Lance's blood. I saw myself in an apron. Remembering that Christmas.

"You read my palm," I said out loud. I must have sounded like a madman.

Remembering the sound of Sheila and Lance upstairs.

Padding up those carpeted stairs now.

Remembering the dinner party, the explosion of sex. Before that night, I had thought of sex as part of the hard surface of life, not something that smashed through, that ripped you wide open. Remembering how it had left me stunned.

Down the corridor. The bathroom. Her bedroom. Every corner swarming with memories.

I stepped to the bedside table and pulled open the drawer where she kept the revolver she had shown me. I used my hand to stir the pencils, the packets of Kleenex, lip balm, penlight, cough drops, tube of ointment, tan and white prescription vials. As if I could make the gun appear.

Leanne.

I rushed downstairs.

"Phone book," I demanded.

Brie got one from a kitchen drawer.

I found the number, Channel Ten. I dialed. I endured the drone of the automated voice as it recited my options. Finally I reached a human being. The woman said she could not connect me with Leanne Corvino. Yes, she was working, but she could not tell me where. She could not give out that information.

I dialed the number of Leanne's cellular phone. It rang a few times before her voice mail kicked in. I left my pager number and hung up.

"Ray, will you tell me what's going on?" Brie demanded. "Is it about my mother? Is it the riot? Is that where you got hurt?"

"Riot?"

"Downtown. It's on television. Didn't you know? I thought that's where you had been."

I stared, my mouth empty of words. Air moved my chest up and down. Her eyes squinted more questions at me.

"Stay here," I said. "Stay inside."

It was all I could think of. The world seemed overrun with danger.

"What's going on, Ray? What happened to you?"

"Don't go out. Please. Trust me, okay? You're right, I'm weak. But trust me."

She stared.

I backed carefully toward the door, and then I was inside my cruiser. I turned on the siren and floored it.

AS I APPROACHED DOWNTOWN, I could sense the city's uneasiness. The quiet of the streets reminded me of the stillness just before a thunderstorm, a kind of seething. Sirens laced the air into a giant cat's cradle of sound that shifted and shifted again.

I turned my radio back on. The electric voices were as familiar to me as my own thoughts. Everybody was on edge, wasting no airtime. Requests for assistance, one after another. Reports of fires, of looting.

All the activity was taking place somewhere else. The first streets I passed were quiet, oddly deserted for a hot summer night. Not many cars. A few people, some of them running.

I swerved to avoid a garbage can overturned in the middle of the road. Nobody around, nothing sinister. Just a can on its side, its contents spewed. Just a sign.

A girl darted into the street. I stood on my brakes. She was only ten or eleven. She stared at me with big eyes. She ran, intent on getting somewhere fast.

Individuals were now merging into crowds. They were headed

toward the center of town, toward the hot glow of Municipal Plaza. Here and there I observed a broken window. I heard alarms, the clanging of burglar alarms and the silly whoop of car alarms.

The gawkers were tired of standing around, tired of watching. Tonight, they were determined to get in on the action. The veneer is thin, brother.

I came to a barricade spread across the road. Some barrels, a couple of old car seats, a stack of discarded tires, all stretched out like a child's play fort.

I had to stop. I unclamped the Remington from the dash and climbed out.

Mad Manny's Television City—the wall of picture tubes glowed with an unnatural brilliance in the darkness. Everyone crowded to see, stood on tiptoe. They pointed and shouted. Shots from different parts of the city cascaded across the screens. They showed flames. They showed cops chasing people. They showed masses gathering downtown.

I started to clear away the debris in the street. I kicked at it, the shotgun cradled under my arm. Then, on all the television sets, the scenes of the rioting vanished and Leanne Corvino's face appeared. I stopped.

She was reporting from a corner of Municipal Plaza. The camera swept around to show a cordon of police guarding the plaza itself. The street opposite was filled with a milling crowd. Some of the store windows along Main had been smashed.

The shot switched back to her. She was speaking gravely, quickly. She looked very vulnerable.

I climbed back into my car. I had to drive slowly, steering around abandoned cars and burning trash.

I came to another barricade, construction debris piled in the street, a car overturned. I got out, locked my cruiser, and abandoned it. I moved along the sidewalk, feeling myself carried by the crowd. No one paid any attention to my uniform, maybe because my clothes were torn up and soiled, maybe because anarchy was sweeping the city that night.

All I could think of was reaching Leanne, of saving her. I tried to run, feeling the pavement pound against my feet. I sucked at the dirty, humid air. I had turned into an old man. My breath made a sound like a death rattle. Sweat stung my face.

I reached Municipal Plaza. The police had cleared the area in front of the government buildings. They stood in a line, shoulder to shoulder, along the low steps that led to the square. Each officer wore a helmet, a face shield, a pouch that I knew contained a gas mask. Each held a riot baton in both hands. In front of them, the street was clogged with people.

Municipal Plaza opens onto Main just before it crosses Market. The Four Corners is still the heart of Mansfield, still the center of the urban glow, a block that never goes dark. That's where I saw the white lights of the television cameras, but to reach the corner I would have to fight through the crowd.

Traffic had long since halted. A bus stood helpless in the middle of the street, its windows smashed. Kids climbed to its roof and threw their arms in the air and shouted to their friends. I forced my way to the opposite side of the street, where the stores were. I climbed onto a car. It was a late-model gray Lincoln, beautifully waxed. Four other people were already standing on its roof, denting it in.

Down at the corner, I caught a glimpse of the Channel Ten News van. It was moving, inching forward through the masses of people, heading south on Market. All I had to do was make it to the corner, catch up with Leanne, warn her, tell her the truth. Just before I stepped down, I thought I saw Sheila farther down the street. Was it her? She wore jeans, a black blouse. Dark glasses hid her eyes. She was gone before I could be sure.

Just as I shoved my way to the corner, a greenish pop bottle rose up from the crowd on Market, turned end-over-end, and lazily crashed down onto the pavement near a group of cops. A running skirmish broke out. More bottles flew, stones. A couple of sergeants tried to organize a ragged line of cops to clear the street. My instinct was to join them, but when they fired a volley of tear gas I had to run with the others to escape the stinging gas. The police didn't follow.

Ahead of me, I again spotted the brilliant splotch of light. Leanne Corvino and her cameraman had climbed to the top of their van. She was broadcasting from there. She had picked an ideal spot to take in the action.

Her presence was attracting a mass of rioters, drawn by the hot beam of the television lights. They gathered around the van, shouting and punching the air.

I caught sight of a dark blouse, black hair. It was Sheila, I was sure of it now. She was strolling along the street ahead of me, almost casual, her hand jammed inside a shoulder bag. There was still an aura about her, a presence that touched me in spite of that maelstrom, in spite of the danger, in spite of the betrayal. She was something to look at.

This would be it. I would grab her and disarm her. I wouldn't have the heart to arrest her. I would just let her know, as the consequences of our actions roiled around us, that we had reached the end of the road.

I ran toward her with lead weights attached to my feet, pushing people aside. I careened into a parked car. Sheila crossed to the sidewalk.

I had covered ten yards when suddenly I found myself flying. The blacktop loomed. It slammed into my chest. My head cracked against the roadway. Darkness poured into my skull.

MAYBE SOMEBODY HAD tripped me. Maybe I had fallen on my own. I came to and rolled over and thought for a moment of staying there, of letting myself sink back into sweet darkness.

I forced myself to move, to climb up from the grave. I managed to stand, to stagger on columns of air. Before I had taken three steps, I knew something was wrong. My service pistol was gone. The missing weight made me lopsided. I looked back, searched the pavement. Of course it wasn't there.

I had trouble focusing my eyes now. They wanted to see double. I was watching a crazy ballroom dance, everyone waltzing with himself. I shook my head, forcing my vision into line. I scanned the crowd, looking for Sheila.

My eyes were used to looking for her, her image was burned into my optic nerve. Otherwise, I never would have spotted her up on the steps of one of the town houses opposite where Leanne was broadcasting. She stood near the heavy Georgian door, almost in the shadows. I started toward her.

I looked again at the news van. I sensed in an instant what Sheila intended. She stood exactly even with Leanne. It would be an easy shot.

In the same moment, her hand slipped from the shoulder bag. The shiny gun glinted in the streetlight.

The pavement went soft under my feet.

Across the way, Leanne was still speaking to the camera. The glow of the television lights turned her into a brilliant vision, like an angel in a school play.

Both of Sheila's arms reached out. One fist cupped the other, just the way I had taught her in my basement a million years ago. She was taking her time, being very careful.

All I could do was shout. All I could do was tear her name from my throat.

"Sheila!" The word consumed me. "*Shei-la!*"

She glanced toward me. Our eyes met. Her mouth trembled for a second. Maybe Frank had told her what he planned to do and she had assumed I was already dead.

But seeing me didn't turn her away from her goal. She again squinted down the sights of the pistol.

I shouted again.

She squeezed the trigger. Let it happen, don't make it happen.

The gun spat its tongue of flame. It jumped. She brought it back down. She fired quickly this time, taking no time to aim.

Both shots missed.

People ducked down, some dove to the pavement. Panic filled the street. You couldn't tell where the sound came from. It ricocheted back and forth across the street twenty times in half a second.

One of the technicians was helping Leanne scurry down from the van.

I watched Sheila descending the stairs. She was going to cross the street and fire point-blank. She held her hand inside the bag again. Absolutely cool. No one was paying any attention to her.

I crossed at an angle, intent on intercepting her.

She saw me. Her face, the set of her jaw, didn't change. She simply turned and walked away from me. I hurried after her. She began to run, taking quick little steps. I stumbled, went down on one knee.

People were sprinting in every direction. I almost missed seeing her turn down an alley that opened just before Main.

I raced forward. I wanted to talk to her. To tell her what? I wanted to hold her. I swear, I wanted to cling to her. I wanted to force everything to come out right. Even now, I wanted to explain away my betrayal. I wanted to make her understand.

None of it mattered. Lance, Lucas, even Frank Kaiser—none of it. I still felt that. Even in the center of that chaos, I realized that I actually did love her. I wanted to tell her that. I wanted to reach her and tell her.

The alley was deserted. As I moved past the corner of the storefronts, the sound of the crowd faded. Now I could hear the permanent low grinding din that drifts through a city at night.

The only light was at my back. My fuzzy shadow crept along ahead of me.

"Sheila?" My voice echoed.

On my right a loading dock held a Dumpster and a compacted mass of corrugated boxes. A fire escape jutted from the wall above me. All the doorways were full of blackness, a landscape of shadows.

I looked up. Past the tops of the buildings, as if I were standing at the bottom of a well in daylight, I could see a single faint star. I remembered Sheila wishing. I know it'll come true. It already has.

The thud was a pickax slamming into my gut. The world went silent except for the sound, a long way off, of a door slamming.

My ears filled with a sharp intake of breath. My own.

The ground tilted crazily. The pavement rose up. I laid my cheek against it. I breathed the smell of hot tar, of deep summer.

It took me a second to realize that I was lying down. Why? Why was I trying to inhale the last oxygen on earth?

I saw her walking toward me up the alley. The jeans, the dark blouse. The black hair. The lovely tan. The eyes. The luscious eyes. The fluid walk. The natural, easy movement of her body. The sway of her hips. The way she held herself. Christ, I loved looking at her.

She was almost standing over me. She was still holding the gun.

Sheila. I couldn't bring her name to my tongue. I couldn't force air through my throat. I wanted to speak to her. I wanted to tell her that in spite of it all. In spite of it all.

Her lips were moving. Soundless. Not angry. Serious. Talking to me. Her beautiful lips.

But her voice wasn't reaching me. I was wrapped in numb silence.

She was raising the gun.

I pointed at her. My hand jerked. Pure reflex.

She lifted her head toward the sky as if the star I had seen had now caught her attention. As if she were anxious to make a wish. Her face changed. She twisted, a graceful half pirouette.

She fell. She fell and fell and fell, as if she would never stop falling. Her body draped my legs. I could not feel her weight.

My hand was detached from my body. It belonged to somebody else. It held the backup gun from my ankle.

I had not decided to shoot her. Like everything else, it had happened on its own. Reflex. An instinct to survive.

I dropped the pistol, reached to touch her hair. My fingers were numb. Cold. My life was leaking onto the pavement.

I closed my eyes. Time passed.

Then the darkness exploded into light. Brilliant white light entered me and filled me.

I forced my eyes open again. Leanne was speaking to me silently, her face close to mine. Over her shoulder, the indifferent, blazing eye of the lens.

I TOLD IT as it happened. I told everything. Sheila, Frank Kaiser, Dante Lucas, Leanne Corvino. I went over it and then went over it again.

I should have caught on right away. I knew the detectives they sent around to talk to me were from Internal Affairs. I thought, well, the major crimes guys would all have been close to Frank. But that wasn't it, wasn't all of it.

Maybe I didn't describe it exactly as it happened. I mean, what I'm telling now is only a version. The details aren't exactly right, not all of them. You can't expect to get all the details right.

Maybe I'm confused about the essentials, too. You go over it enough times and you're no longer telling what happened, you're telling a story. You're telling a story about a story. The way you say it shapes the way you remember it.

HERO COP SHOT. It has a nice ring to it, doesn't it? That was the headline in the local tabloid.

I didn't think much about it at the time. I didn't want to look at the newspapers. I didn't want to know. I never turned on the television that came with my room. Its blank screen stared at me from just below the ceiling, held there by a mechanical arm and a swivel.

So much happens in a second, it would take a lifetime to tell about what happened in that one year I knew Sheila. A story is only a ghost of the truth. I tried to be as honest as I could.

They wanted something else. It was all public relations to them. Chief Preston came to visit me while I still had the tubes in. They were going with a different story.

"You made a mistake," Preston told me. "A bad mistake. But we're going to give you a second chance. We believe you deserve it."

I had made a mess for the department and they wanted me to help straighten it out.

Frank Kaiser was expendable. Frank killed Lucas. It was only a small step to say he killed Lance Travis, too. He and Sheila planned it. His marriage breaking up, the strain, he snapped. The two of them plotted the whole thing. Kaiser shot Sheila as a ruse. They both conspired to frame Jerome Johnson. When Leanne and I began to suspect, they planned to kill us, too. Blood lust.

I had been forced to kill Frank in self-defense. That's how it would be. I had hated to do it. It had shaken me, the way my best friend had betrayed me. But I'd had no choice.

I had saved Leanne's life. I had killed Sheila before she could kill. I was a hero, a hero once again.

Jerome Johnson would be released immediately by court order. The city would negotiate with Carr, lay a big settlement on his client. They had insurance for things like that.

It would be good for the department, good for the city, good for the mayor's reelection.

The riot, that was a wake-up call. It hadn't done that much

damage—some broken windows, a few buildings burned. The media had blown it out of proportion. It would spark an era of renewal in Mansfield. The mayor was already setting up a commission to work with the city's minority communities. Real progress was sure to come of it.

That was their story. I could sign on if I wanted. Or I could stick with what I had told the detectives and do hard time. It was up to me.

I'm no hero.

The footage—graphic footage, I'm sure they called it—of me and Sheila, the hero cop and his assailant, our fresh blood mingling on the street, had gotten a lot of coverage, local and national. That's what I was told.

Every day another dozen bouquets of flowers arrived at the hospital. Flowers, candy, cards. Cards from Canada, from Arizona and Idaho, one from Luxembourg. I had the nurses distribute all the flowers and gifts to other patients. I didn't want them in my room.

Marriage proposals. Can you believe that? Women I had never met wanted to marry me. A woman in Kentucky wrote that she owned a horse farm, that she had the means to take care of me. One from New Jersey sent me a Polaroid of herself in a bikini. Nice-looking, too.

I didn't want flowers. I wanted to lie there and stare at the ceiling. I could think of nothing better to do for the rest of my time on earth. Lie there, make my mind blank, and stare at nothing.

Faces floated past me. Elaine Kaiser. "What happened, Ray?" she asked me. "What happened to him?" I guess she blamed herself. I tried to reassure her. I had always liked Elaine.

Mayor Catlett. He said the chrome words that politicians use.

Leanne Corvino. She kissed me with her sweet, smiling lips. You saved my life, she said. I owe you.

Stonewall Carr came by. Even him. I was a good cop, he told me. He struck me as a very nice man, very sincere.

Brie came. Of all of them, I think she smelled the truth. But she brought me cookies she had made herself. She said people were treating her well. She had decided to focus on premed when she went to college. She wanted to be a doctor. A representative of the insurance company had already been in touch. Since nothing had been proven in court, she had the upper hand as far as the money. They were going to let her keep part of the settlement. She said she was planning to give most of it to charity. I wished her luck.

By the time I left the hospital, Leanne had already been offered a job with one of the networks. I see her on the tube once in a while now, you probably do, too, reporting from some godforsaken place.

After I had had some time to recover at home, they held a ceremony at city hall. That was part of the deal, part of the public relations. They gave me another medal and I shook a lot of hands. I shook Jerome Johnson's hand, but his eyes looked at me coldly.

The bullet is still lodged near my spine. It has cut down on my mobility. It gives me a lot of pain. I can't ride patrol anymore.

They kicked me up to detective. I'm beginning to like it. They have me working with young people, trying to steer them off drugs, help them make something of their lives. It gives the department some favorable ink. I think I do some good, too.

I remember the night I came home after getting my award. I could smell autumn in the crisp air.

The sky was good that night. I set up my telescope. Venus floated near the horizon. I knew terrible storms were swirling on the veiled planet. Tremendous bolts of lightning were shooting from clouds of acid. But that night it glowed like a vision in the west. A creamy, lovely, hopeful vision.

I still think about the street, I still think about when the action would start and everything would just shine.

I still think about Sheila.